The Murder Came Later

a novel by
Lew Duddridge

Also by Lew Duddridge

"The Best 70 Years of my life," "It's all down hill from here"
Published by Orca Book Publishers, Victoria BC Canada. ISBN 920501-13-3
May be viewed in its entirety on website http://www.ourrotts.ca/e/toc.aspx?id=2429

By the University of Calgary Digital Library of Local Histories.

"Who Cares Now"
Published by Borealis Press, Ottawa Canada, ISBN 0-88887-249-6

"Friends in picture and verse:
Art work by Hilda Duddridge, Poems by Lew Duddridge, Self Published

Order this book online at www.trafford.com/07-0235
or email orders@trafford.com

Most Trafford titles are also available at major online book retailers.

Note for Librarians: A cataloguing record for this book is available from Library and Archives Canada at www.collectionscanada.ca/amicus/index-e.html

Printed in Victoria, BC, Canada.

ISBN: 978-1-4251-1825-9

www.trafford.com

North America & international
toll-free: 1 888 232 4444 (USA & Canada)
phone: 250 383 6864 • fax: 250 383 6804 • email: info@trafford.com

The United Kingdom & Europe
phone: +44 (0)1865 722 113 • local rate: 0845 230 9601
facsimile: +44 (0)1865 722 868 • email: info.uk@trafford.com

10 9 8 7 6 5 4 3 2

Credits

To my wife Hilda—
My inspiration

To my children and grandchildren—
You are what life is all about

To Adrian Lowe—
For your editing ideas

To friends I met along the way

Introduction

The brothers Clinton and Richard Drake graduate as pilots in the Royal Canadian Air force. It is late 1942 and the war is at its height. They are posted overseas, and Richard becomes a Lancaster bomber pilot and Clinton a Spitfire fighter pilot.

Clinton is shot down near London England, but lives to shoot down enemy aircraft.

Richard's Lancaster is shot down over Germany. Richard escapes and makes his way back to England and finishes his tour. His crew becomes prisoners of war.

The War ends, and they return home. Mavis, Richard's war bride arrives three months later, and they make their home in Grandeur Saskatchewan.

Clinton returns still a single man, and attends the University of Saskatoon, Graduating as a Chartered accountant

Clinton opens an office in Saskatoon, and travels once a week to Grandeur to do the accounting for business places in Grandeur. Once of his customers is Mavis and Richard's machinery dealership.

Richard buys a helicopter, and adds crop dusting to his farm services.

Grandeur is home to a small group of Nazi sympathizers, who are slowly but surely getting bolder. Their dislike of the Royal Canadian Legion and veterans in general, is surfacing.

The outspoken President of the Women's auxiliary of the Legion is murdered, and Sergeant Doyle of the RCMP faces many roadblocks on the way to the discovery of the murderer.

The community is in shock when Richard Drake dies in a fiery crash of his helicopter.

Clinton Drake took Aircraft Accident investigation during the war, and brings evidence to Sergeant Doyle which points to possible murder in Richard's death.

Kurt, a Nazi sympathizer falls in love with Joan, she had been engaged to Richard before he met Mavis. They marry, and Kurt's love is tested to it limit by two murders.

CHAPTER ONE

Flight Lieutenant Clinton Drake

"I'm alive!" I had said it a hundred or more times over the last sixty days. It was hard to believe, but I was alive. And I had flown my last sortie.

It was an indescribable feeling, but just at that moment the muscles in my cheek twitched slightly. Of course the doctor had warned me to expect these little spasms. Giving me the standard medical exam which was given to every pilot on his discharge, the doc had said, "Clinton, you may have that twitch for a while. But don't worry, it will fade away, now that the war is over. It's all about stress, you see." It made sense. I had certainly had my share of close calls. I remembered the first two nights after a particularly close one. They were absolute hell. My body alternated between sweating, shivers, and facial spasms, made all the worse by the fear that this was how things would be from now on and forever. But the terror had passed, leaving only the slight twitch.

"My God," I muttered to myself, half-aloud. What's a twitch? Seventy-five percent of my squadron are dead. I'm lucky. I'm headed home, in fact I'm only minutes from the home that I was sure I would never see again.

I had been on the Atlantic Ocean from Liverpool to Halifax for five days, and now, after four more days on the train, the lack of exercise, both physical and mental, was beginning to take its toll. I had my brother Richard with me, and no end of other soldiers, sailors, and airmen, but talking to all of them was not the answer. It would take many weeks, months, maybe even years to get my mind and body off the roller coaster it had been on for the past three years.

Was I trying to tell myself that the hell that came with my wartime activities had ruined my life? Did it mean that I would never be the same, that I could never again find comfort in a place like Grandeur, Saskatchewan, where I had grown up? I refused to believe it. If anything I felt a strange exhilaration. Home was suddenly uncharted ground, another challenge to be overcome. "You will be all right, Clinton Drake," I told myself.

Life had not been dull in the months since the war ended. The Royal Air Force had found things for me to do almost to the day that I had left for Canada and home. I had made no end of trips flying Spitfires and Hurricanes from the continent to Great Britain. It was wonderful being able to fly my aircraft and not having to worry about being shot down, but the difference was a little jarring. Only a few weeks earlier, I was shooting and being shot at. I had shot enemy aircraft out of the sky and I had destroyed enemy tanks on the ground. The words of the medical officer were still loud in my mind. "You don't go through what you've been through without paying a nasty price.

You can do everything to try and forget, but your near-death experiences will sneak up on you. Don't be surprised if many nights you wake up screaming and bathed in sweat."

For now my thoughts were all pleasant ones, however. I thought back to my training days in North Wales, on the Miles Master. I remembered that exciting moment when I graduated from the Master to the Spitfire. My instructor had appeared at the door to the flight room. "How do you feel, Drake?" he had asked.

"I feel fine, sir." It was the only thing to say, of course, but in truth I felt nervous. As my instructor pointed at an aircraft bearing the markings "TAS," I realized that I was about to have my first real contact with a Spitfire fighter. Before putting on my parachute I took a moment just to stand and stare at it. It was the stuff of every pilot's dreams: a machine as beautiful as it was deadly, the clean lines of the fuselage matched by the elegant simplicity of the Rolls-Royce engine nacelle. Most important of all, there were no dual controls. After many hours of dual instruction on the Miles Master my instructor had deemed that I was ready to fly alone. My God, I asked myself, could I really fly the Spitfire? Never in my life had my nerves played so many games with me.

My instructor's voice snapped me out of it. "You have one hour. Good luck."

I adjusted my helmet, did up my harness, and sat dazed in front of a massive array of instruments, trying desperately to remember what my instructor had said when we flew the Miles Master the day before. Certainly this was not the first time I had sat in a Spitfire. But all the dials, contacts, and levers rammed into such a confined space seemed unfamiliar and confusing at that moment.

In my confusion I fell back on the cockpit drill, which I knew by heart. The letters HHTMPFFGGS all meant something. Hood, harness, trim, mixture, pitch, fuel, flaps, gills, gauges, switches. Everything was set. The mechanic closed the hood behind me and I was trapped. "This is it," I told myself. "Don't screw it up." I signaled "all clear contact." I manipulated the hand pump and the starter button. Slowly the propeller began to turn, and then with a sound like a cannon the mighty Rolls-Royce engine roared to life. Black smoke, streaked with long blue flames, erupted from the exhaust stacks. The aircraft shuddered but gradually settled as the engine tuned itself in. I waved "chocks away." The mechanic pulled the blocks from in front of the wheels, I opened the radiator shutters wide. As I felt my aircraft begin to roll forward I checked my brakes and the flight controls for freedom of movement; all was well. So I taxied carefully over to the runway, following the standard zigzag pattern which a Spitfire pilot learns is the only way to see forward. I could see the ground controller in his little shack on the edge of the runway. From here he controlled all aircraft movement with his Aldis lamp. His light flashed green and I continued onto the runway. Another green light followed. I had been cleared for takeoff.

My heart pounding, and sweat trickling down my neck, I lowered my seat and slowly opened the throttle. Bits of old advice filtered into my brain. "Don't put the stick too far forward; that huge propeller is almost touching the ground as it is." The Spitfire surged forward and I corrected the incipient swing. I jockeyed the rudders. And then, as if by magic, the magnificent machine was in the air, the runway markers flashing by on either side. I held it straight and raised the undercarriage, throttled back and adjusted the propeller pitch for climbing. The training I had taken in the mockup of the Spitfire was working! I was doing fine.

Oh! how light on the controls this unique machine was! The slightest movement of the hand and it virtually leapt across the sky. I was now experiencing what thousands could only imagine. Gradually the speed went to my head and I grew bolder. I eased the stick forward to try a dive. Three hundred, three fifty, four hundred nautical miles per hour. The ground was really hurtling towards me now. Such speed began to scare me and I pulled the stick back. But the sudden change in direction drove my head into my shoulders. My eyes blurred under the enormous strain of G-forces, I could feel my face being stretched, my lips forcing their way into my teeth. So it was clear that I still had some learning to do.

As the Spitfire shot skyward once again, I shook off the G-effect and regained my composure. For the next thirty minutes I worked through my flying exercises. I was still heavy-handed, but time and practice would sort out my problems. For now all I needed to do was return to base and put this lovely machine back on the runway safely.

I went through all my pre-landing checks: brakes, undercarriage, mixture, pitch, fuel, flaps. I opened the radiator shutters wide, throttled back, selected the propeller fine pitch, raised my seat and opened the hood. But all was not well with the approach. I could not see where I was to land; the broad exhaust stacks of the Spitfire's enormous engine were blotting out the whole runway. And because of the tremendous pressure of onrushing air, I could not stick my head outside the cockpit for a better view. I was a prisoner in my own Spitfire. I made slight turns to port and starboard, from which I finally caught flashes of the runway. I lowered the undercarriage and flaps. The runway rushed up at me at what seemed an impossible speed. Stick back, back, back, desperately back! Then, with a painful jolt, the aircraft touched down. It rolled awkwardly down the runway. A touch of left brake, a touch of right, zigzagging again to get a better view forward. At last I swung off the runway and stopped. I had flown the mighty Spitfire.

Back in the present, in the Grandeur-bound train, I snapped out of my daydream and looked down at my twin brother, Squadron Leader Richard Drake. There he was, slumped over his seat beside me, half-asleep. And then I suddenly realized that the train had reached the outskirts of our old hometown.

"Richard! Richard, do you hear me?" I blurted out. "We're almost home, Richard! Thank you Lord, we're nearly home!"

Squadron Leader Drake had definitely made a name for himself during the years of war. His face was no longer that of the boyish young man who had left Grandeur three years ago. The strain of wartime flying had left its mark. The mark was not unpleasant: it was a mark of achievement, of trials endured and stresses overcome. Over six feet tall with broad shoulders to match, no man wore his uniform with greater class than Rich. More than once I had watched

Richard enter a dance hall during the war, and seen how many pairs of eyes followed him wherever he went. But for all his charisma, brains, and good looks, none of it had gone to his head. For this reason there was no way I could feel jealous of the big lug. Well, not *too* jealous; I was only human.

We had both wanted to be pilots, we both had the necessary schooling to be eligible, and we both managed to pass all the various medical tests that were required for consideration. And like every pilot, we both wanted to end up in Britain flying a fighter plane. But it was here our paths had diverged a bit. Whereas I made it into a Spitfire, Richard ended up as a bomber pilot.

I had respect for my twin brother, but I knew that in many respects we were vastly different. Richard was a born athlete who had loved socializing even before the war. He had never missed a dance that followed the local ball tournaments. I remembered Joan Hanson, the pretty girl who Richard had been engaged to when he left Grandeur for overseas. I could easily have dated her myself. Why the two of them had broken up was a complete mystery to me. When asked about it, Richard always seemed to beat around the bush. This made me suspicious. I knew Joan's parents were just small farmers, living about ten miles out from Grandeur. I wondered if maybe Rich had come to feel that Joan's family was somehow not grand enough for him. Anyway, it was not very long after that breakup that I stood as Richard's best man when he married his Mavis. Now as we rolled into Grandeur I found myself wondering again how Joan Hanson had handled the split. Was she even still living in Grandeur?

I had not followed in the footsteps of Richard where marriage was concerned. It was true that I had gone on a number of dates with a lovely Welsh girl. This started when I was doing my first tour in Spitfires, patrolling the area around Swansea in South Wales where German Junkers and Stuka dive-bombers had been raising hell. Sometimes these patrols went on too long for us to make it back to base, and then we were allowed to fuel up and stay overnight at Fairwood Common. It was on one of these unscheduled stays that I met Megan.

It had been an especially hair-raising day. Dear God, I would never forget how the German Messerschmitt came hurtling straight at me, his guns already blazing. He finally broke to the right but far too close for comfort; I could smell the heady odor of explosives. Then I spotted a Junkers 88 moving rapidly below me, obviously getting ready to drop his load on our steel mills at Port Talbot. I threw my Spitfire into a steep dive. I had the advantage of height, speed, and the sun behind me. But the strain on my beautiful Spitfire was terrible. Every rivet seemed to complain, and the aircraft groaned alarmingly as my speed came dangerously close to the red line. I knew I was running a huge risk. But I knew I had to avoid the Messerschmitt and stop the 88. The force of the dive slammed my head against the headrest and seemed ready to tear my guts out of my belly. But with each second the Junkers grew larger in my sights. It was clear that the pilot had not seen me. No doubt he was concentrating on his intended bomb drop. Then suddenly the enemy aircraft filled my field of vision. We would collide! I squeezed the firing button. The Junkers shuddered crazily. Bits and pieces of it came away. The German pilot flung his stricken plane into a turn. It was leaking a thick stream of smoke, black and oily, so I broke to the left to avoid the mess. I never saw a parachute open. The Junkers pilot died with his plane. The excitement and the thrill of victory vanished. I felt no triumph, only sadness: enemy or not, one of my own special kind had just died.

I was running low on fuel, so with the Junkers out of the way and the Messerschmitt nowhere to be seen, I headed for the landing strip at Fairwood Common. From here, after filing my mission report, I was driven into Swansea itself where I found lodging at a pub. Megan was the pub owner's daughter. It happened that I had instructions to take off again at first light, which left no time for drinking or dancing. But I promised Megan that I would drop in to see her again the next time I landed my aircraft at Fairwood Common, and I kept my word. Megan was nineteen, beautiful, and under fairly strict parental control. We spent three enjoyable hours at the Patti Pavilion, and I had her home an hour before midnight just as promised. It was obvious that Megan wanted the relationship to continue. Unfortunately I had what some Canadian pilots might have called "confused priorities." How could I have resisted the advances of a girl with such an engaging smile? Well, at the time my reasoning was simple: statistics showed that by the time I completed my tour of duty with my Spitfire squadron, only one in five of the original pilots would still be alive. It seemed unfair to make a commitment of any kind to a woman like Megan given those odds.

But most Canadian airmen did not feel that way. Though eighteen thousand Canadian aircrew would lose their lives in the European theater before the war was done, an even higher number than that ignored the odds and married British girls.

My memories of Megan were interrupted by a dig in the ribs.

"What the hell are you into right now?" Richard demanded. "You have a far away look in your eyes."

"I was thinking of your lovely bride Mavis, then my mind drifted back to Megan. What an idiot I was, not to go back to see her after my tour was over."

"You're right. You were an idiot. I met Megan, remember, when you and I went to Swansea on our way to visit Auntie Marion at Pontardawe. The girl was obviously rather fond of you. And she certainly had all the right parts in all the right places, if you'll pardon me for saying so. God only knows what kept you from doing what comes naturally. Some fighter pilot you are."

"Knock it off, smart ass. If you met Megan, then you know how strict her folks were." The train rumbled on. I shrugged. "I'll get out of this rut one of these days. You're not the only one who knows how to play the mating game."

Richard had joined the air force first. Six months later I gave notice at the bank in Grandeur and two months after that I was in the Royal Canadian Air Force, too. The simple fact was that I could not let Richard get ahead of me. My father had never urged either one of us to enlist, but he was proud when we did. Everyone was caught up in the drama and adventure of the war. I had no doubts about what we were fighting for. Hitler was bent on conquering the world; now he would pay the price. My first posting was to the Manning Depot in Brandon, Manitoba. It bore no resemblance to the posters that had invited me to join the RCAF. We were billeted in the old winter fair building. Dubbed "The Horse Palace" by some of the airmen, it was a huge building filled with steel double-decker bunks, which were about as comfortable as you would expect. It was a long way from the comfort and warmth of our farm home.

I had never seen such a motley crew as I met at Manning Depot. By the end of my first day some fifteen hundred airmen filled the "Palace." They were all shapes and sizes. Boxer shorts, dirty shorts, or no shorts at all. There were Greek gods, skinny guys, and plump guys. There were shy guys, brazen guys, and guys just like myself. There were brooding men, shouting and cursing men, and those who attempted to project a bravado they did not really feel. There were those who hid their private parts and those who flaunted them. There were those whose private parts were almost hidden in their pubic hair. I didn't stare at those who were less well endowed than myself, but I couldn't help feeling a tiny surge of self-satisfaction when they came into view. As for those well-hung chaps who flaunted their gorgeous georgies, I tried to ignore them. In all this I realized how completely naïve I really was. Never in my life had I ever come close to a scene like this. In high school we were modest in the locker room, but this was different. By turns I was scared, confused, and at times exhilarated. I had always cherished my privacy, but in this environment there were many times when a well-placed towel was all I had for protection. As time went on, I shed my towels, and Manning Depot unfolded in a way that even a shy farm boy could manage.

My first sleep soon arrived. The lights went out and the men shuffled about to find some comfort in those strange double-decker metal bunks. They stretched row upon row, the length of a football field. I wondered if others were experiencing the same jumble of emotions that I felt. In the darkness it was possible to pretend I was alone. The sheets were hard, but the bed was bearable. For a few minutes there was complete silence. Then out of nowhere a guttural voice cried out, "Fuck the east!" Instantly, as if led by a choirmaster, the reply came, "Fuck the west!" Soon the great hall was rocking with catcalls and four-letter words. None of this was especially shocking to me: suspicion of the eastern elite was in the blood of Prairie folks, and easterners returned the compliment by calling us "stubble jumpers." The exchange of epithets in the great hall was finally broken by a yell from the corporal. "Go to sleep, you bastards!" This settled the place down, and men did a final turn under their blankets. It was to become a nightly routine, strange but somehow comforting.

As Grandeur grew ever closer, my thoughts were in turmoil, haunted by the memories of the past. I had left Dad at the train station almost exactly five years earlier. It was a carbon copy of hundreds of other stations across Canada. Dad was a sentimental man, but not in an obvious way. When we said our goodbyes he gripped my hands and then squeezed my shoulder once. I left him alone on the platform. Mum had not come to the station to see me off. She held her emotions even more tightly than Dad. I had said goodbye to her in the farmyard as bravely and calmly as I could, and she did likewise, but what she did when Dad and I left the farmyard I could never know.

Mum and Dad had good reason to be afraid. Richard would eventually be shot down. Most of his crew escaped by parachute, but Rich's parachute was so badly damaged by shrapnel that he had to stay with his burning plane all the way down. Amazingly he managed to bring it to the ground with some semblance of control. Even more amazingly, he alone of his crew evaded capture and returned to England, to fly with his squadron again. My wartime experience was different but just as remarkable: I did two tours as a fighter pilot and lived to talk about it. It was all history now, but in that history the word 'luck' had played a major part in bringing Richard and me back to Grandeur.

Richard nudged me out of my daydream and whispered, "We're there."

This was the moment for which we had hoped and prayed a hundred or more times. My mouth was dry and I could feel my heart pounding. My legs were rubber.

My brother, as usual, kept his head. "Come on, grab your bags. Let's get into the slipstream of that conductor. He's heading for the door." I didn't have a chance to reply before the screech of steel wheels sliding on steel rails overwhelmed everything. But it didn't matter. Richard and I were like five-year old kids on Christmas morning. "Home, home," I said out loud to no one in particular, and Richard smiled at me.

I was not a religious man, but in my own quiet way

I was thanking God for our safe return to Grandeur. The first few minutes after I stepped from the train were shrouded in a haze. It was unlike anything I had ever felt before. I would seem to levitate one second, and then stumble to earth the next. It seemed like all Grandeur was there, Mum, Dad, good friends, vague acquaintances, and many people I couldn't have named if I'd tried. The hugs, the kisses, the shoulder-pats, and the congratulations were wonderful, but in my daze it was as though I had stepped into a dream. Was I really in Grandeur? In my confusion my mind took an unlikely refuge in yet another memory from the war. I was in the air over London in my Spitfire when a Messerschmitt burst out of the clouds. I should have lost my life that day. There was a burst of cannon fire, and before I could react my propeller had disintegrated and the Rolls Royce engine of my plane was on fire. I sideslipped in a desperate effort to keep the flames away from the cockpit. But other damage to my aircraft steepened my dive. For a moment the aircraft was uncontrollable, and I was too low to bail out. My aircraft finally reacted to the backward pressure on the control column, but I was almost touching the treetops as I came out of the dive. I felt utterly drained by my struggle with the terrible wrenching G-forces, but there was no time to rest, the Messerschmitt was still on my tail. I had to get my plane down or die in the attempt. The next burst from the German's fighter cannon missed, and while he was coming around for another shot I put down in a farmer's field. My Spitfire was burning furiously. I knew the gasoline tanks would explode at any second. I jumped and hit the ground running. A few seconds later I was knocked down by the explosion. Nevertheless I would, and did, fly again.

It was all in the past now. I was safe again with all my family and friends in Grandeur. Words would not come that could express my feelings regarding my hometown. After leaving the platform and making my way back to the house with Mum and Dad, the joy completely overwhelmed me and I found myself doing something I had long ago promised to do. I left the house quietly, and alone, and unashamedly knelt down to kiss the ground. Tears flowed down my face. It was not just that I was home; it was that I had come home after having served my country and done what had to be done to keep it safe.

The doctor had said the terrors of war would fade, and he was right, but it would take a long time, and being back in Grandeur was no magic cure. For a long time I was still trapped in the terror and I wondered if it would ever leave. One minute I would be staring across a familiar field, and the next I would be back in the cockpit, keying myself up to launch yet another attack. This time we were going to attack out of the sun, which would surprise the gunners below–or so we hoped. With a bit of luck, we would be in and out before they had time to line us up in their sights. I cast a swift look behind me to see if the rest of the flight had formed up as they were supposed to in close line to my rear. It was vital that when I dove, they followed instantly, as if linked to me by a chain. At first my hand was trembling violently, but instinct and training took over. I gave my instruments one last check, tightened my safety straps and huddled down in my seat for better protection. My fingers stopped shaking.

Now they were in perfect harmony with the controls. The wings of my Spitfire were like extra limbs. My body was a part of the machine. The powerful Rolls Royce engine seemed to vibrate in my very bones. Not for the first time I was seized by the thrill of combat. Then I threw the stick forward and the Spitfire accepted the challenge. The rest of the flight at my back was swept along with me. Almost immediately the gunners below opened fire and the sky was filled with deadly missiles. Scarlet red flashes appeared on all sides, rocketing and buffeting my aircraft violently. Unscathed by the barrage, my Spitfire plunged down and down. Yet at least two of my mates had been hit; I saw one of the stricken Spitfires stagger violently as a purple fireball exploded behind its tail. I could see the pilot trying to level out, but to no avail. Within a few moments his plane was descending almost vertically. This put an enormous strain on the wings. A few seconds more and both were swept off, fluttering to the ground like autumn leaves. The end for the shattered remains of the aircraft came far below in a mighty, vicious burst of flame. The war, and so much more, was over for that poor pilot.

My application for university was accepted in the fall of 1945 and time seemed to fly. I was given permission to start classes later than was usual, but this meant I really had to get my butt into gear for the balance of the year. I nevertheless managed to spend many weekends on the farm with my Mum and Dad. I couldn't believe the change that had taken place in my lifestyle. I still enjoyed driving a tractor or a combine, but I now had no interest in becoming a farmer, even though I knew the days were not far off when my parents would have to leave the farm.

I recalled tracking down Richard the day before his wife Mavis was to arrive in Grandeur. "How are you bearing up?" I hollered, just a bit louder than was necessary. There was a twinkle in Richard's eye and he knew that I was there for no other reason than to give him a hard time.

"I'm bearing up very well, thank you. I suppose you've come to give me some advice on how to handle myself when Mavis arrives tomorrow?"

"The thought crossed my mind. Maybe you should wait at home and let me meet Mavis at the train station. That way you could conserve your strength." I grinned. "And I'd bring her to you eventually."

Richard laughed sardonically. "You're a smart ass."

"I'm just trying to look out for you."

"Don't worry about me. If I've got more than I can handle, you just spend some time thinking of the excitement I'm going to have trying to handle it. But it's nice to know my brother spends so much time thinking of my well-being. Why don't you scout around and find yourself the kind of trouble you think I'm going to be having tomorrow night."

Richard was nothing if not a cocky bastard. I loved him, but at that instant I was sorely tempted to throw Joan Hansen's name at him, to ask why, if he was such an expert with women, he couldn't make his relationship with her stick. But I thought better of it. And when Mavis arrived, she was just as I remembered her from the wedding in England.

CHAPTER TWO

Squadron Leader Richard Drake

My train was only thirty minutes out of Grandeur, Saskatchewan. I had not been home for three years, since the tenth of September, 1942, and there had been many times during those three years when I doubted that I would ever see my home again. But here I was, my twin brother Clinton beside me, watching the prairie sweeping by, in the happy knowledge that not far ahead there was a train station with my parents and who knew how many other well-wishers waiting for me. If only Mavis could have been with me! Unfortunately it would be another month before my British wife of eleven months would be allowed to leave Wolverhampton and join me in Canada. The very thought of Mavis filled me with so much joy that it almost surpassed the happiness of returning safely to my hometown. And that return was certainly something of a miracle. Not only had I completed forty bombing missions in my Lancaster bomber, I had been shot down, evaded capture, and managed to make my way through Germany and France to rescue.

I gave my brother Clinton a dig in the ribs. "Are you

finished your dreaming yet? I was just watching you and tried to read your mind, but I got nowhere."

"Oh, I was thinking about a lot of different things. I think I'd like to go to university, maybe get a degree as a chartered accountant."

"That's pretty fast thinking, isn't it? We're not even home yet! Since you seem to have all the ideas, what do you see me doing?"

"I imagine you in some kind of a business. And I'd do your books."

"My God, Clint, you do have an imagination." He didn't respond, and I thought he might not have appreciated my attitude. "Well, there's nothing wrong with that, I suppose. Anyway, all I can think about now is not being with Mavis on her twenty-first birthday. Sending her a telegram was not exactly what I had in mind. But it's the best I could do."

Clint was typically blunt. "Just find a nice house for her to move into once she gets here, and she'll forget that the two of you were ever apart."

He was right, of course. It was well past time for me to figure out how I might put food on my new wife's table. But how would I ever settle down to an eight-to-five job after what I'd been through? My obvious path was to go into farming, or possibly university like Clint, but neither option really appealed to me. It was just as well that I had been careful with my pilot's salary. I would be able to buy Mavis the home she deserved. But as for the rest, I hadn't got a clue.

My mind and my memory still struggled with the day I left Grandeur. Joan Hanson, my fiancée, had been there with my Mum and Dad and other well-wishers.

Joan and I had spent the previous night alone together at the Hanson house, and our petting and lovemaking had been moving into new and unfamiliar territory. Joan seemed determined to take me beyond boundaries that we had previously respected. I was not ready, and I said so, bringing the encounter to an abrupt end. Since that night, I had associated with dozens of men who seemed to live for their next sexual experience. So why had I missed my opportunity with Joan? In the months that followed it crossed my mind that something else was holding me back. Could it be that I didn't really want to marry this girl? As the whirlwind of the war overtook me I could hardly remember our engagement. And then I met Mavis. I couldn't blame Joan for being bitter; the letter that came when she returned the engagement ring had a rather nasty bite to it. But if Joan was to continue feeling that way, perhaps it would be better for all concerned if Mavis and I lived somewhere other than Grandeur.

The train had reached the outskirts of Grandeur. I nudged Clint again to bring him out of his daydream and stood up and gathered his kit bag and various belongings together. There was a gift for Mum, and another one for Dad. I straightened my uniform and adjusted my cap. There was an almighty squeal of steel on steel as we made our way to the door between the two carriages. Then the conductor brushed by us and opened the door. He placed a metal stool on the platform. We stepped down, and there they were, Mum and Dad, looking exactly as they did three long years earlier. When the tears and hugging had subsided, other well-wishers stepped forward to welcome us home. The owner of the "Grandeur Weekly

Journal" was present for the occasion and cameras were clicking. It was a strange feeling to be the center of attention like this. But it felt right, too. Clint and I had both earned some congratulations. Like the old saying said, we had gone off as boys, and the war had made us men.

Like Clint I had experienced some bad nights lately. Would Grandeur folks ever be able to relate to the last three years of our lives? How, for example, would I ever be able to communicate the terrors of mission twelve to the Ruhr valley of Germany? At the very moment my bomb aimer had called "bombs away" over the intercom, another of my squadron's Lancasters, next on the bombing run and with all its bombs still on board, received a direct hit and disintegrated in a huge explosion behind us. My own Lancaster, having just dropped twelve thousand pounds of bombs, was so light that the force of this explosion threw the aircraft totally out of control. The instruments went crazy. The engine stalled. The plane veered left and into a spin. It was true that I had gone through training on how to recover from "unusual" positions while flying on instruments. This was night, however, and it was wild out there. No bomber crew looked forward to raids on the Ruhr. It was the home of steel mills and the main hub of manufacturing in Germany. It was home to more German fighter squadrons than any other area in Europe, with the greatest concentration of searchlights and radar-controlled anti-aircraft batteries. Yes, it was wild out there. We seemed to be plummeting through hell; I had on full right rudder, I had pulled all power from the four engines, and the control column was fully forward, but still the air speed indicator was on the red line and my altimeter was unwinding mercilessly. It was only with agonizing slowness that the hundred foot of wingspan began to respond. I eased the control column back ever so slowly, back, back, until my air speed was at two hundred twenty nautical miles per hour, and I could afford to ease the power on again. That was one story I would never tell my parents.

So what stories could I tell them? One could not be avoided: the tale of my forty-one day escape through Germany and France after being shot down. It had already filtered back to Canada, albeit in heavily edited form. I might be able to play it down if I was having a beer with my chums and the question came up, as it undoubtedly would. But with Mom and Dad it would be different. They knew the Royal Air Force had given me a special leave to recuperate after my escape to freedom, but they could only guess about my condition and how long it had taken me to return to flying duties. They knew my letters to them had been subject to strict censorship; they would now want those gaps filled in. Why did this fill me with such dread? Because of the sheer horror of the story. It was bad enough that I had to live through it. I could not and would not subject my parents to the pressure and the stress and the horror of those forty-one days.

Which made it all the harder for me to understand what had come over me on the fourth day of my recuperation leave. I had thankfully accepted the hospitality of Mavis's parents, intending to stay with them until the air force doctors declared me fit to return to flying. In the meantime Mavis had been granted a special leave of her own due to the circumstances surrounding the illness of her fiancée. Every morning and every afternoon, come rain or shine, Mavis had me walking. On the fourth afternoon we sat on a park bench for a rest. We never had any shortage of things to talk about, but this day was different. "Could you tell me about your escape?" she asked quietly. At first I thought it would be enough just to touch on my experiences before we got on with our walking. It didn't work out that way. I don't remember where I started, or exactly what I told her, but as I talked and talked a weight seemed to lift from my shoulders. My tongue was on a mission that had to be completed. I told of the terror that gripped me, the aching hunger and the terrible stomach pains, the headaches, the unrelenting closeness of death. It was once-in-a-lifetime therapy that allowed me to tell my story to someone that I loved and trusted, and with whom I already knew I wanted to spend the rest of my life. I had not known it beforehand, but some unconscious part of me must have realized that I needed to unload the memory from my mind at least once if I was going to have any chance of living a normal life again.

Mum and Dad were extremely understanding and slowly but surely I adjusted back to peacetime. I spent much of my time during the weeks before Mavis arrived trying to figure out what I was going to do with myself. One day I borrowed Dad's truck and went into Grandeur. I ran into some old friends and agreed to join them at the hotel for a beer. This was a mistake. Some of the old regulars were there, and there was no way I could restrict myself to only one glass of beer as I had planned going in. I was up to four glasses before I left. So I was pretty loose when I sat down that night to write my daily letter to Mavis:

Darling Mavis. I have just come from the pub. They're called beer parlors over here, by the way. I've told you a lot of good things about Canada and Saskatchewan, but believe it or not, women are not allowed in our beer parlors. Yes, it's stupid, and a wee bit archaic. It's changing, though. In Alberta, the next province over, they now have beer parlor rooms set aside for ladies and escorts, where women can go as long as they are chaperoned. If you're reading this at bedtime, I'm sure the last two sentences will make you laugh yourself to sleep. While you're in that bed, grab the pillow and pretend it's me. On second thought, that might be hard on the pillow. Tomorrow, I'm going house-hunting. I'll do my best, but I'm sorry to say that we still don't have indoor plumbing here in Grandeur. I know I told you this before, but it's still true. The water comes into our house in a pail and goes out in a pail. The toilets are still in wooden outhouses at the end of a boardwalk. They do not flush. Yes, you have to come back into the house to wash your hands. But darling you can be sure that when I next get my hands on you, you won't care whether we have running water or not! And if it makes you feel any better, apparently there's going to be a vote to authorize the sale of debentures to pay for building a sewer and water system very soon. It won't be ready by the time you get here, but I'm sure it will be here in time to save our marriage.

Your loving husband Richard is getting sexier and hornier as the days go by, but he has a special mechanism that only allows his sex drive to work with one girl. Maybe you've heard of her, she's a beautiful girl from Wolverhampton named Mavis. That's the girl I'm talking about and dreaming about. I started this letter by telling you I had been in the pub. Glasses of beer sell for ten cents here in Grandeur, and it would take at least two of our glasses to make one of your pints. Now you know I'm not a big drinker. But they love us chaps who were over in England during the war so much that we cannot buy a drink for ourselves. And they have a special love for the air force guys, so you can imagine how hard it is to have just one drink. I had to have four before I could make my escape. So you see, for all the negative things I might have said about Grandeur in this letter, the fact is that the people themselves are very friendly. They will love you, Mavis. Certainly there is a small town attitude, where everyone knows almost everyone else, but I think your personality is made especially for a place like this. You are one in a million and I am so sure it will all work out. My major project will be fighting off those damn farmers when they meet you. Maybe one of the wealthy ones will try to have me done away with, just to be able to get at you! Well, I think that's a problem I can handle.

All my love, Richard.

PS—I've shown your picture around a wee bit. Ask your mom if it's too late for you to have a sister.

I began to look for a home. I struck gold when I found a nice old house on a corner lot, owned by a man who was just retiring from one of the companies that bought up grain from local farmers. He knew the Drake family well and knew of me, and seemed to like the idea of an air force veteran buying his home. So he reduced the price to thirty-nine hundred dollars, and even agreed to leave behind many items that could come in handy for newlyweds. We shook hands on the deal. With that, Mavis and I had a home. Furniture would be a bit sparse for a while, but more would come as soon as we got on our feet.

About a week later my mom took a message from Art Wilson. Art was another old friend of the family, and the owner of a garage and farm machinery dealership. He wanted to know if I would meet him for lunch the next day. Why not, I thought. When I got there it turned out that he had more on his mind than idle chitchat. Art told me that he and his partner Jim were tired of the business world. They were well over sixty years old, and wanted to take it easy. He asked me point-blank if I would be interested in buying them out and taking over the dealership myself.

For a moment I was too stunned to speak. I was very interested, but where would I get the money? Art waved this worry aside. He said that he and Jim were willing to accept a down payment and then carry the balance of the loan themselves. As if that were not incentive enough, he told me that the deal would include three adjoining parcels of land in which they had purchased a fifty percent interest a few years earlier; the remaining fifty percent was held by another Grandeur businessman, Russ Kessler. And as a final sweetener, Art offered to stay on for at least six months and maybe a bit longer in order to teach me the ins and outs of the operation. Tempted as I was, it was not a decision I could make without Mavis, who was not due to arrive for another two weeks. Both Art and Jim understood, and they suggested that in the meantime I should spend some time at the garage to get a better sense of what the business was all about. I jumped at the offer; and that very night I wrote another letter to Mavis.

Darling Mavis. Things are happening. It is only about two letters ago that I mentioned that I was still trying to figure out what to do with my life in terms of work. Well, a very interesting and I think exciting opportunity has just been thrown in my lap. My mum received a phone call from Art Wilson, a businessman in Grandeur. He and a partner operate a sales-and-service centre for farm machinery and cars and trucks (lories, to you). He's a great guy. Before the war, I would drop in to see him all the time. Anyway, I've seen him a couple of times since coming home, but today he really surprised me. The man has spent almost his whole life in building up his business, but he and his partner are now old and ready to retire. Neither of them have any sons to take over for them, so they would like me to buy them out. They have no illusions about our finances, but for whatever reason it doesn't seem to matter to them. Maybe it's my war record, or maybe it's just how friendly I've been to Art over the years. Whatever the reason, they seem to have real faith in me and are ready to take a gamble.

Don't worry, my love, nothing will be decided until you get here and we have a chance to talk about it. I'm going to spend some time at Grandeur Ford and Farm Equipment (that's the name of the business) and I will let you know the kind of vibes I get from being around there. But I've got to admit my gut is already telling me this is a great opportunity. Yes, I know I've got to be careful. But the last time I had such a positive gut feeling was when I met you, and look how well that turned out. Good night, sweetheart. With all my Love,

Richard.

On October 4th, 1945, I received word that I was to go to Regina and be officially discharged from the air force. With that my war was officially over. I would be lying if I said that I did not have a pang or two of regret when I watched the stroke of the pen that formalized my return to civilian life. I was already a little nostalgic for the perks that came with being a Squadron Leader: constantly being saluted and called "sir," having a batman look after my every need, and the power to give orders and have them carried out more or less instantly, to name just a few. I had become accustomed to being a somebody. Now I was just Richard Drake again. It would take some getting used to. But at least Mavis was finally on her way to join me.

The last few days of our separation seemed to last a lifetime. My thoughts were Mavis, Mavis, Mavis. The war had been a terror, but it had given me a beautiful, thoughtful, and loving wife. Her telegram from Winnipeg on our last night apart gave me such a lift that I could hardly believe it. I tried to put myself in Mavis's mind. She had never even seen me in civilian clothes, only in the uniform of a Squadron Leader in the Royal Canadian Air Force. There were no medals, no DFC, no squadron leader rings, no one saluted me now. I was just a farmer's son in regular slacks, shirt, and jacket. When Mavis got off that train, would things be different? She had lived for the first twenty-one years of her life with running hot and cold water. I would take her to a home with no running water, no inside toilets. Just a two-story, three-bedroom house on a nice, quiet, well-treed corner lot.

I knew that I had to knock these thoughts out of my mind. I had total faith in Mavis. In her own way she was a tough girl. Deep down I knew that our love was strong enough to see us through almost any difficulty. We would have a bathroom in the house as soon as the sewer and water mains were put in, which I understood would be quite soon. In the meantime, Mavis would get used to the big washbasins sitting on the little table in our bedroom. Grandeur women were accustomed to washing themselves with a washcloth and soap, and then pouring the dirty water into a pail beside the little table. Perhaps the most shocking thing for Mavis would come one morning in wintertime when she woke up and found ice in the water jug; a temperature of forty degrees below zero–Fahrenheit–could easily lead to situations like that. But brave young wives had come to Grandeur long before Mavis and made it work. She had read my letters and knew what was waiting for her.

I was amazed at the number of people who came to the station to meet Mavis. A part of me wished that they had all stayed home so the two of us could be alone, but I was also proud and glad that so many people were interested. I wanted her to see that Grandeur had a small town mentality and that she was welcome. Naturally my parents were there, and Clinton had driven down from Saskatoon. I glanced at my watch. The train would arrive in a few minutes. I could feel my heart hammering. And why was my mouth dry? I marveled at the hold this little British girl had on me. I heard the train whistle at a railroad crossing on the edge of town and the familiar sound of a steam engine. Finally I could see the smoke from the big old coal-burning locomotive. The engineer was applying brakes and the slack was being taken up in the couplers between the carriages. Mum, Dad and Clint pushed me to the front of the well-wishers, who gracefully moved back three or four feet so that the family could be closest to the train. It was clearly not the first time the conductor had seen such a homecoming. He managed to stop the coach with the door right in front of me, and after opening the door he stepped out with a special little stool. Then as if by magic Mavis was in my arms. We hugged and kissed and slowly I pushed Mavis a few inches back so that I could look directly into her eyes. "Darling, I'm in a fantastic mood." Mavis squealed a little squeal of delight and hugged me again. I was now so excited that I could hardly breathe. "Mavis, you've done it again," I whispered. "You've taken my breath away."

"I love you, Richard. And I've missed you so much." She put her hands on my face, and rubbed away a little tear that had appeared in the corner of my eye.

There were a few more moments when no more words needed to be said. But I knew this was not only my moment. "There are a couple of people I want you to meet, Mavis." With that, we turned around and I called out, "Mum and Dad, this is Mavis."

It was an unforgettable scene. My mother never spoke a word, but stepped forward and gave Mavis a hug. Dad did likewise and kissed her cheek. Clinton, a little more awkwardly, shook her hand. But his voice was warm. "Welcome home, Mavis." It was a signal for the whole crowd to start clapping and cheering.

CHAPTER THREE

Emma Jones

Art and Jim greeted me warmly as I walked into Grandeur Ford. I had worked there full-time during the holidays in July and August, and now that I was back to school, I still came in every Wednesday and Thursday from four to seven in the evening. My duties were pretty basic: cleaning cars and trucks, sweeping garage floors, and pumping gas. When they were really short-staffed I worked behind the parts counter. I could not have asked for a better pair of bosses than Art and Jim. Now Art told me that he would be going down to the train station in a few minutes; the Drake twins were coming home from the war.

There was admiration in Art's voice, which didn't really surprise me. I did not know a lot about the war because my dad was too old to join up, and there were no boys in our family, but being from Grandeur I had heard a lot of praise for the Drake twins. Over two hundred soldiers, sailors, and airmen had enlisted from our town. Twenty-five or more pilots, navigators, and other aircrew had been killed. But the Drake twins were very close to being celebrities for what they had done. Clinton was a fighter pilot with one of the famous Spitfire squadrons. He had shot down five German aircraft and won the Distinguished Flying Cross. Richard had flown bombers, been shot down, and by some extraordinarily skill or luck managed to make his way across occupied France and back to England. He too had won the Distinguished Flying Cross. Richard's engagement to Joan Hanson had been big news in our little town. I was only fifteen at the time, but I remembered how the story had buzzed around my school. It had seemed so romantic. I knew Joan Hanson, and I happened to be at the railroad station on the day Richard came home on leave after receiving his wings. I would never forget how handsome he looked. There were very few girls who would not have jumped at a chance of a date with him. Then came the explosive news that sent the school gossip to a fever-pitch. Richard Drake had married a girl in England. Everyone naturally wondered what had happened between Richard and Joan. I had not talked to her, but mutual friends had told me that she was not taking it too well. In fact the word was that she was more than a little bit annoyed with Richard. But nobody really seemed to know the circumstances, so who was I to judge? Grandeur was a small town, so I figured I would hear the truth eventually.

None of this had altered Art's high opinion of Richard. He had told me before how he had known Richard since he was a little boy, when he would come into the dealership with his dad James Drake. It was not long after the Drake twins returned from the war that Richard started coming in to see Art again. The visits became more and more frequent, and one day, during a coffee break, I overheard that Richard was interested in buying the business. Art and Jim had started the business many years earlier, and were ready to enjoy a well-earned retirement. But they wanted to be sure that what they had built would pass into the right hands. They could think of no better man than a war hero like Richard Drake. I soon learned that Richard wanted a heart-to-heart discussion with his wife Mavis before making a final decision.

I was busy cleaning up a vehicle when Richard brought Mavis to see the garage. She seemed like a lovely person in every respect, with a beautiful smile, a shapely figure, and the ability to make a room feel warmer just by stepping inside. Everyone who met her loved her. After Richard and Mavis's next visit, which took place in the office and lasted for well over an hour, Art walked by and whispered to me, "it's a done deal."

The change of ownership took place very quickly. Under the terms of the deal Art would stay on for at least six months in order to familiarize Richard and Mavis with the unbelievable amount of information that was needed to operate the business. All of the staff who had worked with Jim and Art would stay on as well. As time went on, I realized that Art's trust in Richard and Mavis had not been misplaced. They worked long hours and took an interest in every aspect of the operation. It was obvious that Grandeur Ford was in good hands.

It was a difficult time for any automotive dealership. The transition back from the wartime economy was confused, many factories were still not producing enough farm machinery, or cars, or trucks, so we didn't have much to sell. But by the third year of the Drake's tenure, new cars and trucks were more plentiful. The business really began to thrive. One afternoon Mavis called me into the office. "Are you happy working with us, Emma?"

"Oh yes, very much so."

"Good, because Richard and I think the world of you. I don't know how much you know of our plans, but we're planning on expanding. We'd like to build another big garage where we could recondition the cars, trucks, and farm machinery that we get as trade-ins."

"Sounds great," I said.

Mavis smiled. "I'm glad you think so. How would you like to run it for us?"

"Me?" was all I could manage in reply.

"I think you'd be more than capable, Emma. Of course you would have to take a special course first, in Winnipeg. It would take the best part of a year, I'm afraid. Would you be willing to do that?"

She suggested I sleep on it. I already knew what my answer would be, however. "I would love to take the course, Mavis," I told her the next morning. "I won't let you down." She gave me one of her warm hugs. "I know you won't."

I studied hard, and my grades were good. In ten months I graduated and returned to Grandeur Ford and Farm Equipment. My new position was supposed to be purely supervisory. I was not a welder or a metal worker or a painter; but I had learned how to cost out the reconditioning work, to see which jobs were worthwhile and which would price a unit out of the market. But there would be far more to it than

I initially realized. My first step was always to look at the amount that Richard and Mavis had invested in the used vehicle or piece of equipment. I would then check out the price we expected to get on resale. This would give me a good idea of how much I could spend on the vehicle or machine in preparing it for market. Quite unexpectedly I had become a key part of the whole operation of Grandeur Ford and Farm Equipment. Such responsibility could be stressful at times, especially if a unit stayed on the sales lot too long because I had allowed too much money to be spent on reconditioning it. But this didn't happen very often, and became a very rare occurrence as I gained more and more experience. Life was good.

CHAPTER FOUR

Joan Hanson

I was in my bedroom, putting on the last of my make-up. I liked what I saw in the mirror. I knew that I had a lot going for me, whether Richard Drake wanted to admit it or not. He was coming home today, after three years away. There was a time when I would have gone to the ends of the earth for that man, but that seemed like a lifetime ago.

I had become engaged to Richard the very same day that they pinned his wings on his uniform at Number Ten Service Flying Training School near Dauphin, Manitoba. James and Edna Drake had offered me a ride to join them at the ceremony. It was a spectacle like I had never seen before and would probably never see again. The premier of the province was there, as well as several high-ranking officers from the air force. The parade of new pilots was done with machine-like precision, and Richard looked so fantastic as he marched past. The Drakes and I were so proud. There was a beautiful fly-pass of twin-engine Cessna Crane aircraft, just like the one on which Richard had trained. There was another familiar face in the parade, too: Rex

Doncaster, who had gone to high school with us in Grandeur, and was now getting his wings as well. One by one the forty-eight graduating pilots marched up to the reviewing stand, the last survivors of a grueling programme which had seen over fifty other men who had entered pilot training at the same time shunted aside. Having "washed out," as the air force described it, these rejects had been moved to other aircrew trades. They would go on to serve their country as navigators, gunners, wireless operators, and bomb aimers. But the glory, as they well knew, was reserved for the pilots.

The parade dismissed, Richard made his way to his parents and me. He was one proud and handsome man with his shiny new wings. He knew that he was to be posted overseas, but first he would have fifteen days embarkation leave in Grandeur. That night there was a huge "wings parade" dance in the hangar. Before it was over we *were* engaged.

When we returned to Grandeur, Richard was treated like a king. He could not pay for a meal in the café, or a beer in the beer parlor, because there was always someone who insisted on paying for him. It was hard for Rich to resist this adulation, especially since he didn't really want to. He was enjoying himself immensely, and I couldn't really blame him. My beef was that I was being robbed of time with him. I loved to see him have a drink or two with his mates, but because of the stupid law barring women from pubs I couldn't be there. On top of that, his mom and dad wanted to spend a lot of time with him as well. The problem was that I loved him too much. Yes, loving too much seemed to be where my trouble started with Rich. He was old-fashioned in his ways. He had the same urges as any other healthy man of his age, but he just wouldn't let himself go. My own view of the question of sex was different. Why shouldn't we enjoy each other as much as we wanted? After all, we were engaged. It was common knowledge that air force men were issued what was called a "French safe," or condom. Having lived by the moral code of the day, I was still a virgin. But I did not see anything wrong with losing my virginity to my husband-to-be.

In all this I don't think I was anything more or less than a perfectly normal nineteen-year old girl. Before Richard my closest call, sexually speaking, was with a guy named Jerry. Jerry was known to be a devil, but even though girls did not see him as husband material, he was a good dancer and great for a risqué date. I knew I was very attractive and this was right up Jerry's alley. On one particular night, I had been talked into one too many drinks. We were in the back of Jerry's car. Jerry knew how to turn me on, and I was very close to throwing caution to the winds. He already had his hand inside my panties when suddenly he pushed my own hand against his slacks. The shock of feeling his erection spooked me, and it was this that saved my virginity. Jerry was not happy with me. "You're a cockteaser," was his bitter comment, and it stung. But I did not regret how I had acted.

My last night with Richard was a night my life could have done without. We were alone on the chesterfield. I was prepared at that moment to let nature take its course. It was clear in my mind. Richard's right arm was around me, I was touching his left hand. But after a while, when it became clear that he was not going to push matters forward, I lost patience. He was going off to war the next day; for all I knew I might never see him again. I could not control myself any longer. I moved his hand so that it rested on my lap.

Richard stiffened, but not in the way I had hoped. He slowly eased both his hands away. "I'm not ready Joan. I'm sorry. Really I am. But the air force doctors have filled our heads so full of all the dangers of sex I just can't deal with this right now."

I started to cry. Richard held me. "Please, Joan, don't cry. Maybe I'm so old-fashioned that I don't deserve you. But what if we made love, and then a few months from now a letter came to me in England saying you were pregnant? Joan, I'm going into a dangerous business. You know how many pilots from Grandeur have already died. My mind is full enough without adding a new worry."

"But Rich," I pleaded, "we're engaged, and I love you. And you're leaving tomorrow. I was only doing what my mind and body wanted to do."

He shifted uncomfortably on the couch. "I'm sorry, Joan. For now, can we put the last minutes out of our minds? That's the best I can do."

The next few hours were the most difficult of my life. Rather than go our separate ways immediately, we sat on the chesterfield holding hands and pretending not to be uncomfortable. What made it even worse was the knowledge that if I had not moved Richard's hand in such a suggestive way to such a suggestive place, we would still have been in each other's arms. We would have been kissing and hugging and planning our future together. Instead I had made the one move that could change my last night with Rich from a night of love and hope to a night of awkwardness and doubt. I still didn't see that I had done anything wrong. We were engaged! I would gladly risk getting pregnant. If it happened, my parents would stand by me. The world was changing. Rich was making a mountain out of a molehill, I was sure of it. But I didn't say any of this to him.

Only the approach of midnight brought an excuse to escape. "Mom and Dad will be here any moment," I told him. "And your train leaves Grandeur at seven in the morning. So I need to get a bit of sleep so I can look beautiful to see you off." I spoke with a forcefulness I did not feel.

"Yeah, and I still have to get all my gear together. I better get going." The words were hardly out of Richard's mouth when noises at the back door turned out to be my parents.

I was in bed by one a.m. and woken up by my mother at five-thirty. "I thought you'd need a bit of time to get beautiful," Mom hollered. She was far more lighthearted than I felt. But I put on a brave face at the railroad station. The way I hugged and kissed Richard, no one would have guessed the strain that had come into our relationship. The train pulled out on time. I stood alone with my thoughts on the platform until Richard's waving arm disappeared. I wondered if the goodbye would have been any different if we had made love last night. Then Mom took my arm, and I was back to reality.

We continued to write each other regularly, but even Richard's letters seemed restrained. As time went by I found myself becoming even more frustrated, if that was possible, and then finally angry. I began to realize that time would not sort out the difficulties that had developed in our relationship. Rich just didn't make sense. Was he tired of me already? Did he want to break it off? Then why didn't he just have the guts to say so? Instead he seemed content that I should make a complete fool of myself waiting for him, just as I had made a fool of myself on the night we didn't make love.

The war news never seemed to get any better. There were further casualties among the flying men from Grandeur. Then came the worst news of all: Richard and his whole crew were missing. His letters to me stopped. I had to ask myself, was this the end? Was the man I had loved so dearly a prisoner of war, or dead? Of course my friends and family were a great support, but they had no idea how the relationship between Richard and me had changed. The last letter I had got from him could just as easily have been written to a sister for all the romantic content in it. He admitted to dating other girls and going to shows and dances. And yet, in spite of everything, I found myself crying over and over again at the thought of what might have happened to him.

I immediately went to see James and Edna Drake. They soon received another telegram with the Red Cross notification of Richard's aircraft being shot down. Six of his crew were confirmed as prisoners of war. Yet there was no record of Richard. His aircraft had burned when it crashed, but his body was not found in the wreckage. So we were all left in a terrible kind of limbo, not knowing whether we should mourn or not. A long, sad month went by without further information. Then, in the middle of the second month, Edna Drake phoned me with the most amazing news. Richard had made his way safely through Germany and France and was back in England. Back with his old air force squadron. He had lived to fly again.

For a while I hoped that this awful experience might have changed Richard for the better. But the first letter I received after his escape, which came about ten days after his mom's call, made it clear that nothing had changed, at least not as far as the two of us were concerned. He was as distant as ever. He said that he hoped he had not put me through too much of an emotional wringer by going off and getting himself shot down. But other than this he did not write a word about the dangers he had been through. Part of the reason, I supposed, was that he knew it would be censored anyway. The letter nevertheless seemed pretty thin. I thought he might have tried a bit harder to fill in the blanks. But that was Richard, always obsessed with following the rules.

I never mentioned to Rich's Mom that her son and I were not seeing eye-to-eye as we once did, but by now I was positive that Richard and I were through. I did not have to wait long for proof. A letter from Richard told me how he had been granted a special leave. He had met a twenty-one year old girl named Mavis Clifton. He was very sorry if he had caused me any pain, but he had to tell me that he had fallen madly in love with her. Then came yet another letter. Richard had asked Mavis Clifton to marry him, and she had accepted. God willing, he would bring her back to Grandeur one day. I read and reread the letter in disbelief. I was still wearing his engagement ring; he hadn't even had the decency to ask for it back before getting engaged to another woman! In a fury I tore the ring off my finger, threw it into an envelope, and wrote a very sharp letter to go with it. I mailed it off to him at once, in care of his squadron.

I was determined not to let the loss spoil my life. In as discreet a way as possible I dropped hints of my broken engagement to everyone I knew. My mom and dad were very supportive, and even Edna Drake phoned to say how sorry she was about how things had turned out. I wondered what I would do next. Should I grab the first good-looking man I met, take him to bed, and suggest an immediate marriage? I knew it was a dumb idea, and yet somehow the thought was often on my mind. Maybe I just wanted to make Richard jealous. In any case, my love for Richard had turned into something very much like hatred. The worst part was knowing how long I had let him walk all over me. If only all these idiots in Grandeur calling him a "hero" knew the truth. But they would not hear it from me. I was done with Richard Drake, forever.

CHAPTER FIVE

Rex Doncaster

The war was over, but I was still flying, having signed on for extra service with the Royal Air Force. Every day there were more people and supplies that needed to be sent over to Germany. It was an easy assignment, especially after what I had been through. I had flown thirty-nine bombing missions, the last on the seventh of March, 1945. I remembered it well, because that was the day my wife Thelma chose to announce that she was pregnant. She had known for a few days but had been reluctant to drop the news on me when I still had a couple more missions left on my tour; one of the most terrible worries for a bomber crew was to be shot down when they were only one or two flights from standing down.

A few days after finishing my tour, Clinton Drake came down to my base to say hello and to meet Thelma, who had moved into rented quarters nearby. Clint and I had gone to school together in Grandeur, and though we were not exactly best friends, I always thought of him as a decent guy. I couldn't say the same of his twin brother Richard. For as long as I could remember he had seemed so high and mighty, as if he were better than the rest of us. We had come very close to a full-blown fistfight in our last year of school, until our classmates intervened. Since that episode we had hardly exchanged a word with each other. So I was not exactly overjoyed to hear from Clint that his brother was going home safe and sound, with his Squadron Leader rings and a Distinguished Flying Cross. I had not won the DFC. In fact I did not even get my commission until I was well into my time in the air force. And Richard, I was sure, would never let me forget it.

My better instincts told me that I was being unfair. I had nothing to be ashamed of. In some ways what I had achieved was even more impressive than Richard, because unlike him I had never finished high school, which was usually the prerequisite to become a pilot. But I had desperately wanted to fly. I pestered my superiors to let me re-muster from ground crew to air, until they gave in and allowed me to take special classes that would give me the necessary qualifications. I studied my butt off; I knew I would get only one chance to pass the flight school entrance exam. The exam date came and the marks I received were satisfactory. I was posted to the RCAF initial training school in Saskatoon. It came as a shock when, during roll call on the very first day, I heard the name of my old nemesis being called out. Although we had not joined the air force together, fate had thrown us together yet again.

We both came through flight training, received our wings at the same ceremony at Dauphin, Manitoba, and then were posted to the same holding depot in

Halifax. But Richard was in the officer's quarters, and I was still stuck with the NCOs. We had orders to sail for Liverpool on the *Isle de France* and once again were given quarters commensurate with our rank. Our last posting together was in Bournemouth, on the south coast of England. From there I was posted to Banff, in Scotland, to continue my training on the twin-engine Airspeed Oxford. I did not hear where Richard ended up. The day after I left Bournemouth the hotel where we had stayed was bombed by Junker 88's, and twenty Canadian pilots were killed.

Up in Scotland I was immersed in training so intense that I had no time to think of anything other than the job at hand. This would have been challenging enough even in peacetime, but we were already in the gun sights of the Germans. One of my chums, flying an unarmed Oxford, was stalked and shot down by a German fighter plane lurking nearby. He was too low to bail out and died in the ensuing crash. Once I had mastered the Oxford, I was transferred to Wellsbourne to learn the Wellington, the mighty bomber with a ninety-foot wingspan. And then I moved on to another training unit and the four-engine Halifax. My first flight on the Halifax was a terrifying blur. I looked at the massive wall of instruments and controls in front of me and wondered how in the hell I would ever learn what all of them were about. But I did, just like hundreds of other pilots who were similarly terrified when entering the cockpit of a Halifax or a Lancaster for the first time.

In many ways the first minutes of a mission were the worst. If an engine failed on takeoff, you were dead. Three engines wouldn't lift a full load of bombs.

The routine of take-off was still fresh in my mind many years later. I set the directional gyro to the intended compass heading and did another instrument check. The pitot heat was on. The bomb doors were closed. Twenty degrees of flaps all set. I opened the four throttles slowly but firmly until the Halifax was straining against the brakes, the engine screaming. I waited for the green light that would be flashed from the control van over to my left. Ok to go! I released the brakes and moved the four throttles forward, leading with the two on the port side in order to counter the torque, then applying right rudder to check the swing. The heavily laden Halifax lurched forward. My eyes darted back and forth across the cockpit, from the rev counter to the directional indicator to the faint runway lights in the distance. I pushed the stick forward to get the tail up as quickly as possible and also to provide better steering. Then, as the tail rose, I pushed the throttle through the gate for maximum power, taking care to ensure that the rudder pedals were centered. I checked the heading yet again. I watched the airspeed creep past ninety, one hundred, and then a hundred and ten miles per hour. At this point I eased back on the stick; and suddenly we were off the runway. There was still danger. Any sudden yank and I could easily stall the aircraft. If an engine chose this moment to quit, as had been known to happen, my crew and I would all be dead ducks. Wheels up, throttle back to climbing power. Revs back to twenty-eight hundred and fifty. We dragged over the treetops for a few more miles, but now we could relax somewhat.

This was the sequence of events, familiar yet still

nerve-wracking, that opened every one of my thirty-nine missions. Inevitably some of these thirty-nine were more memorable than others. Probably the most memorable, and horrifying, was the flight we made one March day. Having guided my Halifax into the air, I turned her gingerly onto the first course and began the climb that would take us to the maximum height of twenty thousand feet. That day I could feel the sweat under my leather helmet trickling down my neck, but the heat felt good after the clammy conditions we had left on the ground. For the next little while, as we continued the long climb towards France, all was calm in the cabin. Then the first searchlights started to appear in our path. These were part of the coastal defenses which stretched the length of the continent: layer upon layer of searchlights and flack batteries guarded every foot of the French coast, and their range extended inland for twenty miles or more. It was always a relief to get through this zone of death unscathed.

The best friend of any bomber pilot was darkness. However, as I crossed the coast of France that particular night I realized that even though it was the middle of the night, it wasn't really dark. A full moon lay on the horizon to the south, playing on a very thin layer of cirrus clouds. Below us at fifteen thousand feet a separate layer of stratus clouds stretched solidly in every direction. It was as though we were flying in a gigantic, well-lit arena. Every bomber in our formation was easily visible against this white backdrop, and beautifully vivid vapor trails streamed in our wake. I could see every rivet on the wings of my aircraft. At first this was merely a curiosity. Then the awful truth hit me: my God, we were flying in what amounted to daylight. I raised my seat and strained against my shoulder harness and the rudder pedals to look back along the length of the aircraft. I should have seen nothing but shadows, but my mid-upper gunner was clearly visible and I could see the turret swinging back and forth.

This was a new and very alarming experience. Never before had I been sent off in such moonlight. Normally I would never see any part of the aircraft except when silhouetted in the glow of a target. I tried to stifle the panic I could feel creeping into my thoughts. My fear only grew as I swung my gaze around the sky. Bombers could be seen clearly everywhere. I could count a dozen on my port side alone. If the German fighters are up tonight, I thought, then we're dead ducks. I tried to calm myself and clicked on my mike. "Keep a sharp lookout, fellas," I warned. "And keep those turrets swinging. It's a zoo out there." The tail gunner acknowledged the message and they all went back to their work. It was not long before the first German fighters swept in for the attack. I watched, helpless and appalled, as a twin-engine fighter flew up the vapor trail of a bomber on my left. In an instant the bomber was in flames that immediately spread to its bomb load, and the end came in a huge explosion that briefly added even more light to the sky. Other bombers were being hit with cannon shells from the ground. I could see fire racing along the wings of stricken planes as they began the long plunge through the clouds beneath us. Parachutes were everywhere as desperate crews tried to abandon the wrecks. Tracers were crisscrossing the sky as the German cannons found their range. At the same time I could see the smaller machine gun tracers from our bombers flicking out of the turrets; in many cases gunners continued to fire even as their stricken bombers fell out of control.

Somehow my own aircraft was not yet under attack. But with the moon and the clouds as they were I knew we were just as much of a sitting duck. Frightened as I was, I had the overwhelming need to do something–anything–to protect my crew and myself. I braced myself against my seat, straining against the harness and arching my body in a desperate attempt to see what was happening in every direction. "Did you see the fighter at five o'clock?" I yelled to the tail gunner.

"I've got him," the tail gunner answered at once. Then he sounded surprised. "Is that you, Skipper?"

"Yes, it's me."

"Do you mean you can see him too?"

"I can see from here to bloody Russia," I shouted back at him. Out of sheer terror my feet actually chattered on the rudder bars. I continued to roll back and forth, searching, always searching. There seemed to be enemy fighters everywhere. Again and again I witnessed the dim shape of a bomber transformed into a fireball that lit up the clouds and then slowly faded as the aircraft disintegrated, the pieces falling to earth. As for my crew they were silent, frozen with fear, and expecting death at any moment. Yet we lived. By some unbelievable quirk of fate we swept through the bloodiest night that Bomber Command ever faced and survived, unscathed.

Then at long last, we were over the target, bomb doors open and vibrating against the air stream. It was time for yet another grimly familiar routine. Air speed steady. Hold at one hundred sixty miles per hour. Hold it. Hold it at twenty thousand feet. Keep your eyes on the flight instruments. Concentrate. Never mind the insanity outside the cockpit. Concentrate! Through all this I waited for the bomb aimer's direction. What was taking him so long? "Hurry up, you stupid bastard, have you fallen asleep?" But the bomb aimer was methodical. He had flown over three hours and defied death to perform this one task and he did not want it hurried. "Left, left, Skipper," the bomb aimer called, and I touched the left rudder. "Left, left," he called again, and this time I jabbed hard on the bar. Sure enough, next it was, "right, skipper!" And finally, "steady, steady, bombs away!"

Not bothering to wait for direction, I snatched up the lever and swung off the target. "Bomb doors closed," I hollered. Pushing the throttles up I continued the turn and settled on our course home. Our route lay across France. The gunners swung their turrets ceaselessly, following the recommended search pattern. Across, up, across, down, trying to cover each segment of the sky in sequence but instantly reversing when they got a glimpse of a shadow or something else moving. Now and again the sky lit up as a German fighter dropped parachute flares to illuminate the bomber stream. Such flares hung for a long time, dazzling white lights that were visible for miles, and if you were close enough they made it possible to see every inch of your aircraft. Even more sinister were the "scarecrows," huge balls of fire the Germans had devised to simulate exploding aircraft and make Allied bomber crews even more nervous. Such things only punctuated the fact that this sky did not belong to Bomber Command.

We made it home that night, but how or why God only knew. Finally, unbelievably, after many more such missions over Germany, our tour of duty came to an end. There is no way to describe the feeling that came over me when it was over. Certainly there were no words in my vocabulary to describe it. To fly to Germany thirty-nine times and face death on every trip was something to which very few people could relate. As I left my last debriefing I was actually congratulated by the military policeman at the guardhouse, who was not known for his warmth. And an officer of the RAF women's division gave me a hug. They, at least, understood the magnitude of what I had done.

The bus driver I encountered a few hours later was a different story. She was a big woman with a face habitually devoid of emotion. I had ridden with her before. On none of these trips had she ever spoken a word in response to a greeting that I sent her way. Still bubbling with excitement after the debriefing, I tried again. "I finished my tour today," I told her as I took my seat at the front of the bus. In response, there was not a hint of a smile, only a grunt. I could not believe she could be so rude. The British people I had met were usually so wonderful. They had saved the world's collective ass, and I had vowed to love them until the day I died. So what was wrong with this bus driver?

"I flew thirty-nine missions."

This time I didn't even earn a grunt.

"Do you know what thirty-nine missions over

Germany is all about?"

"Move back," growled the bus driver.

"Bitch," I muttered under my breath, but loud enough for her to hear. I decided that with an attitude like that, she must be a conscientious objector. She would have been run off the job were it not for the extreme shortage of labour caused by the war. I pulled the cord as we neared my stop. "Good night," I said sarcastically to the bus driver as I stepped off the bus. I wondered, what must she be like at Christmas? Oh, to hell with her, I concluded. Notwithstanding her attitude I still felt like I was walking ten feet off the ground. And I knew that my wife was waiting for me at home.

I had met Thelma for the first time not long after I got my own crew. My squadron had been suffering through a lot of bad weather and my crew and I were frequently stood down. That left a lot of time for courting. I had never been known as a shrinking violent where women were concerned, and my track record of getting what and who I wanted was pretty good, to say the least. I knew that falling in love and getting married might be an exceedingly dumb move when I still had twenty-five missions to fly over Germany. But there was something about Thelma that made me want to throw caution aside. We were married within a few months, in a ceremony at Stratford-on-Avon, with my navigator as best man, and the rest of my crew in the audience.

The day I finished my tour, Thelma was beside me even before I was through the door. "Sweetheart," came her voice from deep within our embrace. "Is it true? Is it really over?"

I hugged her even harder. "Yes, Thelma, I'm home for good." I didn't see any reason to spoil the moment with any more details. In fact my squadron had lost a crew in a particularly cruel way, when an engine quit at the instant of takeoff and the place dropped out of the sky. She didn't need to hear such things now. I kissed her and grinned. "Pour me a drink."

She laughed and scurried off to get a glass. I flopped down on our faded couch and watched her, and everything about her seemed to radiate joy. Yes, life was grand. Little did I know that in a few more seconds it was about to get even better.

She flopped down on my lap, causing my whiskey to wobble dangerously as she handed it over. "Rex," Thelma began somewhat slyly, "I have something to tell you, now that your tour is over. You're going to be a father."

"What? How?" I burbled.

She laughed again. I had asked a very silly question.

"But I thought..." I was still fumbling for words. "Well, you know, what with all the stress I've had lately, I haven't been... we haven't had much... I mean, I didn't think there was much chance."

"I know," she said simply, brushing a stray hair off my forehead. "And I didn't take it personally. But Rex, you have no idea what it was like to sit here at night, all alone, knowing that the man I love might never come back. I'd imagine your aircraft in flames, and you fighting to control it, while your crew bailed out in their parachutes. God, Rex, it really tore my guts to shreds."

"I know, Thelma, I know. But that's all over now."

I struggled still to come to grips with the news

about the baby. I was thrilled, but a baby so soon was not what Thelma and I had planned. She had made it clear to me before that she wanted to put off getting pregnant for a while after the war. She thought it would be better if she took some time to work in Canada, establish herself as a secretary, and then we might have fewer money worries. As far as I could remember we had always taken precautions. On the other hand it was always said that none of the contraptions in question were foolproof. In any case Thelma had clearly had a big change of heart. It would slow up her arrival in Canada, of course. But we could work around any difficulties. In that moment I had no doubt whatsoever that everything was working out of the best.

I slapped her playfully on the backside. "So I guess this means our hanky-panky tonight will be worry-free!" With equal playfulness she was about to pull away in mock outrage. But I pulled her back with another kiss. "No, love, stay here and cuddle with me, because your cuddles are what I need. I've had enough flying, talking, guessing and second-guessing for a lifetime."

My crew and I were granted a wonderful three-week leave. Over this period Thelma and I finally found time for a honeymoon. And one week after I returned to my squadron, the war was over. The commanding officer of the station granted me another week of leave, after which I shifted to flying VIP's and supplies to occupied Germany. More than ever my thoughts turned to the future. I still had memories of my experiences with aircraft engines. I began to wonder about the possibility of taking further training and getting my license to work as an aircraft mechanic somewhere in Canada. Flying supplies to Germany was an interesting job, but with the war over it could not last much longer.

When the cargo missions came to an end, I headed home to Grandeur. It felt wrong to be leaving without Thelma beside me, and the tears flowed freely on both sides, but rules were rules. The authorities would not transport a pregnant wife until she had given birth and the baby was two or three months old. So Thelma had to stay in England for a while longer. In the meantime I promised to keep her informed about all my plans.

Apart from this, my homecoming to Grandeur was everything I could have asked for. I was treated like a king. I did not have any difficulty signing up for an aircraft mechanic's course and off to Winnipeg I went, finding a small bachelor place close to the college I would be attending. The course went well. As soon as I knew when Thelma and our baby would arrive, I started looking for a place we could truly call a home. This was not easy, since the local college, like universities across Canada at that time, was swamped with thousands of returning veterans. My good luck held, though, and I managed to find a pleasant enough apartment that satisfied all of Thelma's needs.

Life only seemed to get better when Thelma did finally join me in Canada. Her first surprise, and it was a very pleasant one, was what she saw in the grocery stores. Rationing was still a part of everyday life in Great Britain, but what little rationing there had ever been in Canada was already long gone. We were in no way destitute. Thelma had a fair amount of money saved from her wartime wife's allowance, and I had been equally sensible with my earnings as a pilot. As if this were not encouraging enough, I was still happy with my chosen field of study. But my chief source of joy came from my baby son. How strange it was to look upon that beautiful baby for the first time and to realize he was my own. He had been conceived against all the odds, near the end of my tour of duty. And post-war Britain was not the healthiest place to deliver a baby. Yet here he was; I would always look upon the little fellow as a wartime marvel.

With my mechanic's exam safely out of the way, I found a job at a flying club in Saskatoon. Thelma had grown to love Canada. What more could I have asked for? Yet as the years went by, my mind played with a little dream. I wanted to start an aircraft repair station of my own. This was not as crazy as it sounded. All of the air force buildings which had been used to train airmen during the war were now in the hands of War Assets, which was selling and renting those same buildings to interested parties across Canada. There was one such building only seven miles east of Grandeur. It was a standard-size wartime aircraft hangar, situated on what was known as a relief aerodrome and designed to take pressure off Number Four Flying Training School in Saskatoon. It was served by three asphalt runways, laid out in the pattern of a triangle. I could not afford to buy the building or even rent all of it, but I thought I might try to rent a portion of it; War Assets had already rented the land surrounding the runways to a neighbouring farmer. Thinking quickly, I grabbed my mechanic's certificate and proof of my wartime service, and caught the train to Winnipeg to see what kind of a deal I could make. Unfortunately my wonderful run of good luck finally hit a snag. Only minutes after I entered the War Assets office, I was told that the hangar had already been sold to another veteran from Grandeur, Saskatchewan. His name was Richard Drake.

CHAPTER SIX

Tom Doyle

It was the day before my thirty-fifth birthday. The life of the Royal Canadian Mounted Police had been good to me. During the five years of war, policing had not been terribly difficult. Canadians, even the criminal element, seemed to realize the country was in the midst of a crisis. Canada's contribution to the war was tremendous (as were our losses) and most people were so busy doing their share for the war effort that they didn't have a lot of time to get into any sort of trouble with the police.

I was not far from my thirtieth birthday when Germany invaded Poland. I had always wanted to fly, so I got permission from my commanding officer to head over to the RCAF recruiting station. But when I explained to the recruiter that I wanted to become a pilot, he looked at my birth certificate and suggested gently that maybe I was a bit too old. He reminded me that serving with the RCMP was a great service to Canada, especially during wartime. So even though I was disappointed, I decided to stay with the RCMP. A number of my younger colleagues joined various branches of the Canadian Armed Forces and would return to the police force when they came back after the war.

The war was over now and a good number of Grandeur fighting men had returned home. The hotel beer parlors were noticeably busier, and there was a considerable increase in rowdiness. My commanding officer told me to be a bit more tolerant than usual. After all, some of these men and women returning from the war had been through hell. Such an easy-going approach by the police could not go on forever, but at that time it seemed like the common sense thing to do, and I was a great believer in common sense.

My stay in Grandeur was winding down when I received word that I had been promoted to corporal and transferred to Melfort, Saskatchewan. I had enjoyed Grandeur. Situated right on the South Saskatchewan River, it was such a beautiful little town. The people were friendly. The farming atmosphere suited my wife and me, since we were both country types. We half-jokingly talked of retiring to Grandeur one day. Actually we would return much sooner than expected. The RCMP, like the Canadian Armed Forces, was full of surprises when it came to postings. You were generally posted to the last place you would have guessed. After only a brief period in Melfort, I was promoted again and sent back to Grandeur where the detachment was being enlarged. The RCMP barracks were new, and we were able to move in immediately. We could not believe our good fortune.

It was of course inevitable that I should have come to know Richard Drake, who was not only a prominent war veteran and thriving local businessman, but also a Justice of the Peace. Most of Grandeur seemed to have a very positive view of Richard, but there were a few snide remarks, too, which I was inclined to write off as envy. Maybe he was a bit stuck up, but you could not deny his success, and given his war record, his name deserved special respect.

There is always a bit of humour to enliven your day when you are a police officer in a small town like Grandeur. A lot of the humour comes from gossip, it must be said. Sometimes the gossip has a darker purpose, especially when a police officer is the recipient. The most recent gossip to come my way concerned Richard Drake and his wife Mavis. Apparently Richard had been engaged to a Grandeur girl named Joan Hansen at the time he left for overseas. They had quarreled just before he left and Joan took it all very badly. Now she was dating Kurt Driger. This was indeed very interesting, because Kurt was the son of John Driger, whose Nazi sympathies were so notorious that he had been required to report to the RCMP twice a month during the war years. Going from a war hero like Richard Drake to the son of a potential traitor was quite a remarkable leap, I thought.

It says a lot about my life commanding the RCMP in Grandeur that sifting through such gossip was one of my more challenging tasks. I was glad enough to leave the major crime to Saskatoon and Regina. My detachment really wasn't equipped to handle such problems anyway. My wife was happy, and so was I.

CHAPTER SEVEN

Mavis Drake

Hallelujah! It was eight a.m., the tenth day of September, 1945. If my calculation of the difference in time zones was correct, Richard had been in bed for about an hour. He'd better be in bed alone, I told myself. Well, I wasn't really worried. I stretched lazily in my own bed, rolled over and hugged my pillow. I had received a telegram from Richard the previous night, alerting me that he would arrive in his hometown of Grandeur, Saskatchewan the next day. I reached for the telegram, which lay on my bedside table. I could not resist reading it again. "Happy Birthday sweetheart *STOP* Time going slow without you but we'll soon be together *STOP* Letter to follow *STOP* Expect to be in Grandeur Saskatchewan tomorrow *STOP* J19801 Squadron leader Richard Drake DFC." I laughed at myself. The telegram was signed simply "Richard" and out of habit I had mentally added the regimental number and the DFC. And why not? He had survived many brushes with death and deserved all the distinction of his rank, if not more.

Richard, asleep or not, was at that very moment

shooting across Canada by train. I missed him so much. I was lonely. There was no reason I should have felt lonely. I knew my Mum was probably in the kitchen. Dad had gone to work, but would be back in the evening. And I would hear Frank dash out the door to school at any moment. Good old Frank! I thought of the day I brought Richard home for the first time. Frank had been thirteen years old, and already in the air force cadets. He went to Mum and announced that even though my new boyfriend was an officer, he was not going to salute him. Mum had assured him that while he was in our house, protocol did not require that Frank salute an officer..

The war in Europe was over now. Of course the struggle had almost brought England to its knees, but it had brought me a wonderful husband with whom I was so much in love that I did not think any words could adequately express my feelings. Boats and trains could not bring us back together soon enough. I would be among the first of the so-called "war brides" to go to Canada. Those war brides in the late stages of pregnancy would be denied passage until their babies were a few months old. But as Richard and I had planned, I was not pregnant.

The next day would be my twenty-first birthday. I had been only nineteen when I met Richard. I would never forget that night. My four girlfriends and I had finished our Sunday shift at the General Post Office in Wolverhampton and immediately caught the train to Blackpool for a whole week of fun at the Blackpool resort. We planned on nights of dancing and days of just lazing away the time. We also expected that hundreds of handsome Canadians, Americans, Australians, and native Brits would be there on various kinds of leaves and passes. The first surprise of the trip came at Crewe. This was where we were to change trains for Blackpool, but the Germans had just dropped a bomb on the area, and trains were not going anywhere. We had no choice but to sit on our suitcases until the all clear sounded.

As the five of us girls sat chatting and planning, I became aware of a Canadian officer who kept glancing our way. He was a smart-looking fellow, very mature, maybe halfway into his twenties. He carried an overnight air force bag. He actually strolled by on a couple of occasions, and I was sure that all this was meant for me. I boldly returned his glance.

I felt older than my nineteen years. This week of holidays had been planned for months, and I was going to make the most of it. I felt a strange twinge of excitement. How amazing would it be if that Canadian pilot turned out to be going to Blackpool, too! My thoughts were disrupted by the shrill 'all-clear' siren. In a minute or so the conductor's whistles started blowing and everyone rushed for their trains. I almost gasped: the Canadian was catching our train, and he was beside me, offering to carry my bags. I accepted, and the six of us crowded into the compartment. After placing my bags on the overhead rack, he sat down beside me. We were at the end of a seat, and along with my two girlfriends we filled one side of the compartment. The other two girls sat directly opposite, with two older women we did not know taking up the rest of the compartment.

The Canadian was the first to speak. He introduced himself as Richard Drake. We all responded with our first names only. My girlfriends and the older ladies started chatting among themselves while Richard and I made small talk. In the background the old train coach groaned and rattled, and the great steel wheels pounded along the joints in the railroad track. Soon Richard's right arm was across the back of my shoulders, his other arm on the windowsill. The arrangement freed up a little more room in the coach, but it also allowed me to snuggle a bit closer to him.

As we talked about nothing in particular, Richard's arm came off the windowsill, across his lap, and rested on my clasped hands. I had never experienced such a forward approach from a man. There was something new and exciting about being nineteen. I let my fingers mingle with Richard's, and let them drop in my lap. I asked Richard all the obvious questions. It turned out that he was just coming off a forty-eight hour pass. He was a bomber pilot; he flew Lancasters. He would be staying on this train until Blackpool, where he would catch another one that would take him back to his base. His right hand was now tucked under my arm, and I could feel his fingers playing against my side. I snuggled even closer and squeezed his hand. Richard whispered that he could probably get more time off the following Friday evening. If the bad weather returned, it might be even earlier. He asked if he could take me out somewhere, on a date. I turned my face towards his and whispered that I would like that. He moved in closer and gave me a little kiss on the cheek. I responded in kind. Much later Richard told me that my kiss had been almost an exact replica of the ones he got from his grandmother back in Canada!

The train pulled into Blackpool, and I was the last of my group to leave the compartment. I made sure that Richard had my address. "Please come sooner if you can," I whispered. In a matter of seconds after leaving the train I noticed that I had forgotten my raincoat, so I turned and ran back. I saw Richard waiting in the doorway, my coat in hand. My God, he's handsome, I thought. He passed me the raincoat, smiled, and then the train started moving again, and he was gone.

I had been on my share of dates. For a six-month period when I was eighteen I had gone out several times with an American soldier. He had become too serious, however, and too passionate. I was already on the verge of breaking it off when he told me he was being transferred to another camp much farther away. Against my better judgment I made one more date with him just before he left. It was a terrible night. He really wanted to get me into bed. "I'm going to the continent," he said. "I could be killed." It was so predictable: I had heard other girls talk about boyfriends in the military who tried the same approach. Anyway, that night the American spoiled any chance of ever having another date with me.

I had a feeling about Richard that I had never had before. I wanted him to come back to Blackpool. I thought that he would, but I didn't have a lot of confidence in my judgment where men were concerned. On Monday my friends and I were goofing around at an amusement park when five British sailors started chatting with us. We made a date to meet them in the same spot at seven p.m., and then we would all go dancing. Around six o'clock we were at our bed and breakfast, getting ourselves ready to go out, when one of the girls hollered, "Richard is here!"

I rushed to the door, heart in hand. It was really him! We shared a little hug and another of my "grandma kisses." My four workmates knew what was going on, and they had no problem explaining the situation to the British sailors. These were five very nice boys, and they would still go dancing. My own evening was heavenly. Richard and I rode what was said to be the world's most spectacular roller coaster. We also went dancing. Richard proved to be a beautiful dancer, and a little tremor went through my body as he pulled me to him in the jive.

"I didn't expect to make it here," he explained over the music, "but the weather over Germany is terrible right now. None of our planes are flying. And I couldn't resist seeing you again."

The band started playing 'In the Mood" and it turned out that it was the jive tune both of us like the most. "Dancing always seems to put me in a good mood, and from now on every time I hear this tune, I'll think of you," Richard murmured in my ear. "Even if I never see you again, Mavis, your face will appear and I'll hear this tune. But I want to see you again in person, and again, and again."

I was utterly transfixed. But Richard wasn't finished talking. "I'll book up at a bed and breakfast just outside the gates of my base, if you'll visit me on Wednesday night. I'm the duty officer that night, but I can find a stand-in for two or three hours, I'm sure. Otherwise I'll be too busy flying to see you until Saturday night. Here," he handed me a scrap of paper, "this is my address so you can wire me when you're going to arrive. Today I heard that I'm being promoted to Squadron Leader. Please come and help me celebrate." Without thinking of what my parents would say, I instantly agreed. "Yes, Richard, I'll come."

We shared one more hug and kiss before I retreated to my bedroom. Richard's last words were wonderfully simple. "Goodnight, Mavis. And don't forget, send me a telegram and I'll be there to meet you."

After the door closed my mind was in a whirl. What had I done? I'd committed myself to go alone to a place I did not know, to be with a man I had just met. But I sent the telegram as promised and Richard met me as promised. There was a pub nearby, but I didn't drink. Richard was still technically on duty, so he couldn't drink either. So for over two hours we just sat on a park bench in the blackout. We talked about a hundred things. Richard gave me a little Royal Air Force brooch, and I promised to wear it. The kisses and hugs started to get a little more intense. I enjoyed the feeling. Richard's hands roamed a little bit, but he didn't push it too far. The ten o'clock curfew at my bed and breakfast came quickly and Richard had to get back to his duties immediately. And because Richard had a special flight scheduled for the morning, I would eat breakfast alone.

My duties at the Post Office in Wolverhampton involved processing telegrams, and I had seen many that made me shudder. How many times had I read, "The Air Ministry regrets to inform you that pilot officer Joe Go has been reported missing over Germany. A letter will follow with more details." To ease my fears Richard had promised to write me every second day, and I would do likewise. I didn't want to think of what I'd do if these letters ever stopped coming. I couldn't deny it any longer: I had been hit by an acute case of love at first sight.

Richard had warned me that he had special duties the next weekend, but he offered to come to Wolverhampton in two weeks if my folks would allow it. I thought of the daring things that I had already allowed myself to do after only one date with Richard. I had said yes to visiting his base and staying at a bed and breakfast nearby. My mother would never have allowed it if she had known. "Those things are just not done, Mavis," she would have said. My girlfriends had given me a lot of encouragement and support, of course, but even with them I was a little afraid to reveal how quickly matters were progressing. Finally I blurted out the whole story.

"He'll be in the room with you overnight!" one of the girls exclaimed.

"Of course not, you silly girl," I replied primly. I sounded a lot more confident than I really felt. Regardless, the girls gave me their unqualified approval. "From what we've seen we all think Richard is a fine man."

I received the promised letters from Richard and answered each one. He had a mission to fly Friday night, but he would come at noon on Saturday. He arrived in Wolverhampton on schedule, and after he had met Mum and Dad, he asked if they'd mind if he took a nap. He had flown all night, he explained, and had barely managed two hours sleep after his debriefing. Then on the train he had been so afraid of sleeping through the stop at Wolverhampton that he had forced himself to stay awake the whole way. Now he really needed a rest. My dad was happy enough to accommodate him, and asked me to show Richard his room.

At the bedroom door I sneaked Richard a kiss, and returned to my parents in a somewhat flustered state. I finally filled them in on the week in Blackpool but I still did not tell them about the Wednesday night I had spent near Richard's base. That could wait.

I did not try to hide how much I was interested in Richard. I was not naive. I was well aware that Richard was right in the middle of a tour of duty and that losses of aircraft and crew were very heavy. My Dad was involved in the recovery of Lancaster and Halifax bombers that had failed to make a safe landing for whatever reason and had seen how badly they were often shot up. I would not soon forget the concern in Dad's voice. "Mavis, darling, I'm not sure you fully understand the danger Richard is in. He may well be a very fine young man, and an excellent pilot, but he's involved in one of the most dangerous jobs in the whole war."

Even with all these warnings, I was on top of the world. I began to look forward to bad weather, because it made flying impossible, which meant Richard's squadron would be stood down, and he could rush down to Wolverhampton to see me. On these days I was the happiest girl in town. I was always able to find someone to take one of my shifts at the office, especially after I took Richard in to meet the telegraphists I worked with. They were all very impressed; some were even smitten. I told Richard that showing him to my girlfriends was one of the riskiest things I had ever done. He answered that I had absolutely nothing to worry about, that no other woman could compare to me. As we walked down the street and away from where I worked, I peeked over my shoulder and smiled. Three of my girlfriends were leaning out the window and watching us walk arm in arm. They giggled encouragingly. Over the following weeks and months some of these same girls would literally lose sleep so that Richard and I could have as much time together as possible; the telegraph office was an around-the-clock operation, and many of the shifts that I missed were in the middle of the evening or night.

It was not long before we became engaged. The sequence of events was a bit of a blur, but suddenly I found myself wearing a ring. I later found out that in fact Richard had taken the time to talk to Mum and Dad beforehand. They had reminded him that I was nineteen, below the legal age of consent; but even though they were not yet ready to give their permission for us to get married, they would be proud to see me wearing his engagement ring. This was good enough for Richard. I was ecstatic. Just before he left to return to his squadron, I looked at my left hand and fingered the engagement ring. "How did this happen?" I asked. He gave me one of his devilish looks. In return I gave him a hug. He was priceless. I loved Richard so much that it almost hurt. Yet it was easily the most pleasant pain that I had ever known. When I returned to work, I walked over to the girls who had been so supportive and held up my hand. They saw the engagement ring and screamed with excitement.

Of course there was still the question of when Richard and I would get married. My parents had agreed in principle, but they were very concerned about their daughter toddling off to Canada, and there was also the real danger that one day Richard might not come home from one of his missions. Wouldn't it make more sense, they asked me, to wait at least until Richard had flown his last mission? I didn't like it, but they stuck to their guns. And until I turned twenty-one, there was nothing I could do. Richard was understanding as always. He asked me when my next time off would be. I told him that I had a free weekend ten days later. It seemed like an eternity, but in the meantime I had a tough assignment: to convince Mum and Dad to let me go to the bed and breakfast in the village near Richard's base. I was sure I could get Dad's permission, but Mum would be a much harder sell. Their reaction was exactly as I expected. At last, on the second day of pressure, Mum gave in, but not without some positive assurances from me. I sent Richard the happy news by telegram and received a "hooray" telegram in return. The date was on.

Richard was able to free himself from all duties that weekend, and met my train at the appointed time. I may not have had Richard's wings, but I was in a mood like a bird ready to take flight. The bed and breakfast was the same one where I had stayed during my first visit to Richard. The lady owner was just as strict as she had been before. She was almost worse than my mother: I had to be in bed no later than ten, and I had to be alone. Notwithstanding these rules, Richard and I managed to enjoy ourselves. There were two occasions when he managed to slip into my room, and our passions came close to the breaking point. I had never had sex before, but I knew that this was the man I wanted to be with for the rest of my life. Richard was just as willing as I was. But we were also very conscious of the guidelines my mother had laid down and neither of us wanted to betray her trust. It was not going to be easy, but we agreed that the only way to get around our problem was to get married. I would be twenty fairly soon. Maybe that would be enough to change Mum's mind. Yet no matter how often Richard and I tried to reopen the subject with my parents, they continued to insist that we could only talk about it after Richard had finished his tour of duty.

During our periods apart, the letters from Richard were my security blanket. Then came a terrible day came when there was no letter. There was no letter the following day, either, nor on the third, or the fourth. I grew frantic. I knew that hundreds of girls in my position had been similarly frantic, and generally with good reason. I tried to reason it out. I knew, from a secret code that we used in our letters to each other, that Richard was going to be flying his fourteenth mission the day after his last letter. If he had suffered engine trouble and went down anywhere in Britain, he would have sent me a telegram. There was no telegram. There was no word of any kind. Notwithstanding our engagement, I did not know anyone in his squadron, and no one in his squadron knew me. I was terribly afraid. In my heart I knew there could only be one answer: Richard and his crew were missing.

My parents did their best to console me. This was exactly the situation they had feared when they advised me to delay the wedding. But Dad had grown very fond of Richard and was determined to get me some sort of news. This was where his job in aircraft recovery came in handy. Normally there would be no way that the authorities would release the name of a missing pilot to someone other than family. The very next day, however, Dad had a call to work in the area near Richard's squadron. Using his credentials, Dan Clifton talked himself into the adjutant's office and asked if he could talk to Squadron Leader Richard Drake. Trusting in Dad's credentials they had not hesitated to inform him that Squadron Leader Drake had been shot down during his last mission. No word had yet been received from the Red Cross as to his fate. Dad then revealed his real purpose in asking for Richard, and managed to have my name and address placed in Richard's file. If nothing else I could now be sure I would be notified as soon as any more information was received.

At last a letter came from the Red Cross. It did nothing to remove the pain. Richard's Lancaster had been shot down. Six of the crew had been captured and interrogated in a POW camp, but Richard, strangely, was not among them. The German authorities had reported to the Red Cross that Richard's bomber had been destroyed by fire, but there was no sign of a body in the wreckage. All of this could mean many things. The worst-case scenario was that Richard had been captured by the wrong people and killed on the spot. A much brighter possibility was that he was hiding out somewhere. I knew that our pilots carried appropriate money for the various countries on their route. They also carried certain survival items, and special food kits. Richard could be in the hands of one of those wonderful groups of people who helped Allied airmen get back to Britain. I could only hope; I had nothing else to go on.

Forty days passed without further news. But on the forty-first day, an unbelievable telegram arrived in our office. I was not on shift when it came. Words could never set the scene I found when I walked into the telegram room. Everyone rushed towards me, huge smiles on their faces. One of my best friends handed me the little piece of paper. It was from the adjutant of the squadron. "Squadron Leader Richard Drake," it read, "is safe and back in England." The rest of the day was like a dream. Despite the rules there were many hugs and more tears, and people were constantly wandering by my station to touch me on the shoulder and whisper words of congratulation. From the post office the news of Richard's survival spread like wildfire. Mom told all the neighbours, and at my brother's school the headmaster was so impressed he ordered Frank to announce it to his whole class. As for Dad, he happened to be away on a major recovery job at Wellsbourne. Mum immediately sent a telegram off to him, care of the RAF station where he was billeted. A priority telegram came back from Dad right away, saying that he had arranged to pay Richard's squadron a visit the next day. "I wish it could be me," I told Mum.

A telegram from Richard himself arrived in the morning. Having worked a late shift I was still asleep. I opened my eyes to find Mum looking down at me, with a familiar piece of paper in her outstretched hand. The message was everything I could have hoped for. "Hello sweetheart *STOP* I'm temporarily in the hospital at my squadron *STOP* I am skin and bones will you still love me *STOP* Will be getting some time off before I fly again *STOP* Ask your Mum if she could put up with a starved boarder *STOP* I love you Mavis *STOP* Richard.' I held the telegram to my breast. "I'll keep this forever," I said.

Mum was what some might call an unflappable woman. She took things in her stride. But now there was a hint of a tear in her eyes. "Can I marry him now, Mum? Will you let me even though I'm not twenty-one?"

She leaned over and kissed me. "You're a crafty girl, Mavis, but we'll see what your Dad says." I almost laughed out loud, because I knew that Dad would have agreed long ago. It was Mum who was gumming up the works.

I had so much to do, and the first thing on my list was to send a telegram of my own to Richard. As promised, Dad was allowed to go to the RAF hospital at Richard's base, and by some stroke of luck he made it into Richard's room just as my telegram arrived. To top it off, Richard's commanding officer was in the room at the same moment. The CO shook Dad's hand. "He's one hell of a man, this Canadian your daughter's marrying," he said.

"Yes, sir, I know," Dad replied.

Soon Dad was back at home and giving Mum and me as much first-hand information as we could handle. "He's lost a lot of weight but he's still Richard," he assured us. Apparently the CO had granted him a fortnight off, but after that he would be assigned a new plane and crew, do some refresher work with them, and finish his tour. Dad saved the best for last. From bed Richard had asked him if he could marry me as soon as his tour was completed; and Dad had said yes. For the first time in his marriage to my mother, he had made a major decision without consulting her. Mum and I were speechless. But Mum was not upset. We both showered Dad with kisses.

Three days later, just before three o'clock in the afternoon, I was at the railroad station in Wolverhampton to meet Richard. I had asked Mum and Dad to let me go alone. I was so proud and so much in love that I was afraid I might look silly to them. There he was, stepping off the train two cars down. "Richard! Richard!" He heard my call. A few long quick steps and we were together. We stood and embraced one another without a word being spoken. Richard kissed me again, and then gently pulled back. "My sweet Mavis. For forty-one days, you and God were what kept me going. Thank you, Mavis."

"Richard, how can I ever tell you how much you mean to me? I love you so much."

"I know, sweetheart. I love you, too, with all my heart.

"You still look tired, Richard. Wait here with your gear while I find a porter and a taxi to take us home."

He looked like he was about to argue, but with a sheepish smile he thought better of it. "Alright, but this babying me can't go on for too long. Already I can feel my strength coming back just being near you again. It must be your kisses."

"Richard, if my kisses can do that, then after two weeks with me you'll be able to lick your weight in wildcats." I kissed him again and dashed off for the porter. Dad had arranged his day so that he would be home with Mum when our taxi arrived at the door. I took a great deal of comfort from the fact that my parents obviously loved Richard, and that we were now all in step. What more could a girl want? Mum intended to make my man as comfortable as possible. Despite the strict rationing of food that had been in place since the beginning of the war, she brought out a lunch like I had not seen for years. I was to learn later that our neighbours and the girls from my office had contributed ration cards for the occasion. It was like rations from heaven and Richard knew it.

Even so, I could see that all was not well with him. "Richard, you are somewhat used up, aren't you?"

"Yes, I do feel rather strange. Our squadron doctor said that all the days and nights I spent without sleep and food will take to time to fade. I just need rest, then I'll be my old self again."

I decided to show him where he would be sleeping. I was not anywhere near as shy and speechless as I had been the first time he had stayed with us. Dad had already moved Richard's luggage inside, so he would have everything he needed. I took his grey coat and uniform jacket and hung them in the wardrobe. "Dear God," I said to myself, "he's so haggard and thin. I should undress him and put him into his pajamas." I blushed at the thought. The day would come, of course, of that I was sure. But for now I just kissed him and left the room. Frank appeared as I came back to the kitchen. Frank's cadet training had prevented him from being home for Richard's arrival and the wonderful lunch that followed. Fortunately there was enough food left over to satisfy even the hungriest fourteen-year-old boy.

I decided I to go to bed and rise early, on the assumption that Richard would do the same. My sleep was very much of the on-again, off-again type that comes when your mind just won't settle down. At about three a.m. I heard noises in the hall. I opened my door just a crack, in time to see Richard return to his room from the toilet. "Go and chat with him," a little voice told me; but another, even louder voice said, "Your mother will kill you." I returned to my bed. By seven o'clock I was wide-awake. I shook out my hair, pulled on my dressing gown, and went down to the kitchen. Mum was already dressed and preparing Dad and Frank's breakfast. "Dad's in the bathroom, Mavis. Richard could be down anytime, and you aren't going to let him see you dressed like that."

"How about less than this?" I teased her, which earned me a friendly pat on the backside and a gentle push up the stairs to my room. The bathroom was empty and in no time I was fully dressed. When I stepped out into the hall, Richard was right there beside me. My heart skipped a beat. I threw my arms around him. "You look much better," I told him.

"I needed that sleep. It was the best rest I've had in forty-seven days, including my stay in the hospital. Anyway Mavis, I couldn't really be myself again until I was with you."

"Whatever you say, Richard, but I hope my presence doesn't always put you to sleep. Now, let's go downstairs."

We entered the kitchen arm-in-arm. "Look what I found wandering around the house."

"Lucky girl," Mum answered. "Sit him down at the table and see if he'd like some oatmeal porridge."

"Good morning, everyone," Richard said. "And

yes, I'd love some old-fashioned oatmeal porridge. My Mum always said that nothing sticks to your ribs better than oatmeal porridge."

"Well, mothers are always right, aren't they, Mavis?" Mom walked up to where Richard was sitting. "Young man, I don't want you to feel embarrassed about eating as much as you want. We understand completely, so let our contribution to your health be meat on your bones." Then she leaned over and kissed his cheek. I loved her for it. After breakfast I spoke up. "Let's go for a nice walk. Do you mind?"

So Richard and I walked, occasionally finding a bench where he could rest. It became a daily ritual. During one of these walks I finally worked up the nerve to ask him to tell me the story of his ordeal. He was reluctant at first, since technically he was supposed to keep quiet about it at least until he had a chance to be debriefed by his superiors. But after a short silence he agreed that I had a right to know.

Richard began by explaining how one by one of his crew had jumped from the crippled bomber. He remained in the cockpit, trying desperately to maintain control of the aircraft until the last man jumped, and then headed aft thinking to make his own escape. It was at this point that he saw how badly his parachute had been damaged. It was useless. He fought his way back to the pilot's seat, and it was a fight, because once again the aircraft was in a spiral. By some miracle he regained control only a few feet above the ground, side-slipping the burning aircraft into a farmer's field. The impact of the crash, the spreading flames, and all the debris thrown around him left him stunned for a moment, but his seat belt had held, and though the cockpit had collapsed, he was not badly injured. But he knew that soldiers and civilians with guns could arrive any minute. So he ran into the field, and suddenly there was an explosion, and more debris showered around him: the gasoline tanks of the aircraft had exploded. About half a mile from the burning Lancaster he came across a pile of rocks, which supported the platform of an old swather. It was about seven feet long and twice as many wide, and that made it a great makeshift shelter for the night. His only fear was that tracking dogs would find him, but they never appeared.

Richard was very quiet as he told me all this, but as the tale unfolded I grew worried he might be tiring himself out again. He waved my concerns away. "No, I need to get it all out," he said. The details were spellbinding. He told of the rations he had carried. He mentioned the special button that was really a compass. He described the close calls where he barely avoided capture, and all the help he received for seven or eight days in a row from people who could easily have lost their lives for helping him. He told me of the stolen train ride that took him in the wrong direction, and how he had noticed just in time to change trains and regain some of the lost miles. There was the night he gained almost two hundred miles by sneaking on the back of an army supply truck; he jumped off just before daylight, and slept in the bush until nightfall. As he moved across the countryside he ate carrots and turnips from gardens, and drank water from hand pumps over wells. The closer he came to the English Channel, the more careful he became. He often found himself hiding in damp, cold places, soaked to the skin, but not daring to steal clothing or shoes from clotheslines or back steps because the loss might have alerted the owners to the presence of a downed airman in the area. On these days the only thing that kept him warm was the thought of getting home.

"There were times that I felt like an animal, and acted like one. I had to learn how to be cunning. This was a game that had death as first prize and I knew it. There were hundreds who would shoot me on sight, and only a few brave souls who would help. But I could never be sure which was which. There was always the chance that people offering to help were actually leading me into a trap. But God was helping me, I think. I was pretty sure I was somewhere near Mannheim, because that was the last position report my navigator had given me. If this was true then I knew that the border of Germany and France was less than a hundred miles away. So my plan was to try and move south and west.

"My mind was full of the stories of other airmen who had lost their planes over Germany or France and made it back to tell the tale. Every airman hoped that their advice would never apply to him. I was down, and now the instructions applied. They went on and on. Do not carry personal papers or anything else that would identify your squadron. If captured, give nothing but your name, rank, and serial number. Beware of anyone claiming to be a Red Cross official who tells you that you will not be declared a POW unless you fill out a lengthy form. Stay off busy roads and avoid transit control points. In remote areas, seek the help of farmers for such things as food and civilian clothing. Do not write down the names of people who help you.

Whenever possible, be tidy and clean. Always look before you leap. But the instruction that really stuck in my mind was the one that said, 'Escape will be easiest if done early.' It was for this reason that I almost played myself out during those first few days. We were each issued with an 'E and E' kit, which stood for 'Escape and Evasion.' It contained a signaling mirror, knife, fishing line, hooks, iodine, bandages, gold coins, and halzone tablets to purify water. This was the stuff that kept me alive for many weeks."

As Richard described it, rescue came just in the nick of time. He had stumbled into a new area, and through a contact heard about a special safe house. By then he was truly exhausted, stressed to the very edge of breakdown. He feared that the house in question was a trap. But he was so desperate he decided to go there anyway. It was a lucky decision. The people in that house turned out to be members of the French resistance, running an escape system for airmen like him. He was questioned at length before finally being accepted for what he was and told that he would be helped. He was to leave immediately. Following their instructions, he hid in a freight train heading for the coast. Then he was turned over to a mysterious fellow wearing the uniform of a Sergeant Major, who escorted him down to a beach in the middle of the night for a pre-arranged rendezvous with two Royal Navy torpedo boats. From here, along with six other evaders, Richard was evacuated to England. "Mavis," he said, squeezing my hand harder than ever, "you can't imagine how I felt when my feet touched friendly soil."

I tried to stop Richard talking. I put my arm behind him and pulled his head to my shoulder. A shudder passed though my body, and I sobbed. But he could not stop. He seemed almost to be in a trance, the words tumbling out under their own power. I would never witness anything like this again. Forty-one days of unrelieved tension were unwinding in his brain. Every incident he described lessened his load of stress, every word he spoke seemed like a breath of new life. And to hear him tell me, over and over again, that it had been the thought of me which kept him going through all those appalling days on the run was almost too much. What a man! I had never imagined that I could love anyone so much.

After unburdening himself in this way, Richard was very much the fellow he had been when I first met him. I noticed the return of his cheeky ways. And everyday, no matter what shift I was on, he would meet me at the Post Office when I came off duty.

Then came the day of our wedding. It was everything that a girl could wish for. Strict clothes rationing was still in place, but after a complicated process of improvisation I ended up with a dress I could wear with pride. We even managed a wedding cake! Richard's crew, joined by Clinton, his twin brother, made up our guard of honour. The reception was unbelievable. Dad made the most wonderful, poignant little speech. Rich's tail gunner told tales about the groom that brought gales of laughter. My brother Frank spoke as well, and embarrassed me no end. He joked that Richard had no idea what I was really like around the house, and went on to paint a frightening picture of my cooking, the state of my bedroom, and several other things I hoped my husband would soon forget. Yet it was Clinton Drake who truly stole the show with his description of my future home among the Eskimos in Saskatchewan.

Yes, at long last we were married. We could then look forward to ten days of honeymoon and freedom from the pressures of the war. Richard was able to get his hands on a nice little car, and was entitled to a small petrol ration, so we followed the Mumbles Road towards Langland Bay Hotel. How we made it is rather difficult to explain. All of the old road signs had been taken up so that parachuting enemies could not find their way. But at least traffic was not a problem. Because of the petrol rationing we were one of the few non-military vehicles on the road. And Richard's uniform was a great asset everywhere we went.

Neither of us could restrain ourselves once we checked into the hotel. We had waited for this day, but now the waiting was over. We were a pair of excited lovers without knowledge other than that which is God-given. Days later, as we became more experienced and comfortable, we thought back and laughed at our own ineptitude. I could not come up with words that would do justice to the love and the strength that flowed from Richard. Surely I was the world's happiest bride. When we were not enjoying each other's bodies we talked, and talked, and talked. Richard had so many amazing war stories to share.

I had only one story that could even begin to compare. One night a few years earlier I had been going home from a late shift when I was caught in the crossfire of a surprise air raid. At the very height of the attack I found myself in the middle of an area that had already been bombed, but where the rubble had been cleared away. All that remained was a small brick wall. I put my hands over my head and lay as close to the wall as possible, praying loud and hard in the faint hope I might somehow live. Shrapnel spat and whizzed blue sparks around me as it struck the concrete I was laying on. As I walked that same route again on the following day, I came upon the spot where I had huddled for protection. I could see the marks that my body made in the earth near the concrete wall. The brick wall was covered with shrapnel pockmarks. How was it that I wasn't hit? This seemed to me one of the many minor miracles of the war. On another day my family and I were not so blessed. A German air raid cost us our home and put Dad in the hospital for three months. Yes, even in our little corner of Britain we got to know an awful lot about the dreadful truth of war.

Finally I was on my way to Canada and Richard. The four and a half days at sea flew by. I was spared the misery of seasickness, but other brides were not so lucky. Despite what I had been led to believe beforehand, some of them carried babies with them on the boat, which made those of us who did not have babies of our own a valuable asset: the little ones needed constant care, whether or not their own mothers were in a state to give it to them. I made lifelong friends in those eight or nine days of travel just by cuddling and changing their newborns.

It was goodbye to pounds, shillings, and pence, and hello to strange money. The various stores near the train depots had watched many trainloads of war brides pass by. They had come to know what we craved; bags of assorted fresh fruit were ready for sale. Overall the Canadian Government had everything wonderfully well organized. At the end of the trip, I realized I would have to have been blind, deaf, and dumb not to arrive safely at my destination.

It became a sort of game to watch my fellow war brides get off the train at each town or hamlet as we crossed Canada. A young lady would step down onto the platform and inevitably be swallowed by a crowd of relatives and well-wishers. Nurses were often there to hold the babies while wives embraced their long-lost husbands. It was harder to see the goings-on when we came to a city like Toronto or Winnipeg, because in those places the girls and their babies tended to be whisked away at once to an informal reception. But in remote northern Ontario, there were two or three occasions when the train released its passenger into the middle of the countryside. There was one especially vivid scene where the train was met by a simple buggy drawn by a team of horses. We could only guess how far that war bride rode in that buggy before she was home.

Soon I was in Saskatchewan. Grandeur was just a few more miles away. I sat in my seat with all my belongings piled around me. I hugged myself, so overcome by emotion that it seemed my heart was beating way up in my throat. Some friends who were going on to Alberta and British Columbia had promised to help me get my baggage off the train. They discreetly left me alone during those last few minutes of my journey. I was filled with excitement and impatience, but also a tiny morsel of doubt. Would he still love me?

The train slowed and the reverberation that chattered through all the couplers as brakes were applied was music to my ears. I had heard that sound again and again for four days and I knew that this time it was meant for me. With my friends carrying my luggage right behind me, I moved towards the conductor who was waiting near the door. He stepped down and placed the familiar stool on the platform. As my feet touched the stool I looked up. There were dozens of people. Suddenly one broke loose from the throng and it was Richard. I could have screamed, but I didn't even have a chance. I was in his strong arms and smothered with kisses. He pushed me out to arm's length and simply said, "Mavis, you're heavenly." Then he pulled me to him again. I felt tears welling up in my eyes, but this was no time for tears. This was a time for laughter and joy. Finally Richard and I let go of each other and turned towards relatives and friends. Almost instantly I felt warm and comfortable. James and Edna Drake looked exactly like the pictures I had seen of them; and just as wonderful as Richard had promised they would be. Richard's twin brother Clinton had come down from Saskatoon to help make my arrival even more memorable. As for all of the others who were at the station, I would have to wait until morning, and a welcoming breakfast arranged in my honour, for the introductions to be made. For now they seemed satisfied to wave and say goodnight.

Rich had borrowed his dad's car to take me back to our new home. Once inside the car, we were instantly in each other's arms all over again. The love, the passion we had been denied would be denied no longer. Rich quickly drove to the house I had never seen and parked in our driveway. The next minutes were another blur and I was grateful there was no one else inside to watch my reaction. My mother-in-law and one of her friends had dusted and tidied up the whole house. Not only that, but they had set out a lunch ready to be eaten! What beautiful people they were, I thought. But lunch would have to wait. Rich gave me a short tour of the ground floor, and with stars in our eyes we moved up the stairs. Our bedroom was the first one off the second-floor hallway. It was a moment like no other. The Rich I held so tightly was more precious to me now than he had ever been. Being out of uniform had taken nothing from him as far as I was concerned. I had not fallen in love with a Squadron Leader in the Royal Canadian Air Force, I had fallen in love with a man. Being reunited with him lifted a great load from my shoulders. We stood hugging and kissing and caressing each other beside the bed. We murmured words of no particular meaning. There was no longer any need at all for the self-help sex books we had purchased at the beginning of our marriage. How much time elapsed I would never know or really care. There obviously was more to life than sex, but I had learned that in every person's life a vacuum that could only be filled by physical intimacy.

My body moved with pleasure at Richard's touch. It was a different excitement than our wedding night. I was not moving into the unknown. I was impatient, hungry for his touch. Yet the act of sex itself was so simple, so wonderful, and so gentle, I felt as though it were taking place on a soft summer cloud. It was like the love I had for Rich. I shuddered as Richard held me tight and I was in heaven. In time we moved apart and gazed at each other without speaking. It seemed that our love had its own understanding. We pulled on our pajamas and went down to the kitchen for the lunch that Rich's mother and father had left for us. Then we went back upstairs ....

We awoke in each other's arms the next morning at seven o'clock. The previous evening, as we left the railway station, Clinton had reminded us to be at the farm for breakfast at ten. There was, I'm sure, a twinkle in Richard's eye as he now repeated the time we were expected. Once there I had the feeling that all of Saskatchewan had come to meet me, every person I met full of warmth and friendliness. Certainly they all seemed very inquisitive but I figured a small rural area in England would be much the same. Even their curiosity was comfortable, somehow. "I'm going to like it here," I told myself. "There are no airs or graces–just my kind of people."

Over the following days I seemed to get to know Richard all over again. The learning was so easy. We visited the business place Richard was interested in buying, and very shortly, with my blessing, Rich made the deal with Grandeur Ford and Farm Equipment. What was my first job? I was told that it was the toughest job that you could take on in that line of work: stocktaking. But we closed the doors for three days straight and got it done. It was an excellent learning process for both of us. We held on to the old staff, and even the old owner, Art Wilson. The fact that Art was staying on for six months was a great break for Rich and me. It helped ensure that from the very first day, our business was a success. Right from the start, I knew that I would enjoy this kind of work, and Rich caught on very quickly, too. It was not long before he was able to incorporate his love of flying into the business, buying a four-place aircraft that would carry him far and wide in search of deals. Life, it could honestly be said, was unfolding in a way beyond our dreams.

CHAPTER EIGHT

Richard Drake

I was on my way home from Carrot River, Saskatchewan, in my Piper aircraft. A few days earlier a farmer had driven down from Carrot River to Grandeur to look at a used tractor I had advertised, and today I had flown up to his place to see the tractor he wished to trade in. We ended up making a deal. It was a beautiful clear day and now, back in my cockpit, all I had to do was make sure I was on the track that I had planned and the plane would pretty much take care of the rest. I would be home for supper, just as I promised Mavis. That left me with plenty of dreaming time.

My mind recaptured the day that Mavis had arrived in Grandeur. My God, I thought, what a reunion, what a woman. I could have searched the wide world over, and there would only be one Mavis, I was sure of it. The memories of her first night in Grandeur still left me with goose bumps. I had been so nervous before meeting her at the train station. I was worried about how I looked; she had never even seen me in civilian clothes before! But Mavis didn't seem to notice. Our love for each other pushed everything else aside. The first hour in our new home was indescribable. I was her captive. She could have me as she wanted me, forever.

It was a lucky day for me when Mavis agreed to us buying Grandeur Ford and Farm Equipment. She fit in so wonderfully well. Not only was she capable of learning the basics, she had the kind of personality that gave our customers a secure feeling. You can't put a price on that kind of trust. It was in no small part due to Mavis that our customers came back, and not only came back, but also spread the good word.

When we made the deal to buy the business, we were well aware that Art had purchased three other lots and a vacant building behind our garage. In one of those strange moments that come along at least once in the lives of most people, he had bought it in partnership with Russ Kessler. "We were in the pub having a beer and it just happened" was the way Art explained it. In any case our agreement with Art stipulated that his share of these properties was part of our purchase, which meant that now I was in partnership with Russ Kessler. At the time I had not given it much thought; I barely knew Russ, and I had no obvious use for the property or the vacant building. But one day my dad heard me mention Russ Kessler and his comments were startling. "You watch that man Kessler, and his father Wolfgang. Believe me, they're not your kind of people."

I had reason to remember Dad's warning only a few months later. One night in early April, just after midnight, I received an emergency phone call. The storage shed behind our garage was on fire. I rushed down there, but nothing could be done to save the building.

According to the person who reported the fire, it had started from the inside of the building. I could not understand how that could be. The place was totally empty as far as I knew. The power supply had been cut off years ago. It was always securely locked and didn't even have windows. Russ Kessler and I were the only ones with keys. How could anyone, even someone bent on vandalism, have made it inside?

Art had told me that when he had gone to Russ to sign the deal, Russ had insisted that they arrange for fire insurance right away. They each took out a five thousand dollar policy on the building, with a premium that came due in July of each year. Now the building had gone up in smoke. It was suspicious, to say the least. When I subsequently received a visit from the insurance adjuster, I answered his questions as best I could. More alarming was when I received a second call from the same fellow. He said that he just wanted to confirm something Russ had been at pains to tell him, which was that I had a key to the building. No one was making any accusations, the adjuster assured me. It was just for the official report. That must have been the truth, because about a month later, a cheque for five thousand dollars came in the mail.

Unfortunately, because the building had been owned jointly, the cheque required Russ' signature as well as my own. Mavis offered to take it over to our "partner." "I'd like to take a look at Russ' operation," she joked.

I replied rather sharply. "You never mind his operation. I'm starting to understand how he got his reputation." But after Mavis made a promise to be careful I let her go.

She was soon back, and her report was reassuring. "He signed the cheque. And he didn't even come on to me! I must be losing my looks!"

"Don't be silly," I told her with a grin. "But seriously, you should count yourself lucky that a guy like Russ doesn't look at you. I don't think I trust that man. By the way, did he ask you about getting me to sign *his* cheque?'

"No."

"Now that's strange. He won't be able to cash it without my signature. So what the hell is going on? The next time Clint is in Grandeur, I'll run the whole story by him."

A week later, Clint was in town and I did tell him the story. He told me to leave it with him. He had the name of the fire insurance company, and he had an idea of how he might get the truth. Three days later, after posing as a chartered accountant who needed information about an insurance policy, he found a willing informant. "The claims are both paid out," the informant said. "Five thousand dollars to Grandeur Ford, and ten thousand dollars to Russ Kessler." So now we knew that Russ had not only secretly doubled his fire insurance, but forged my signature on the payout cheque. The obvious conclusion was that he had set fire to the building.

I was furious, but Clint warned me against doing anything hasty. "Think it over, Rich, and carefully. Russ is smarter than you think, and right now it's your word against his. He can say that you really did sign the cheque. You'd actually have to prove it's a forgery. And if you dare say that Russ burned down the building, a building that hasn't been used for years, he could easily make a monkey out of you in court."

That night I went through the whole scenario with Mavis. It appeared to both of us that we were between a rock and a hard place. We decided to wait until Clint's next visit to Grandeur before settling on a response. How would it look for two Grandeur businessmen, both selling cars and trucks and farm machinery, to be at each other's throats in court? I would probably come out with egg on my face, and Mavis and I both knew it. If nothing else I wanted to confront Russ in private and ask him when it was that I had endorsed his cheque. But Mavis gave me her special look and I put the idea out of my mind.

When Clint came to town, we talked it over again and realized that it was absolutely a no-win situation. "He's a crook!" Clint said bitterly. "And according to Dad, he learned most of his tricks from old man Wolfgang. Maybe we gain more by not saying a thing."

It was just as well that I had plenty of other matters to occupy my mind. Mavis was pregnant. I wasn't exactly shocked, and she told me I had no reason to be. "Bedtime with you is a no-holds-barred time of day," she teased. "I might as well throw away the damn diaphragm. It's just a joke with you." This was all said in fun, because we had always agreed that we wanted two children, and there was no financial reason not to get started given how well things were going with the business. As it turned out, Mavis had no problem at all with her pregnancy. Melanie Jane Drake was born on December 22, 1952, the most beautiful little girl I ever saw. My only regret was that I did not get to see her until she was already an hour old. I had been sent home because the nurse thought that nothing was going to happen for at least twelve hours; it then took them a good forty-five minutes to track me down. When I finally burst into the room, and saw my lovely Mavis holding our baby, I felt a pride that no man who has not been a father can hope to understand.

James and Edna Drake were simply ecstatic about the arrival of Melanie Jane. They had waited a long time to be grandparents. As my mother said, it would have been a much longer wait if they had to rely on Clinton to do the deed. I would never forget the day that Mavis put our little baby in a sled and pulled her over the ice and snow down to Grandeur Ford. The customers had come to love Mavis, and their love was compounded when she arrived among them with a three-week-old baby. It was not long before Mavis and Melanie Jane were everyday workers at the garage.

One day Mavis casually mentioned her worries about Rudy Schroeder, whom I had promoted to sales manager about two years before. Rudy had a way with people, and even if he wasn't my favourite person, I thought he was good at his job. But Mavis had noticed that he seemed to be living far beyond the salary and commission that he received from us. I never mentioned it to Rudy, but I took Mavis's concern seriously. I had learned to trust her instincts. I promised to keep a closer eye on him.

Meanwhile another plan was forming in my mind. A few miles out of Grandeur, on the main east-west road, there was a fine aircraft hangar. During the war it had served as a relief airport for the big training base near Saskatoon. There were long runways and the parking lot was paved. It occurred to me that this place would make a great flying club for Grandeur. I had kept the idea to myself, because I did not want to get into a bidding war with other entrepreneurs. Yet as an air force veteran with an above-average war record, I had a bit of special leverage with the War Assets people. I guaranteed to them that I would only buy the hanger in order to turn the building and property over to a properly selected committee of local pilots for the same price. I was not looking for a quick profit. After the usual bureaucratic delay I received the call: I was to go to Winnipeg to sign a contract. Mavis was as thrilled as I was. We could already see Jim Johnson as chief flying instructor of the new club, and his wife Glenys as the office manager. I flew to Winnipeg and returned home the proud owner of an aircraft hangar, complete with runways and adequate parking. I kept my word to War Assets and transferred ownership to the club at cost; the minutes of our first meeting were forwarded to the government as proof. I chose not to sit as a director, but I was one of the first five people to rent space inside the hangar. Seven other aircraft owners rented a parking space outside. The Grandeur Flying Club was off to an auspicious start.

The first social event of the club was a sold-out affair. I was presented with a beautiful plaque commemorating my contribution to the business and social life of Grandeur. To top it all off, I was made the first honorary life member of the Grandeur Flying Club. Mavis gave me a congratulatory kiss. What more could I ask for?

CHAPTER NINE

Russ Kessler

I felt no remorse. The war was not my war. I was of military age in 1939, but my father had found ways of keeping me out of service. To be really honest, I was supporting the German side, both mentally and financially. Yes, over two hundred men and women from Grandeur had served in the Canadian forces during the war, but that was their choice, not mine. Their love of Canada meant nothing to me.

I was proud of my dad. I could write a book about my dad. He seemed to me a genius in so many ways. He actually had two patented inventions to his credit, both of them to do with giving vehicles better traction in icy conditions. But what really set Wolfgang Kessler apart was that even in the middle of the Canadian Prairies he was a German through and through. I would not be surprised if he did things to help the German cause that I never knew about. I never questioned him about it, because I thought he would be uncomfortable discussing such matters even with his son. Whatever he had done, he was my hero. Among my friends, only Kurt Driger seemed to feel the same sort of feelings for his own father. Maybe it was a German thing, I thought. Did every community the size of Grandeur have German citizens who preserved the love of the Fatherland that Wolfgang Kessler felt? It was an interesting possibility, and my mind immediately recalled the names of Punch Stuka, Pete Heider, Rudy Schreiber, and Kurt and John Driger–all good friends, and all good Germans.

Staying out of the war had been a smart move for me in more ways than one. This was when my dad's craftiness came to the fore. The Canadian Air Force had an urgent need for dozens of large aircraft hangers, and Dad's technical wizardry allowed us to bid on these projects with a high rate of success. Once Dad won a contract, he would find ways of squeezing extra money out of the government without actually doing anything extra on the project. His reasoning was simple–if the Canadian government insisted on allowing dummies to run their affairs, then he would do his best to get his share of the easy cash. It would be fair to say that we were among the strongest supporters of the British Commonwealth Air Training Programme–but not for the usual Canadian reasons.

It would also be fair to say that I did not have what most people would consider high morals. But who decides what is moral and what is not? It could also be said that I didn't have good business ethics, but once again, how do you judge ethics? My business was cars and trucks and farm equipment. I was an excellent mechanic, having learned the trade at a very early age from my father. The turnover in my shop was fairly good, but during the war there had been very few machines coming in from the factories for civilian sale. Of course I knew they would start to come once the war ended, and then the demand for all these machines would be high, maybe higher than ever before. And that was what happened. For a long time I was able to ignore suggested retail prices and set my own obrates as high as I liked. I found many other, less obvious ways to make money as well. If a customer of mine was asleep at the switch, and didn't realize that I had pulled a fast one on him, then whose fault was that? I was always very careful to make sure that my customers did not catch me out on something, even when I was pulling a fast one on them, if for no other reason than that I wanted them to come back. I found women especially easy targets. I knew a lot of tricks, and the more tricks I played, the more money I made. And if a woman came on to me, I was always ready, willing and able. It happened much more often than "moral" people imagined.

When I was nineteen, I got away with what some people would call rape. I was out on a drinking party, and at first this girl was allowing me a lot of latitude in my sexual advances. But when her panties came off, she suddenly decided that she wanted to stop there. I did not stop. When she screamed and hollered, I threatened her to the point where she was incapable of even considering a report to the police. I drove her home, pushed her out of the car, and never heard of the incident again. My friends and I still chuckled about it once in a while. What did the girl expect anyway?

At the moment there were no women involved in our gang. My wife Sadie was a dead loss, and seemed to want to know as little as possible about who I associated with. Why couldn't she be more like my own mother? Mom had loved Dad with every fiber in her body, and knew how strongly he supported everything Germany was fighting for. I also had my doubts about Kurt Driger's wife, Joan. Everyone in Grandeur knew that she had once been engaged to Richard Drake, the so-called war hero himself. I had done my best to ignore the rumours of his exploits, and those of his equally "heroic" brother Clinton. It was said that Richard had led a squadron of bombers or some such, while Clinton had flown fighters and shot down five enemy aircraft. Both of them had won medals for their trouble. How many poor Germans had they killed? And yet the Drake twins were now local celebrities, while a grand old man like John Driger was a pariah just for hollering "Heil Hitler" in the wrong company. So much for Canada being a tolerant country.

Reflecting on such injustice was enough to make me bitter, especially when I considered the fate of my cousin, Gustov Kessler. Gus lived in a small town about a hundred miles west of Berlin. I had never met him, but I had seen pictures from when he was in the final stages of his education. In August 1939, on the verge of his nineteenth birthday, Gus joined the Luftwaffe. After that we did not receive any more pictures. In fact there was no news of any kind for a long time. It was not until early 1943 that we learned, through the Canadian Red Cross, that Gustav Kessler had been killed in action. There was no further explanation. I knew he had been a pilot, and suspected that he had been a fighter pilot. Suppose Gus Kessler had crossed paths with one of the Drake twins? Suppose Gus had attacked Richard's bomber and come out second best? Or suppose Gus was in one of the five aircraft shot down by Clinton Drake? The mathematical odds of either scenario being true seemed ridiculously low, but I didn't take much comfort from this. I remembered Richard Drake before the war. He was a star baseball pitcher, the guy who always won a ribbon at track meets. He was always a cocky bastard. I dreamed of the day I'd be able to bring him down a peg or two. The day had not yet come, but it would. Of that I was sure.

The mere sight of Richard Drake was enough to put me in a bad mood, especially when I saw him strutting around with that English wife of his. I wouldn't have minded a wrestling match with her. Sadie and I had a beautiful home, but there was nothing to match it in our marriage. I could no longer overlook how much her attitude had changed. She had reached the point where she didn't bother to pull any punches with me about anything, trusting that the new divorce laws would keep me from doing anything to retaliate. "Can you recall the last time we had sex?" It was one of Sadie's favourite sneers. "It doesn't matter, but it was almost three years ago, and that was the night you raped me. Ironic, isn't it? You raped me, and I conceived. Now we have two beautiful daughters. How an ugly animal like you could have fathered such beautiful girls is a mystery to me."

I could stand no more and walked out of the house rather than argue. It was humiliating. In my father's day there would have been a simple enough solution to this. "I'll find a way of keeping my daughters and losing my wife," I vowed.

One of the greatest shocks I had suffered since the end of the war came when I learned that

Richard Drake had bought Grandeur Ford and Farm Equipment. I could not bring myself to believe that the great hero would last long as a businessman. Yet the shocks kept coming. It turned out that Richard's new wife, Mavis, would be working the business with him half-time; and that Art Wilson was going to stay on to show both of them the ropes. That bastard Drake seemed to have all the luck. It only made me even angrier to remember that I was saddled with him as a partner on those three vacant lots behind his garage. But soon enough it occurred to me that I might be able to use the "partnership" to my advantage.

Soon after Drake took over from Art, I poured myself a stiff drink of scotch and phoned my insurance agent. I claimed to be reviewing my policies. I gave the legal description of the property that Richard and Mavis had just purchased in partnership with me. I stated that I had a new plan for the property. Would it be possible to increase the insured value to ten thousand dollars, and include it as an adjunct on the policy I already held? Since I was one of their biggest policy owners, the insurance company was happy enough to agree. I hung up the phone, refilled my glass, and congratulated myself on pulling off the first phase of my plan. Phase two would come a month or so later, I decided. And so it turned out. What made the whole transaction that much sweeter was that the great Richard Drake was totally oblivious to what had happened right under his stuck-up nose.

The years flew by, and the aftershocks of the war continued to fade. I continued to do well, but there was no doubt that I had lost customers to the Drakes. This was hard to accept, and then came the news that

Richard Drake had purchased a hangar and intended to sell it back to a new "Grandeur Flying Club." I just couldn't stand how the guy kept finding new ways to lord it over the rest of us. It was time, I thought, to make a grand gesture of my own. Although I had absolutely no interest in learning to fly, I offered the new club an interest-free loan of seventy-five thousand dollars for them to purchase aircraft. The club, of course, leapt at the offer, and even granted me an honourary social membership–which happened to be the same honour they had just bestowed on Richard Drake.

Membership of the Grandeur Flying Club proved to have benefits that I never anticipated. It quickly developed into the busiest social club in town, and gave me new insight into men I thought I knew. I had a pleasant surprise when, in the course of idle conversation, I discovered that Punch Stuka and Kurt Driger shared my views on the Royal Canadian Legion. And they were not the only ones: Punch and Kurt spoke of a Pete Heider who farmed east of town and who also disliked veterans. I knew Pete, having sold him various farm machines, but I had never realized that the man was on the same wavelength where the war was concerned. There was no way that men like Peter Heider or Kurt Driger, with a love of all things German and Nazi, were ever going to buy anything from Richard Drake. I soon learned, though not from Kurt himself, that he had an even more personal reason to detest the man. Kurt had married Joan Hanson, the woman who Richard had cast off in favour of his oh-so-English Mavis. There were rumours about town that Kurt had absorbed all of Joan's bitterness at the way she had been treated.

Truth be told, I found such concern for a wife's honour rather hilarious. As far as my wife Sadie was concerned, I would have been thrilled if she fell for some other guy. It would have given me just the leverage I needed to run her off at last. I had no doubt that I could replace her in short order if I really made up my mind to do so. I already had my eye on one other woman in particular: Judy Strome, who was one good-looking gal, and if the rumours were true, very "modern" in her thinking about sex. I had not had much success with her yet, but I figured it was only a matter of time.

CHAPTER TEN

Kurt Driger

My dad John Driger had phoned me and asked that I come home for a day to give him a hand with the farm. So there I was on the train, thinking about the last trip home to Grandeur when I was suddenly pulled out of my thoughts by the sight of two fellows at the front of the half-empty railroad car. They were obviously in the air force, with prominent rings on their jacket sleeves. One of them, I noticed, had one more ring than the other. They both had pilot's wings and a row of ribbons below the wings. They were both exceedingly smart-looking men, who were obviously proud of their appearance. As the train pulled into the station at Grandeur, I watched them stand up and start gathering their gear, then move into the area between the two cars. I moved forward as well. I saw the conductor pick up his trusty stool and ease himself out in front of the two pilots. As the train came to a grinding halt, he opened the door and placed the stool on the platform for the convenience of his departing passengers.

The two men in uniform had to be Richard and

Clinton Drake. I had heard of them on another recent visit to Grandeur, when I had overheard the owners of a local garage talking about a local family with two sons in the air force, both pilots, who had been decorated for heroism, and who were due home very soon. Yes, these two officers had to be the Drake twins. Everything the garage owners had said seemed to fit as the two stepped off the stool. They were hugged from both sides by an older man and woman who were obviously their parents. Without a greeting party of my own I hung back and watched as a host of other well-wishers surged forward to add their own hugs and handshakes to the festivities.

A few minutes later I left the station and walked to the parking lot where Dad was waiting. I mentioned the episode to him, and the net result was a less-than-pleasant reference to Canadian war veterans. This was not surprising. My father John Driger made no attempt to hide his hatred of the allied war effort, from me or anyone else for that matter. In 1942, after he drank too much in the local beer parlor, he had been overheard talking in glowing terms about Nazi Germany, capping it off with a loud "Heil Hitler!" Inevitably he was picked up by the RCMP, and from then on he had been forced to report to them every three weeks. At the time I had kept my own mouth shut. But I was in full agreement with my father's views.

When we got home, I went immediately to my room and changed into my work clothes. My thoughts drifted back to the previous night and to Judy Strome. She was another Grandeur girl in Saskatoon, taking a course in commercial practice, and as arranged we had met in a little café on Second Avenue. She had led me to a corner booth, and when the Coke came she opened her purse and produced a neat metal flask. Wearing a mischievous grin she drank down about half of her Coke, and threw in a good slug of rum. She did the same to my glass as soon as there was room. When we downed our drinks, the waitress brought two more as requested. The exact same sequence of events ensued, and as we drank our second round of spiked Coke, Judy took my hand in hers and rested it on her knee. Then she slowly moved my hand up her leg. Very soon I could feel her warmth through her panties.

All this was foreign to me and, to put it mildly, rather unique. I was accustomed to girls pushing my hand away, not assisting it to where it wanted to be. I had never been on a date where the breaks were coming so thick and fast. The odd date had led me on a bit, and sure, I'd been with a couple of girls who were out-and-out cock-teasers, but when the going got close to real sex, they invariably turned it off. The stigma of getting pregnant before marriage was still very strong. So my knowledge of what to do next was limited. In the confines of the rather dimly lit booth Judy had allowed her pleated skirt to slip up her leg. I slipped one finger under the edge of her panties and she moved ever so slightly under my hand. She whispered in my ear, "Should we go to my place before we go dancing?" None of this added up. In every other respect Judy seemed to be distinctly shy. She was very quiet in group settings, and had been only moderately chatty before we sat ourselves in the booth.

We left the café, hailed a cab, and within ten minutes we were at Judy's small but comfortable apartment. She locked the door, threw her jacket on a chair, and moved towards me, throwing her arms around my neck, pulling my face down to hers. She was obviously miles ahead of me in this game; I had never been on the receiving end of such passionate kisses. But I was prepared to follow her in every move she made, unbuttoning my shirt, slipping it over my shoulders, and pulling it out of the top of my slacks. Soon her blouse was off her shoulder and on the floor. By then she had unbuttoned the waist button of my slacks and made quick work of the zipper. I reached for her bra fastener, but knowing nothing of the mechanics of bra clips, it came as a relief when she reached behind and unhooked the bra herself. I did my best to stifle a gasp as her small but lovely breasts came into full view for the first time. But being new at this game I soon had an even more embarrassing problem, as my erection started to force my shorts forward.

I stepped over the clothing on the floor as we slowly shifted in the direction of the bed. Judy's hands were on my waist, and her fingers were on the waistband of my shorts. She eased them down, and they fell over my knees to the floor. My passion was taking over, and my hands were on hers. My fingers caught the waistband of her panties and I slipped them off. She pulled me onto the bed, gently maneuvering my face to her beautiful breasts. By instinct I began to kiss and nuzzle them. Judy's hips were on the move, and her inner thighs were rubbing hard against me. I didn't want any of it to stop.

Soon I was at the point of no return. I had masturbated in the shower so an orgasm was not entirely foreign to me. I was alarmed at first as I realized that within seconds I was going to lose control, but I needn't have worried, because Judy was about to do the same. As if by magic, our bodies convulsed together violently and then we were still. Little twitches passed through my body, and I hugged Judy tight, feeling her hot breath on my chest and stomach. I did not care in the least how long it took for her to finish the job, which she so obviously enjoyed. In the course of the proceedings I had come to rest on my back. She now closed my legs and spread hers. Shoulders thrown back, beautiful breasts thrust forward, she lowered herself onto me once more. Was this a dream? No, it was real, and better than any dream. Judy was in complete control. In a way I felt like an intruder on her performance, but I was not about to complain. I was sure that these last moments would be in my memory for a long, long time to come. Whatever woman I ended up with, Judy would be a hard act to follow.

The following Saturday I was in a café in Grandeur when I happened to come across some old friends from my days at school. They announced that they were going to the weekly dance at the town hall; would I like to come along? A girl named Joan Hanson had joined the group and I was immediately attracted to her. We shared three or four dances, and since she was unattached, I offered to take her home. She agreed to see me again, but it could not be until the next weekend: she explained that she would be busy all week taking a course in Regina.

It all worked out as planned. We shared dinner at the Royal Café before going on to another Saturday night dance. In the middle of the evening I was struck by how very comfortable and relaxed I already felt with this girl. But even so, there were a few subjects that I had no intention of bringing up. In fact I was dreading what I would have to say if and when the subject of my father reared its head. Not that I was embarrassed. I just didn't want to scare Joan off before we really had a chance to get to know each other.

I was rather annoyed with myself as I realized how often I was plagued with a guilty feeling about my lack of military service. I could easily have satisfied all the requirements for aircrew training in the RCAF. I was physically fit, I met the educational prerequisites, and I even had a lifelong desire to learn how to fly. But there had never been any question of me volunteering. My father had literally bought me out of military service, going so far as to lie about the amount of land I owned. Of course I owned it now, but I hadn't done so when Dad made the declaration to the recruiting board. My dad was still paying a price for his political views. I sympathized with these views, but I was extremely careful about who might be within earshot whenever I discussed the subject of Nazi Germany.

The issue was likely to be even more complicated with Joan. I had already heard the rumours of her old romance with the heroic Richard Drake. The subject first came to my attention over a beer with Russ Kessler and some of my other friends, when Russ made a caustic remark about the return of the Drake twins from the war. "It looks like Joan Hanson came to her senses just in time," he added in an aside not meant for my ears. "At least she won't have to marry him now." Having finally met Joan, I decided to let her keep that part of her life to herself as long as she wanted, just as I would never mention my one-night stand with Judy Strome. Every life had to have a bit of intrigue, after all.

Joan was certainly all woman. She was in no hurry to go home after our date. As yet we had not had even a single alcoholic drink, but she made no objection when I brought out a mickey of vodka to go along with a couple of bottles of orange pop. And though she was no Judy Strome, she was not averse to a bit of sedate, decorous and exploratory lovemaking. I had no regrets. For all the excitement of being with a girl like Judy Strome, I could be fairly sure that I was not the first man she had worked over. It was hard to imagine Judy settling down and accepting the quiet life of a farmer's wife.

Over the next month our dates became very frequent. Joan tended to keep her hands to herself, but she seemed to have no problem encouraging me to take liberties. Near the end of our second month of dating, she asked me if we could take a trip to the city. There was a special sale she wanted to check out, and she thought that afterwards we might see a movie. In fact it was to be a far more dramatic trip than I expected.

We got out of Grandeur early and were on the outskirts of the city by about two in the afternoon. Since women were not allowed in the beer parlors, Joan suggested that we pay for a hotel room where we could have a drink before we went shopping. I thought this sounded great. But the rules of hotel registration were strict; how would we convince the desk clerk to let us in? To this Joan had a simple and somewhat surprising answer: we should just register as "Mr. and Mrs.

Kurt Driger." So that's what we did, and sometime later, as we finished our second glasses of vodka, I realized that we wouldn't be leaving the room any time soon. I had the feeling that Joan had planned everything, that she knew exactly what was going to happen. We both knew there would be sex before the evening was out.

We never got to Joan's sale, and we never got to the movie. Despite Joan's lack of experience, she was never in a hurry. She was obviously determined to make the moment last. As for me, I was almost in a trance, oblivious to the specific chain of events. I did not really know whether I had undressed myself or whether Joan had done it for me, but there came a point when all of a sudden I was aware that we were lying on the bed naked. Time stood still. Joan's arms were around me. Other than passionate kisses, she did nothing further to excite me, but nothing to discourage me either. At that moment I could not keep myself from thinking of Judy Strome. It was strange, but then she was the only other woman with whom I had shared this experience.

Joan's eyes were closed tight and she was flushed. Her breathing was far from normal. I could feel my own heart pounding as I moved over her. It was not over quickly. There was a slight moan from Joan as her membrane parted, but she did not hold back. She reacted to every movement I made. She was a full partner in this unique experience. Again, my mind involuntarily flashed back to how Judy Strome had positioned herself above me on the night I lost my virginity, how beautiful her breasts had looked as she moved. So I swung Joan's body so that she was straddling me, and her own beautiful breasts started moving in concert with her thighs and hips. Joan's movements were even more strenuous and intense than Judy's had been in the same situation. Her eyes were still tightly closed. There was a series of quick gasps, and inexperienced as I was, I was sure that Joan was having her first orgasm. In the afterglow, her head on my shoulder, Joan whispered in my ear, "Let's get married." Without a moment's hesitation, I whispered back, "Just name the day."

I could feel her smile, though given our position I could not actually see it. But as the minutes passed, and she said nothing more, I could feel something else, as though she were struggling with something deep in her mind. I waited, and finally it burst out. "Kurt, did you know that I was engaged to Richard Drake?"

I nodded, but said nothing. The whole story started to flow out of her. "I started dating him when I was nineteen, and our last date was the day he left for overseas. I won't bore you with too many details, but he hurt me deeply. Not physically, no. That would almost have been easier to get over than what he did to me. I didn't do anything to deserve how he treated me. I never believed that I could hate anyone, but being with him changed all that. He left, and I waited, thinking he would come to his senses. Then he told me that he had met another woman. That's when I knew that he never really loved me. I don't know why he ever gave me the engagement ring. I don't think I was ever anything more than a stopgap, which he needed to break the stress and tension of his flight training. Then when he was finished with it, he didn't need me anymore."

I listened to her with a rising anger, and pity. How could any real man use a woman the way Richard Drake had used Joan? But the fact that she was willing to talk about it with me also made me very happy. I felt like I could now trust her completely. "Joan," I said, "since we're sharing secrets, there's something I need to tell you, too. You must have heard about my father, John Driger, and his court appearance." Joan nodded. That was a relief. "Well, you should know that I believe in my father. I love Germany every bit as much as he does. Can you handle that?"

The pause before she answered seemed to last forever. But it was worth it. "Kurt, I love you. And the war is over, isn't it?"

My heart sang. That afternoon we had broken the ice in every conceivable way. I could really see myself marrying this woman. We made plans for another trip to the city, and it came off very much as before. But this time we bought an engagement ring before booking the hotel room. The ring only seemed to add fuel to her desire. So it turned out to be another very enjoyable afternoon.

CHAPTER ELEVEN

Rudy Schreiber

It had been six and a half years since I came to Canada. In mid-February 1939 I had left my beloved Berlin with my father Hans Schreiber, a mining engineer who was heading for a stint in Saskatoon. We planned to be home within six months. Then one day in Saskatoon Dad suffered a heart attack and died. Three days later the war started. All of my many attempts to get back to Berlin while the war was on had proved fruitless. In the meantime my mother had died during an air raid on Berlin, and my only brother, a decorated officer in the SS, had died of wounds suffered in France. So even though the war was now over, I had nothing to go home to.

This day I had overheard my bosses talking to Emma Jones, another employee of Grandeur Ford. Everyone, it seemed, was heading down to the station to welcome a couple of veterans home. These two, Richard and Clinton Drake, were both supposedly war heroes. It was common knowledge that about twenty-five Royal Canadian Air Force pilots from Grandeur and the surrounding district had died as a result of the war. The Drake twins could be added to the list of casualties for all I cared. If they were real smart, I told myself, they would go back to England for more training. Why? Because Nazi Germany was bound to rise again. No one in Grandeur, with the exception of my wife Anna, knew anything of my background. But my heart had never left the Fatherland. And when the Third Reich won the next war, I would take my dad's body back to where it belonged.

How many times in the last year had I repeated that promise to myself? I had made the greatest mistake of my young life back in January 1939. Dad, nearing retirement age, had often claimed that he'd like to finish his career with a really key assignment. Then one evening he came home bubbling with excitement. The words spilled out of him. "Our company has just been contacted by a firm looking to develop a potash mine in central Canada. The bosses want me to go out there for a few months and make an assessment for them!"

I was immediately infected by my father's enthusiasm. Though just about due to join my brother in the SS, I had the urge to join Dad on what seemed likely to be his last adventure, and when I asked him if I could, he was overjoyed. "With you there to help me, we might even make it home a month sooner."

We arrived in Saskatoon in high style. Dad's company treated us royally. I had the finest auto that could be rented. We stayed in the Bessborough Hotel, which was Saskatoon's best. My dad's work ethic, coupled with his personality, cleared away all obstacles, and we made rapid progress. By the end of June, we were in a position to inform the home office of a possible completion date. We had every reason to hope that we'd be back in Berlin no later than mid-August. By mid-July, however, I started to worry. Dad was going at it too hard. Too many field trips and too many late night meetings. He was falling behind the schedule he had set for himself. On July 30, Dad asked me to drive him to the hospital. I was parking the car when he slumped forward in his seat. He had suffered a heart attack. But I got him to the emergency ward in time. He spent the next three weeks in bed, and the doctors only released him on condition that he continue to avoid stress. This proved impossible. The news from Germany was not good. People began to speak of war. Dad refused to believe that his man Hitler would start a war unless he was terribly provoked, and I felt the same way. Ignoring the doctor's orders, he made plans for us to start the long journey home as soon as possible. We never even made it to the Saskatoon train station. On August 28, Dad had a second, even more massive heart attack, and died.

Suddenly I was alone. Within a few days Canada was at war with Germany, and Hitler had imposed a total blackout on communication into and out of the Reich. The staff at the Bessborough did their best, but it proved impossible to get any sort of message out, either to my family or the company back in Berlin. I had no alternative but to bury my father in Saskatoon. In spite of everything my situation could have been worse. Dad, perhaps having had a premonition about possible delays, had secured a sizable advance on his salary from the company and deposited it in trust with the manager of the hotel. The manager helped me set up a bank account in my own name, and released the money to me.

During my long stay at the hotel I had come to know many of the employees quite well, but none so well as Anna Hiebert. We had gone on several dates during the summer. It turned out that she was German, and had only been in Canada for four years. Anna now pointed out that hotel living was very expensive for a person who no longer had an income, and suggested I stay with her until my life got back on an even keel. She had a couch in her living room that would make a comfortable enough bed, she told me. But soon I found myself off the couch and in her bed. She was everything a young man in my situation could wish for. At first she was miles ahead of me in the bedroom, but she told me I was a fast learner and that she would keep me forever.

I was smart enough in the ways of the world to know that Canada being at war with Germany created special problems for me. Although I kept my love of Hitler very much to myself, my heart ached to serve beside my brother in the SS, the elite guard of the Fuhrer. But try as I might I could not find a way to get back home and serve. Every way I turned I found a roadblock. I thought of joining the RCAF as an air gunner, which involved a relatively short course of training, and then defecting to the Luftwaffe once I got to Britain. But then it occurred to me that the air force would trace my background, and once that happened I'd be in hot water for sure. So I gave up the idea. It was lucky for me that Canada did not have a cut-and-dried system of conscription.

I had come to trust Anna completely. The sudden outbreak of war had ruined her own plans to return to Germany, and we were very much on the same page about Hitler. We decided to go to a rural area, because we knew the armed forces recruiters were sensitive of the need to protect agriculture, and so were more likely to leave us alone there. I answered an ad for a general maintenance man at a Ford dealership in Grandeur. My expertise was limited, but with so many men rushing off to join up, no employer could afford to be too picky, and I got the job. To cover myself I told my new employer that I had tried to join the military, but had failed the medical exam because of a weak heart. I kept my ears open for any scrap of conversation that might indicate a kindred soul. But with a name like Schreiber and the German accent to go with it, I had to be careful about asking too many questions.

I was enjoying a beer in the Riverview Hotel one evening when a break of sorts came my way. I was alone, and sensed someone standing by my chair. "You're Rudy Schreiber, I believe."

"Yes, I am. And you are?"

"Kurt Driger," he replied, "can I buy you another?"

"Yes. Will you sit with me?

Kurt mentioned that a friend of his, whose name was Pete Heider, had been doing some business at Grandeur Ford, and had read my name on the staff bulletin board.

"Pete's parents and my parents were all born in Germany, and we gambled that you might have arrived in Canada under much the same circumstances." I sensed that this Kurt Driger fellow had already consumed more than a few pints, but what he said next still shocked me. "I'll tell you how German my dad is. He drank far too much right here in this beer parlor about four months ago. I had a bad feeling and tried to get him out. But before I could get him through the door he turned back and hollered, 'Heil Hitler!' In front of all these people! The next day, the police were at the farm. Now he has to report to them every three weeks."

This was how I learned the story of John Driger. It was rather heartwarming for me to hear that there were others nearby who shared my feelings. I was still cautious. I kept my own story vague. When they leaned hard on me with pointed questions, I lied my way out of it. In mid-1943, Kurt introduced me to Russ and Wolfgang Kessler. They were contractors who had sold their construction business, and were returning to Grandeur to take over the John Deere and General Motors dealership.

Anna did not immediately accompany me to Granduer. She and I had agreed that she should stay at her job in Saskatoon until I could find definite work for her in my new town. Fortunately the fact that so many young Canadian women had joined the war effort had the effect of opening up opportunities for Anna. A good job came up in the school board office in Grandeur, and after sailing through an interview, she was hired. It was not long before the school board realized the extent of her ability and she was given a substantial increase in salary. Reunited and now living as Rudy and Anna Schreiber, we congratulated ourselves on how well life was treating us. And with men like the Kesslers, the Drigers, and Pete Heider in the neighbourhood, we felt strangely at home, as though there was a little corner of Germany here in the Canadian wilderness.

Then the war ended and all the veterans started returning home. Big changes were soon taking place at Grandeur Ford and Farm Equipment, where new Massey Harris equipment and Ford cars and trucks were starting to flood in from the factories again. By now I had graduated to selling repair parts for the owners Art and Jim, and I also had a hand in both new and used whole goods sales. There was still something missing from my life, however, and I knew what it was. I could not believe that Hitler was dead. I yearned for the day when Germany would rise again and have its revenge, and I was determined that I would be there when it happened. Kurt Driger and I spent hours lamenting the murder of our relatives at the hands of the Allies. Kurt was fascinated by my stories of the Fuhrer, with whom I had been captivated since a very young age, and whom I had actually heard speak in person. In spite of everything that had happened, I was still convinced that a man like Hitler was what Germany needed.

It was therefore no coincidence that a rather unique chemistry developed between Wolfgang Kessler and me. Almost everytime our little gang of patriots came together the two of us would end up in deep conversation. Early on I confessed to Wolf that I had lost a brother in the SS, and I could see how affected he was by the story. It was hard for men like us not to hate men like the Drake twins, although logically we knew how unlikely it was that Richard or Clinton had played any role in the deaths of our loved ones at home. For whatever reason, those boys came to symbolize everything we resented about Canada.

So I could barely stand it when Grandeur Ford and

Farm Equipment was sold, and the new owner, my new boss, turned out to be none other than Richard Drake. When I told Anna what had happened, she had no doubt about what I needed to do. "You've got to get out of there, Rudy. We don't need you working for that bastard war veteran."

I was not so sure. "That was my first reaction, I'll admit. But this might turn out to our advantage. I might be able to get some useful information for our gang. Besides, the salary is as good as I'm going to get. Who knows? As a salesman I might find a way of skimming off a bit extra here and there. How smart can these new owners be? They aren't even German!" Anna and I shared a good laugh at the thought, which was only partly in jest.

CHAPTER TWELVE

Joan Hanson

I had finally come to terms with the realization that my life was not going to be shared with Richard Drake. True, withdrawal pains would bug me for a while yet. I was surprised at how suddenly my feelings had flipped from love to something very close to hatred. I knew of all the wonderful things Richard had accomplished during the war. But whatever quality of character had seen him through combat had deserted him when he chose to break out engagement. I had moments of extreme bitterness towards Mavis Clifton, who I had never met. I told myself not to stress myself with such silly thoughts. If I had made a mistake it was a mistake that many other girls had made long before I came along. Who knew why we fell in love with certain people? And who could say why we fell out of love with them? The first real test of my life after Richard Drake was not long in coming. I met a good-looking man named Kurt Driger. As early as our first date, he was far more aggressive than Richard had ever been. I was intrigued enough to ask Grandma and Grandpa if they knew anything about him. They had nothing bad to say about Kurt, who lived only two or three miles away with his parents. According to Grandpa, the Driger family was quite wealthy and always had been. "But John, the father, is very German," Grandpa warned me. "I heard it got him into trouble recently."

My dates with Kurt became more frequent, and I enjoyed it all. For a long while nothing too serious happened, but I could feel myself steadily warming up to him. Kurt never discussed his German background. I noticed that he tended to change stations on the car radio whenever war news came on, but that didn't bother me. I assumed that Kurt had heard about my broken engagement to Richard Drake. Yet if he did, he never mentioned it. What we did discuss were things like farm life and marriage. One day Kurt mentioned that his mom and dad had bought a house in Grandeur, and that as soon as they moved the farm would be his.

I could already imagine him as a hard-working, successful, handsome farmer and husband. It didn't hurt that he loved to laugh and was an excellent dancer. One Saturday we decided to drive to Saskatoon for shopping and a movie. Kurt had bought a mickey of vodka. "We can't drink our vodka in the car," I pointed out. "Why don't we get a room?"

"But the hotel will never let us!" Kurt protested. Sometimes he was so naive it was adorable. "They'll never know," I assured him. "Just book it as Mr. and Mrs. Driger." Kurt grinned sheepishly and did as I suggested. Then we went to our room. After the second vodka and some petting, I came to a firm decision about what I wanted to happen. We did not shop, and we did not go to a movie, but it was an evening that I would long remember. Kurt seemed to be a man of some experience, but I was not about to question him on it. I had read what I believed were good books on the subject of physical intimacy, and one title in particular just about summed up everything that was on my mind: "Don't Let Birth Control Spoil Your Sex." I had planned this evening accordingly. We were sitting on the edge of the bed when I eased myself out of Kurt's arms and asked him if my suggestion to book the hotel room had made him think any less of me.

"Of course not, Joan, you're a beautiful, intelligent woman, and I can't believe I'm lucky enough to be here with you like this."

There was only one more thing to be said. "Kurt, I just want you to know that I've never been to bed with any other man. Do you believe me?" Kurt's answer was to take me in his arms. Within seconds I knew without a doubt that this was the time and the place. I did not contribute too much to the foreplay. My contribution was more in the way of yielding to Kurt's advances. The very fact that I wanted it to happen seemed to prepare me completely. I was consumed by passion, and somehow I knew that Kurt was completely aware of it. The power of sexual desire amazed me. It was no wonder that shotgun weddings were so common. Kurt's hands seemed magnetized. My body moved willingly to his touch. I was still only partly undressed when he moved over me. There was a split second of pain, but I pulled Kurt to me. We lay for about five minutes and then began to make love again. This time Kurt maneuvered our bodies in such a way that he was beneath me. My legs were spread and I could feel his heat. The pleasure reached new heights. I knew I was in control. It was odd, but at the decisive moment the word "orgasm" actually flashed before my eyes. I knew it was happening. I lost control of my body movements, and nature seemed to take over. There was a rush of heat. I moaned with the ecstasy that coursed through my body. Finally, in sheer exhaustion, I was still.

As we cuddled, the sense of intimacy was overwhelming. The timing may not have been ideal, but I could no longer hide my past from Kurt. I had to talk about Richard. So I let loose with the truth, about the broken engagement, and how much I had been hurt by the chain of events that led to the breakup. I was so relieved when Kurt did not seem at all surprised or upset. He told me that he knew all about it and that I had nothing to be ashamed of. Then it was my turn to listen. What he proceeded to tell me, as we lay there naked in bed, was a challenge to my whole mind and body. He brought up his father, John Driger, and how he had been taken to court by the RCMP for his suspiciously pro-German behaviour. Kurt admitted that he sympathized with his father. He was obviously worried about what I would think of him. What could I say? I had already realized that I had strong feelings for Kurt. I wanted to make a life with him. The truth was that I wasn't sure what to think at that moment. But I didn't want to hurt him, either. So I told him a little white lie, and assured him that as far as I was concerned the only thing that mattered was that the war was over.

Soon enough we showered and headed back to Grandeur. I leaned against Kurt all the way, but our conversation was very limited. For some infuriating reason the face of Richard Drake kept popping into my mind. I knew I had made a big decision. I had told Kurt that I wanted to marry him, and he had told me to name the day. Was I crazy? I couldn't help remembering how madly in love I had been with Richard, how badly I had wanted to marry *him*. With Kurt it felt different. Maybe that was to be expected. Maybe first love really was special, never to be repeated. Did that mean I wasn't in love with Kurt? Was I marrying him just because I wanted to be married? Or was it even worse than that? Could I be marrying Kurt just to prove to myself that Richard no longer had a hold on me? It was all so confusing. It would have been confusing even if Kurt had not admitted that he had inherited his father's Nazi sympathies. What on earth was I supposed to do with that information? Take it away, and what was left was a man who had everything that a marrying girl would want. Oh, everything would have been so much simpler if it was only a question of love! But by the end of our long drive back to Grandeur I had resolved to have faith in the decision I had made. If it were meant to be, then God would help me make it work.

The following weeks saw our wedding plans made. John Driger said he would pay every penny of our expenses if we would go to his beloved Germany for our honeymoon. Kurt didn't say anything, but as he looked at me I knew the answer he wanted to hear. So I gave it to him. "Yes, Dad, we'd love to go to Germany." At that point Kurt had tried to remind his dad that, from what he'd read, Germany was still in a shambles as a result of the war. John would have none of it. "You'll be fine," he said. I took comfort in the fact that at least I was with a man who could speak the language. It would be an experience, there was no doubt about that. How many Saskatchewan girls would be able to say they had spent their honeymoon in Germany this year? Even so I had my moments of doubt. In fact there were times when I was downright scared.

The wedding was beautiful. I was a beautiful bride and I knew it. The gifts we received were out of this world. And we were treated wonderfully while we were in Germany. Kurt's relatives tried to shrug off the effects of the Second World War, but I was wise enough to know that Kurt had been warned of the areas that we should avoid, the areas with the greatest devastation. Instead we visited beautiful rural areas, and small, non-industrial towns where the Allied bombers had not struck. All too soon the honeymoon was over, and we began our lives on the Driger family farm a few miles from Grandeur.

Everything we had in our home, and every vehicle we drove, was the very best. We did not have a cent of debt. But every car, truck, and tractor we owned came from the dealership operated by Russ Kessler. My dad had never had anything good to say about Russ. He was a womanizer and a smooth operator, my father had said. I only understood what he meant when Kurt sent me to fetch some spare parts for the first time. I met Russ face to face and I could sense his eyes undressing me. He made me feel naked.

Kurt had often told me of his lifelong desire to own and fly an aircraft. The establishment of the Grandeur Flying Club seemed to spur Kurt on. He became the proud owner of a four-seater Piper aircraft and received flying lessons from Jim Johnson, the chief flying instructor and manager of the club. A whole new world had suddenly opened to my husband, and he seemed happier than ever, which in turn made me happy. I loved the freedom of the farm, and relished Kurt's obvious love for me. It was a very good life for both of us.

CHAPTER THIRTEEN

Rex Doncaster

The fact that Richard Drake, of all people, had beaten me to Winnipeg, and made a deal with War Assets for the hangar that should have been mine, was a real blow. Why was it, I asked myself, that our paths always seemed to be leading the two of us in the same direction? The only difference, and this was the bit that really rankled, was that Richard Drake always seemed to get to the destination first.

I was still brooding over my disappointment at losing the hangar to him when, a few days later, the phone rang. It was Richard Drake. This was surprising enough, but he completely shocked me by asking if he could come to Saskatoon to see me. I agreed to meet him at my house at three o'clock the following afternoon. I was still stunned when I broke the news to Thelma. "I can't believe that Richard Drake is coming here. What could he possible want?" Thelma understood my feelings. I had told her the whole history of my dealings with Richard Drake. In any case he had asked if I would mind if he brought along his wife Mavis, another war bride, just like my Thelma.

Three o'clock came and Mavis and Richard arrived. Richard's first words were warm. "It's great to see you, Rex. It's been a long time." He held out his hand. I took it. "I hear things are working out well for you," Richard continued as we settled down in the living room. "Mavis and I have nothing to complain about, either. Actually our business in Grandeur is working out far better than we could have hoped." There was more small talk in this vein, but I was relieved when Thelma came in with the tea tray and took the burden of conversation off me. She certainly knew how to be gracious to guests. "Mavis, I've heard so many wonderful things about you from people Rex and I know in Grandeur," my wife said. "It's nice to finally meet you."

Mavis flushed. "Well, Thelma, that's so nice of you to say. I'm rather ashamed at how long it took for us to get together like this. Richard and Rex have known each other since they were children, after all. Let's just make sure that our next get-together happens a great deal quicker."

"I couldn't agree more. Now, what do you take in your tea?" The women chatted on for a minute more before Thelma turned to Richard. "We girls seem to have plenty to talk about, and I know you wanted to see Rex. Perhaps Mavis and I should go to the kitchen?"

"No, Thelma, that's not necessary. What I came to ask Rex is hardly top-secret stuff. I've recently closed a deal on the old RCAF hangar east of Grandeur. What I want to do is use it to form the first real flying club in town. I've already set up a management committee, which will take over the hangar for what I paid for it. I'm not in this to make money, believe me. The only conditions I insisted on were that Jim Johnson be appointed the club's chief flying instructor, and his wife Glenys be the secretary and office manager. And I also asked that I be allowed to approach you about becoming chief mechanic."

I simply could not believe my ears. Richard went on to explain that if I accepted, I would control my own department. What was even better, any profit from the sale of aviation fuel would be mine. In the circumstances I thought it best not to reveal how I had tried to purchase the very same hangar. Was it possible that he already knew? Was this offer his way of throwing me a bone, so to speak? The last thing I wanted was pity from Richard Drake. But the offer was an amazing one. I needed time to think.

"Richard, I'm sure you can understand that I can't give you an answer before I've had a chance to talk it over with Thelma," I said. "If you don't mind, I'll call your office around four o'clock tomorrow afternoon. Do you have a business card with you?" He happily handed over his card, and when lunch was finished, Richard and Mavis went on their way.

That night I had a very full discussion with Thelma. We liked the idea of living in Grandeur. I was still suspicious, but whatever Richard's motives, the offer was too good to turn down. So when I picked up the phone the next afternoon, my answer was yes. And I had to admit that Richard sounded genuinely pleased.

Thelma and I didn't waste any more time. We were anxious to get down to Grandeur as soon as possible. It was just the sort of place where we wanted to raise our little family. We bought a comfortable home and I got down to work at the Flying Club. It felt great, finally, to be my own boss.

From day one, the Grandeur Flying Club was an unqualified success. Clinton Drake, now a fully chartered accountant, was hired to come in once a week to check the cash flow. Glenys Johnson, as Richard had intended, became responsible for the mechanical logbooks that came with each aircraft that I serviced. The subsequent addition of a second mechanic, Punch Stuka, made the care of these logs even more important. If any kind of an accident occurred with an aircraft that either one of us had worked on, as chief mechanic I would automatically have been deemed responsible for the work that had been done unless the logbook stated otherwise. But I had no worries about Punch: he seemed to be very capable and efficient from the moment I hired him.

Richard Drake soon shocked me yet again by announcing that he had purchased a Hughes 300 helicopter. He was going to Oklahoma in order to get training on the machine, which he would fly all the way home. This news meant a new challenge for me, too, because I had no experience of helicopter maintenance. Yet Richard, now apparently in the habit of coming to my rescue, offered to pay for me to spend some time in Toronto learning the ins-an-outs of this special type of aircraft. I leapt at the chance.

Even before Richard arrived home from Oklahoma with the helicopter, an unusual attachment had arrived for the craft. It was an aerial spray kit, consisting of two tanks, two spray booms, nozzles, pumps, and a lot of wiring. Richard had not mentioned it, but obviously he was planning to get into the business of crop spraying. There were already fixed-wing aircraft in this business, some Grandeur farmers having hired them to come in from other towns to spray for weeds or insects. Now Grandeur was to have something new and innovative of its own. Within a few weeks an unfamiliar high-pitched whine could be heard coming from the east. Richard and his Hughes 300 helicopter had arrived. It was a three-passenger machine with a three-blade main rotor and a very noisy tail. Richard did a neat turn into the wind and set down on the tarmac well away from the fixed-wing aircraft. When the blades had wound down, everyone who happened to be at the hangar that day pressed forward to congratulate Richard on his purchase, and to ask for a ride.

Richard, as usual, threw himself into this new venture without delay. He purchased a supply of grasshopper poison. While in Oklahoma he had watched how to convert a Hughes 300 helicopter into an aerial sprayer, and this knowledge came in handy as I worked to install the spray kit. In the weeks to come I would often watch him take practice runs, spraying the field near the hangar using just plain water. It became clear that using a helicopter was a great way to spray for weeds or insects.

Punch Stuka continued to prove himself an excellent aircraft mechanic. I had absolutely no complaints about his work. However, there was something about him that made me uneasy, something I could not explain. One day I had overheard him talking to Kurt Driger in German. They were behind Kurt's plane, and another aircraft's engine was being tested outside, so they had no way of knowing that I could hear them; but the mere sound of German left a bad taste in my mouth. On another occasion I stopped for a beer at the Riverbend Hotel. Punch, Russ and Wolfgang

Kessler, Kurt and John Driger, Rudy Schreiber, and Pete Heider were sitting around a table together. Punch waved at me, so I walked over to say hello. They all acknowledged me with a word or two, but I was not invited to pull up a chair. It was as though there was an imaginary wall between the group and myself. I was now in an uncomfortable position. I didn't want to sit alone but there was no one else in the pub that I knew. I chose to excuse myself, with the excuse that I had dropped in for some off-sale and had to be on my way.

From then on I could not shake a feeling of foreboding. I knew Punch from having hired him, and Kurt from having so frequently serviced his aircraft. But it occurred to me that I had never seen any one of the guys in their group at a Royal Canadian Legion meeting or a Remembrance Day service. I wondered if the "wall" I had sensed at the pub might have something to do with my wartime service. It was a very disturbing thought, which raised more questions than it answered.

We had a stretch of rainy weather and Richard asked me to do a thorough, fifty-hour inspection of his helicopter. His new business as a crop sprayer had grown like gangbusters. Even as I went through the mechanical motions my thoughts were frequently elsewhere. Thelma and our children were about to head off on a long summer visit to England. It had been my suggestion, but like all good wives she was concerned for my welfare in the three months she would be away. She was right to worry, but not for the reasons she thought. I had always been cursed with a wandering eye. With Thelma waiting for me at home I was able to keep it in check, and I prided myself on being a one-gal man. But I didn't trust myself in her absence.

Sure enough, Thelma had been away three weeks when temptation reared its ugly head. I ran into Judy Strome at a pub. She made a point of telling me that she would be at the next club social on Saturday night. The message was clear. I knew I ought to put it out of my mind and give that social a pass. But way down deep I knew I would not.

CHAPTER FOURTEEN

Kurt Driger

I was having a quiet beer with Pete Heider. He asked me what I thought of Russ Kessler. I laughed. "Russ? I know him like I know the back of my hand. He's a crafty son of a bitch, but then so am I. Let's just say I wouldn't leave him alone with my girlfriend or my wife."

Pete laughed, but his laugh was bitter. "Well, he can have mine. Mona and I are still civil to each other, but I'll see her down the road the first chance I get."

I took another swig of beer. "Anyway, Russ isn't a bad guy. Actually we have a lot in common. He learned German from his dad, just like my dad taught me. And Wolfgang Kessler is as proud of the Third Reich as my dad is. Your parents came from Germany, didn't they, Pete?"

"Yes, they did. That's how I learned the language. I've never made a big thing of it, but I refused to join any Canadian war, especially a war against the Germany that Mother and Dad taught me to love." Pete drained his glass and stood up. "Now I must go and pick up my wife. Her church meeting should be just about ready to break up."

After all the talk about Pete and Russ' marital problems, I could not resist congratulating myself on my wife Joan. We had no secrets from each other. Our honeymoon in Germany had been a dream. Content to let nature take its course, we had agreed not to use any contraceptives. I think we were both a little surprised when Joan did not immediately become pregnant. But I wasn't concerned. "Oh well," I said, "if it takes more effort to get you pregnant, I'll be happy to do my part as often as it takes!"

"Me too," Joan responded with a smile.

I had plenty to be happy about. Married life on the farm was even more rewarding than I had expected. Farm life seemed to suit Joan, and she was a great helper in every way. And yet it annoyed me to think of how often Richard Drake's face continued to appear in my mind. No other person in the world had such an effect on me. It didn't make any sense, I realized. I could hardly be angry with Richard for making a marriage commitment to Joan and then jilting her, because if he hadn't treated her that way, I would never have had the chance to marry her. So what was my problem? Maybe it was nothing more than the idea that Joan had once loved someone other than me.

The formation of the Grandeur Flying Club sent unexpected new opportunities my way. I had wanted to fly almost since I could walk. My desire was so strong that in the early part of the war I had talked to my dad about finding a way of getting me into Germany, and into the German Luftwaffe. It soon became obvious that this was impossible, so I gave up on the idea. But the war was over now, and there was no longer any reason why I should avoid taking flying lessons here in my adopted land.

Flying lessons and the associated coursework on the ground started at a perfect time for me. The harvest was done, and I had no other pressing calls on my time. Joan was enthusiastic. As soon as I completed my first solo I was hooked. Jim Johnson made it clear early on that he thought I would have no difficulty getting my private pilot's license. So even before the end of my training I began to search out ads for used aircraft. I came across a used Piper Supercruiser, which Rex Doncaster, the club's chief mechanic, agreed to check out for me. When he could find nothing wrong with it, I completed the deal and immediately rented a parking space at the Flying Club for my new toy. The more flying I did, the more I liked it. With each hour in the air my regret at not having been able to serve in the Luftwaffe during the war only grew. But I consoled myself by remembering that if I had joined the Luftwaffe, I would probably never have seen Grandeur again. Far more importantly, I would never have met and married Joan.

Of course before Joan there had been that amazing encounter with Judy Strome. It was probably just as well for me that Judy had chosen to leave Grandeur soon after our night together. I was well settled into marriage by the time she made her reappearance, which happened in rather a strange way. Rex Doncaster had become so busy that he had taken on an assistant, Punch Stuka. I had never met Punch before, but we were soon introduced at the hangar. By his accent I had the feeling he would prove to be a good guy to know, and so it turned out. He became a friend. But I still wasn't altogether sure about him until one evening, when Joan was at a meeting of ladies from church, and all of us Grandeur Germans got together at the Schreiber house. So there we were, Russ and Wolfgang Kessler, Rudy and Anna Schreiber, Pete Heider, Punch Stuka, my dad, and me, sitting around talking, not an English word to be heard. We were drinking hard liquor, which made tongues even looser than usual. Then Punch made a remark that sent shivers of German patriotism up and down my spine. I had been describing my honeymoon in Germany when he leapt up and literally hugged me in his excitement. "My father's land!" he hollered joyfully. Further discussion quickly revealed that Punch, like the rest of us, had purposely avoided military service, despite the fact that he was the right age and in perfect health. "How could I take up arms against any German?" he asked me. I knew exactly how he felt, and said so. It was clear that Punch had the makings of a great member of our gang.

Then I noticed the clock. Joan, thinking I would be spending the evening at the pub, had said she would pick me up there as soon as her meeting was over. "Fellas!" I exclaimed, "I've got to meet my wife at the pub in ten minutes, so I'm off." To a man, they were in the mood to follow me. What could I do? So we all went for another beer that none of us needed. Pete, who was slightly less intoxicated than the rest, suggested that we leave the German language at Rudy's place. I gave a sigh of relief when they grudgingly agreed. As we stumbled down the alley at the back of the hotel, my booze-soaked brain was well aware that this was the last thing my marriage needed. The guys were still talking in German. But maybe that was no bad thing: at least it would ensure that Joan had no way of knowing what we were talking about.

We entered the pub and found a table for seven, Anna Schreiber having stayed home. The guys were feeling no pain. We sat down and ordered a round. From then on everyone kept their word, and not a word was spoken in German, and nothing was said about war veterans or the Canadian Legion. Joan was still nowhere to be seen, but I was no longer too worried about what she would find when she came in. And then, totally out of the blue, Judy Strome walked into the bar. She saw us and came straight over to our table. I almost choked on my beer. The last time I had seen Judy, she had taken me to bed. "Hello Kurt," she said with a sly grin, as if we met each other every day of the week. She was a cool customer, and she looked great. I knew that every man at the table was admiring her. Then came another thunderbolt. Punch stood up and introduced Judy as his wife. As if I did not have enough to think about, Joan picked that moment to appear at my side. Joan knew most of my gang and said hello. Then she went over to Judy and started talking to her. Only later would I learn that the two of them had already met at the Flying Club.

Sitting quietly in the car while Joan drove us home, it occurred to me that sooner rather than later I was going to be in big trouble with my wife. What would she have thought if she had seen me at Rudy and Anna's place? Whether or not she could understand German, I couldn't imagine her approving of what we had been talking about. I could never introduce her into that sort of scene and expect it to go well. So if I really valued my marriage, I had a choice to make: I must either leave the gang, change the gang, or change Joan. But how could I do any of those things?

I felt helpless. I was suddenly torn between my love of Joan and my deep-seated feeling for everything that was German. As I eased myself out of the car I was so drunk that my feelings began to dribble out of my mouth. "Please help me Joan," I pleaded with her, albeit under my breath. Naturally she misunderstood and rushed around to give me a shoulder to lean on. But I was perfectly steady on my feet.

CHAPTER FIFTEEN

Mavis Drake

As the months rolled by, I became more and more concerned about our sales manager, Rudy Schreiber. For example, he made a habit of using one of our demonstration cars as his personal vehicle. This was not necessarily unusual behaviour for a sales manager; but I had a feeling that in some strange way he was abusing the privilege. Rudy's wife Anna definitely saw herself as a high roller. She was constantly heading to the city with a carload of friends, and always in our Ford demonstrator. In this and many other small ways, Rudy and his wife seemed to me to be living beyond their means. I had also overheard a rumour that Rudy Schreiber was one of several German-speaking men who frequently met at Russ Kessler's garage–men who all supposedly shared a nostalgia for Nazi Germany. But this seemed too bizarre to believe. In any case I did not make too big an issue of Rudy's conduct with Richard, because the business was showing a respectable profit, and I was quite sure that Richard would have noticed if there was anything definitely wrong with the accounts. I began to

wonder if I was being unfair to the Schreibers.
I also decided not to worry Richard with the crazy rumours about Nazi Germans at Russ' place, at least not for the moment. My husband had more than enough on his mind, I thought. In the years since the war he had evolved into a forthright and successful businessman, always on the lookout for new ways to make money. In early 1960, I learned of his latest idea. "Mavis, I think we should get into helicopters," he announced one evening as we sat at the dinner table. It had occurred to him how useful a helicopter would be for crop spraying. I saw no reason to disagree. I trusted Richard's instincts completely.

All went well as planned. In a month he had obtained his license and was back home, spraying farmer's fields. The first season was an exceedingly fortunate one. There was lots of rain, and the farmers found it difficult to get into their fields with wheeled equipment. Rich had more work than he could handle. And it was work that paid handsomely. The helicopter also gave Rich and me unexpected time together. Helicopters were few and far between, so we would frequently be invited to show off our Hughes 300 at local sports days and country fairs. The Grandeur Legion Branch would sponsor us in return for a share of our take: I sold tickets, and Richard gave rides. It made for a nice break from the daily routine. Similarly, when Richard called on farmers to sell farm machinery, he often made a practice of taking their family members up for rides. Many deals were closed in this way.

Richard and I were together in the helicopter one afternoon when a disturbing thought popped into my head. "What would happen if you lost power, or had an engine failure?" I asked him. At that instant we were cruising at seven hundred feet. Richard offered to demonstrate the procedure. He switched off the power. "Keep an eye on the rotor RPM." I did; it was about six hundred revolutions per minute. Suddenly he hollered, "Collective down!" and we dropped like a stone. I was interested to see that our downward fall was keeping the RPM of the rotor at about six hundred. We were very nearly on the ground when Richard selected "collective up," and with a precise movement of the cyclic flared the helicopter onto its skids. We slid into a perfect landing.

I was a little shaken, but impressed. Richard assured me that he practiced this maneuver at least once a week. "Smart thinking," I was quick to tell him.

Because her department was so well organized, Richard borrowed Emma Jones to be his right-hand man with the weed and insect control part of our business. She studied up on combining amines, esters, and other products to create the most effective mixture. Emma soon hired another part-time lady, Maggie, to assist with the marking while Rich was spraying the field.

Emma was a wonderful friend to me. We seemed to think alike in so many respects, and our business and social lives were often one and the same. One day she mentioned how Richard had shown her the same autorotation maneuver he had demonstrated for me. She was equally amazed at how simple and effortless he made it look. It made us both worry less about Richard than we might have done otherwise.

The Grandeur Flying Club continued to be a roaring success. The dances and parties were wonderful.

Rich and I loved to dance, and so we seldom missed one of these events. They were a breeding ground for gossip, but of course that was part of the fun. Judy Strome and Punch Stuka kept tongues wagging, and so did Anna and Rudy Schreiber. Early on Richard had pointed out Kurt Driger's wife. She was none other than Joan Hanson, the girl to whom Rich had once been engaged. Kurt was a relative newcomer to flying, but he was apparently not short of money; and why would he be? He had made lots of it while fellows like Richard and Clint were away doing their bit to make sure the German language did not become a compulsory subject in Canadian schools.

I tried to put myself in Joan Driger's boots. I could only imagine how I might have reacted if I had been engaged to a fellow and then been ditched for who knew what reason. Of course I didn't blame Richard, but I knew how hard it must have been to lose a man like him. I did not see how I could go on living if Richard were ever taken from me. It was unthinkable on so many levels.

The fifteenth of June, 1962, was a dark day for Grandeur. Mabel Wickham was the assistant to the postmistress at the Grandeur post office. She was thirty-five years old, a very attractive lady, a war veteran, and president of the Royal Canadian Legion Women's Auxiliary. She had written several articles in the local paper reminding Grandeur of the sacrifices made by its servicemen and women. A few days earlier she had been seen getting into a dark car near the ice cream shack on the east end of town. She had not come home that night. Naturally her mother had contacted the police. On June 15, Mabel Wickham was finally found: her dead body was uncovered near a little-used road. It was the kind of thing that just did not happen in Grandeur. Neither Emma nor I could understand how it could have happened. Emma, still unmarried, was especially shaken. "Mabel and I were so alike. We were the same age. Why would she have gotten into a car with someone she didn't know? I don't believe it. She must have known, or thought she knew, this person. And only a really strong man could have overpowered her. It's terrifying to think that this man is still somewhere near us."

The police set up warning signs, requesting women to come forward if they had experienced any kind of nasty run-in with a man during the previous two or three years. The signs were explicit. They made it clear that even those incidents that might not have seemed very serious at the time might help find Mabel's killer. Very quickly rumours started swirling around town that one or two women had come forward with stories of their own.

But after that months went by without any more news, and the frustration at the police detachment rose to a boiling point. "I never bring the subject up when Sergeant Doyle and I are doing business," Richard told me. "Just mentioning it puts him in an ugly mood."

Meanwhile I had another thought-provoking encounter with Rudy Schreiber. Richard was doing some routine service work on the helicopter. We had moved it into the big door at the back of our garage, and Richard had the covers off the drive belts so that he could give the idler pulleys a special check-up. Rudy had wandered in and seemed extremely interested in this unique and simple drive system. I couldn't put my finger on it, but there was something about his questions that struck me as odd. I found myself thinking back to that old gossip, which I hadn't shared with Richard, about Rudy Schreiber and the supposed German gang who occasionally gathered at the Kessler garage. I must talk to Richard about this, I decided.

The forecast for the following day was for wind, but Rich didn't have much faith in the local weatherman. He intended to go on with his work regardless, and excused himself immediately after supper in order to check a few things on his helicopter out at the hangar. If it did turn out to be windy, well, every farmer knew you couldn't spray if the wind was blowing. But otherwise he wanted the machine completely ready for an early morning start. He promised me he would not be too long.

For once the weatherman was right. Thursday morning proved far too windy for any kind of crop spraying, and Rich quite sensibly came back in and worked around the garage. He had plenty to do, even on the ground. Farmers seemed to have the ability to dream up new troubles for their machines all the time. "I love it," Rich confessed to me. "There's something awful nice about being needed."

I felt a sudden irrational need to hold him close. "Just remember, love, that your daughter and I need you as well. I've watched you, in that helicopter of yours, roaring over and under telephone and power lines. All I ask is that you always be careful."

CHAPTER SIXTEEN

Judy Strome

It was sometimes hard for me to believe, but yes, I was a native of Grandeur. I had completed high school there with above-average grades and decided that I would like to study accounting, though at a level somewhat below that of a chartered accountant. I also thought it would be a good idea to learn some secretarial skills. All of this required me to move to Saskatoon. It was in Saskatoon, near the end of my coursework, that I met a chap named Punch Stuka. I was in a beer parlor with some girlfriends when Punch and three of his own pals came over to the table. I was no shrinking violet where men were concerned. As the evening progressed I heard Punch say that he was an aircraft mechanic, and how he had taken a job in Grandeur. This caught my attention and I suggested the two of us should meet again at the beer parlor the next night. It turned out that Punch was heading to Grandeur very soon to look for a place to stay. I proceeded to make one of the dumbest offers of my life: "Find a place for two, and I'll come with you." Looking back I couldn't understand what I had been thinking. Sure, he spoke intelligently and was handsome as hell, but I barely knew him!

When we set up camp in Grandeur, we found it easier to tell everyone that we were married, though in fact we weren't even engaged. My relationship with Punch was a strange one. I was drawn to him in a very unusual way. He was a good drinking buddy, and a perfect partying friend, but there was no relationship at bedtime. It was bizarre. I had never been in bed with a man without having sex with him. Punch and I never talked about it. Of course I wondered. On the other hand I realized there were advantages to our situation. So I accepted the way things were between us without argument. In a way it was refreshing not to have to worry about sex.

Punch did not get drunk every night, although he seldom missed an evening without a drink. I could absolutely depend on Punch going overboard at least once a week. On those nights, I was on my own. But I came to expect it, and Punch's benders gave me a chance to pursue my other interests, sexually-speaking. I enjoyed the continuing power I was able to exert over most men. One of the few to resist me was Richard Drake. I tried to make time with him at one of the first Flying Club parties I attended. He didn't give me one iota of encouragement, however, so I cooled it. It was obvious that he only had eyes for his wife Mavis. I had to admire his loyalty.

Unlike Punch, I was far from being a heavy drinker. I loved to feel daring and devilish every so often, but I did not like to feel any loss of control. I didn't see any sense in drinking so much that I couldn't dance. And I didn't see any sense in drinking so much that I couldn't keep a conversation going, either highbrow or lowbrow. I always wanted to be clear-headed enough that my comments made some kind of sense. The truth of the matter was that I tried to be a smart drinker, and a smart person. For this, and other more obvious reasons, I was far from being loved by the other women in the Grandeur Flying Club. I had heard the whispers: "No man is safe," they said, "when Judy Strome is around."

Punch was quite the opposite of me in this respect. He bordered on what his friends feared was alcoholism, but he was one of those amazing characters who seem able to avoid hangovers no matter how heavily they drink the night before. There was no doubt that his job would have ended abruptly if his drinking had even slightly affected his work as an aircraft mechanic; there was no way that he would have been given a second chance if his work on a plane was ever faulty. But his work was always spotless. I suppose this was one of the things that kept me interested in Punch.

To have said that I was completely happy with my lifestyle would have been a lie. I knew that this was not a normal way to live. No doubt Punch was a big part of my problem. There were many times when I wondered how I had ever got myself into this mess. Although we continued to live together amicably enough, there was something about him that scared me, and maybe it was this fear that caused me to stick with him for as long as I did.

There was one wife around the club who never had to worry about me being a threat to her marriage. Her name was Sadie Kessler. Her husband Russ thought he was God's gift to women, but I wasn't very impressed.

Actually I couldn't stand him. He just reeked of dishonesty and craftiness, two qualities that could put me off the most gorgeous man on earth. And Russ was a long way from being gorgeous. I had danced with him at various club socials, and on at least three occasions he took the opportunity to proposition me. On the first two occasions I had let him down gently, but the third time, fed up and frankly disgusted, I told him as bluntly as I could that I was not interested in the slightest. His response left me amused, but also a little afraid. "Rumour has it," he said, "that you're an easy piece. And believe me, I know more about turning on a woman than any guy you've ever met. You'll find out soon enough." I couldn't believe any man could be so crude. I considered myself a true modern woman, maybe even ahead of my time. I knew all the techniques and I wasn't afraid to use them. But this was too much. From then on I wouldn't even dance with Russ.

My life and all of its problems were suddenly pushed into the background by the murder of Mabel Wickham. Such a thing was totally foreign to sleepy, happy Grandeur. Rumours were piled on top of rumours, but in the end word came down that Sergeant Tom Doyle had found Mabel's body beside a remote country road. A special squad of the RCMP from Saskatoon had arrived to comb the site for clues. I had only known Mabel vaguely, but the whole incident rattled me in a personal way. I had got into my share of strange cars over the years. I wished I had some kind of pipeline into the investigation. I thought of that handsome young Corporal Tim Holden I had seen in town. Now I had extra motivation to get to know him better.

Friday night came and I was watching TV in the bedroom when Punch walked in. I instantly sensed trouble. He had been drinking, but was not stupid drunk. He could not blame what happened next on alcohol. He paced around the room like a man possessed, shouting at me, making no sense. He seemed obsessed about finding his flask, the silver one he habitually kept filled with booze. He kept shrieking, "Where is it? What have you done with it?" When I tried to calm him down, he actually slapped my face. At that moment I made the decision I should have made long before: I was moving out tomorrow. As soon as Punch left for work in the morning, I phoned a lady friend and explained my problem, and she offered me a place to stay while I looked for an apartment. I moved fast. I took the day off work, rented a small storage locker and pickup truck, and moved all of my personal stuff out of Punch's home. Before turning the key in the door for the last time I wrote a long thoughtful letter and left it on Punch's mantle. With that our strange relationship was finally over.

Punch took it all very well. He did not go off the deep end, or phone me at work, or in any way make it difficult for me. Somehow, in spite of the previous night's rage, I was not surprised. Punch was a man of many dimensions, and when another side to him appeared, it was almost to be expected. In the weeks ahead I would struggle to explain to myself the phenomenon that was Punch Stuka. I came to the conclusion that the only way to understand his behaviour was that either he was a homosexual, or a man that suffered from some other, and far weirder, sexual deviation. I was relieved to be free of him.

CHAPTER SEVENTEEN

Tom Doyle

I settled in well as the officer commanding the detachment in Grandeur. For a long time nothing major came along to complicate my life. Once in a while there would be a misplaced child, or a call from a frantic mother that a teenage son or daughter had not returned home as planned. But this was the extent of the serious calls that the detachment received.

So when such a call came in from a Mrs. Wickham, saying that her daughter Mabel was late coming home, I wasn't overly worried. Mabel was well known as a responsible woman. She was president of the Royal Canadian Legion Auxiliary. She was a war veteran as well as being the assistant postmistress. Then the Wickham story worsened. Mabel did not come home the following night, either. I sent Corporal Tim Holden over to Mrs. Wickham's home to take a more detailed report. In a small town like Grandeur news spread very fast, and calls started to come in from people who claimed to have seen Mabel getting into a dark-coloured car, not far from the ice cream shack on the east end of town.

On Monday evening I contacted Rich about some unrelated Justice of the Peace matters, and the topic of Mabel Wickham inevitably came up. He made an interesting comment. "You know, Tom, last night I went out to the hangar to check one or two service items on my helicopter. I happened to pass by that old road that comes from the south near the Sandish Farm. It was strange, because I almost never see anyone on that road, but last night a dark car came barreling along it and slid right in front of me through the intersection."

"Did you see who it was?"

"No, I didn't. It wasn't really a dangerous incident. I avoided him easily. At the time I thought it was just some young buck who had a new driver's license and his father's car. But then I heard about the dark car that Mabel supposedly got into, and I started to wonder."

I shrugged. "At this point it's impossible to know. Maybe that car you saw was involved somehow, but maybe it wasn't. If only Mabel would smarten up and phone her mom." Then a dark thought crossed my mind. "If she can, that is."

Richard looked glum but said nothing more.

"Anyway, from a police point of view, I damn well have to take a negative approach to all this. If Mabel Wickham still hasn't turned up by noon tomorrow, I'll post signs asking the public for information.

As it turned out I could not bear to wait until noon on Tuesday. Before the local painter was even out of bed, I called him and got him working on the signs. "I don't like this," I said to one of my constables who I met coming back from an early patrol. "This girl has been missing too long. Could you stay on duty for another hour?" Together we posted the signs in conspicuous places. The request was for more than whatever news people might have about Mabel; I asked any woman who had recently been propositioned or offered a suspicious car ride to please come forward. It could be taken for granted that by nine a.m. ninety percent of Grandeur's population knew that Mabel was missing.

No sign that I had ever commissioned ever brought a quicker response. Soon after lunch I was called to the phone. "Sergeant Doyle? My name is Neva Graham. I saw one of your signs. Can I come in and talk to you?"

"Yes, of course, come in immediately. Or if you'd prefer, we could meet in the parking lot next to the RCMP building."

Neva Graham's story was unlike any I had ever heard, in Grandeur or anywhere else. She came to the parking lot as we had arranged on the phone, and she was very distraught. In fact she could hardly put two words together and it took a good deal of prodding to get them out of her. But her intensity overpowered my doubts. As she spoke, her eyes seemed to drill into my brain. When she was eighteen, she had been walking on a road on the outskirts of Grandeur. A car came along and offered her a ride. She did not know the driver. As she rode with this man, he opened two cans of Coke, and after producing a flask of rum, carefully poured some in each can. She did not object; she had drunk rum and Coke before, and liked the taste. They drove on, east of town, drinking and chatting. The driver offered her a second round of rum, but she said no. It was at this point that Neva's story took a nasty turn.

"I can remember exactly where he turned off the main road," she told me, her voice now so flat it was as though she were in a trance. "He went south by Sandish Farm. I'd been there before on drinking and petting parties. He turned the car around by a small grove of poplar trees, maybe two miles down the prairie trail. Then he stopped the car. He put his arms around my shoulders and pulled me towards him. I became hysterical. I tried to pull away from him, I fought him as hard as I could. But it was no use. He opened the door and dragged me from the seat and out onto the grass. I screamed and screamed, but no one lived within miles of there."

Neva was crying now, great sobs wracking her body. "He pulled my dress up over my head, and ripped off my panties and bra. And he raped me. Right there in the grass. I bled, I thought I was going to die, that he would finish with me and kill me. But he didn't. He picked me up and threw me back into the car. Then he put an arm around my neck and gave it a terrible wrench. I thought I would pass out, strange colours were flashing before my eyes. But he released his grip and warned me he would do it again if I wouldn't promise to keep everything he had done to me a secret. He started to apply pressure with his arm again, and I screamed that I wouldn't tell anyone, ever. Then he drove me into Grandeur and let me out."

I passed her a tissue and she wiped her eyes. She was calmer now. "I had to come and see you. Yesterday, after I heard about Mabel, I drove to the spot where I was raped. I can't explain it, maybe I'm crazy, but I just have this feeling that Mabel may be lying there in those trees. Now, Sergeant, if you don't mind, I'd like to leave now. And please, please, don't let my visit here become public knowledge." I assured her that I would never share what she had told me with anyone. With that, she stood up, and refused to speak another word. I watched her walk across the parking lot and drive away. I knew that I should have questioned her further, pressed her for a better description of the man who raped her. But my gut told me she had told me everything she was going to, at least for now.

There was no question what I was going to do. Neva's story was begging for action. I would go out to the abandoned prairie trail that ran south of Sandish Farm. I sent a message for the two officers who were out patrolling to meet me there at once. It was not difficult to locate the stand of poplars that Neva had described, though it was a much larger area than I had anticipated. I came across a slight indent in the ground that was full of rotten leaves and other broken bush and grass that had accumulated over the years. A coyote or dog had been digging there and had pulled away some leaves. A human leg was exposed. I radioed my office, and had them put in an emergency call to the office in Saskatoon. Without giving any further details over the air, I asked that the RCMP special investigation squad from Saskatoon meet me on the main road east of Grandeur as soon as possible.

It took several hours for the squad to arrive, and the wait gave me a lot of time to think. Richard Drake's story, of the black car racing down the deserted prairie trail, gnawed at me. This was the road that Richard was talking about. I would have to talk to him again. What if the dark car that slid out in front of him was driven by the murderer? Something else occurred to me. Richard had made it clear to me that he couldn't identify the driver of the car he saw; but what if the driver had somehow recognized Richard? I would have to warn him to be careful. But I wasn't really worried about him. Richard Drake had faced far worse things in life, and I was sure he could look after himself.

The RCMP special squad finally arrived, and I led them over to the scene of the crime. They would turn every blade of grass at the murder site; every inch of the ground for many yards around would be scoured. The coroner was expected at any moment, and the body would not be moved until he authorized it. If the investigation continued past nightfall, then lighting would be arranged, or failing that, a guard would be placed on the site and the forensic analysis would continue in the morning.

While the experts did their work I decided I was going to track down Richard and let him know the situation. I tracked him down at the Flying Club hangar where he was just about to do some sort of maintenance on his helicopter. He was stunned and very sad after hearing that I had found Mabel, dead. Remembering my pledge to poor Neva Graham, I didn't give him too many more details, other than to say that the signs I had posted, asking the public for tips, had done their job in record time. The truth was that I would never quite understand the instinct that led Neva Graham back to that spot out by Sandish Farm. It was as though her own nightmarish experience, years before, had given her an insight no one else had. I was determined to catch Mabel's killer, but I prayed to God that in doing so I also would be able to give Neva the peace of mind and the justice that she had been denied for so long.

The following day I received a preliminary report on the findings of the RCMP experts. It stated that the partially clothed woman found in the field had been raped before she was killed. The pathologist estimated that she had been dead for forty-eight hours when found. She was blond, five feet seven inches tall, approximately thirty-five years old, with a long-legged full figure. She lay on her back, one arm flung behind her head, the other twisted under her body. The only bruises or blood seemed to be on her fingertips. Her head was twisted awkwardly to one side. The cause of death was a broken neck. She carried a driver's license that clearly stated her name, and her heart-broken mother had already been summoned to confirm that this was indeed Mabel Wickham.

The crime scene squad had discovered two other items of particular interest. One was a rubber cover, such as could be found on the brake or clutch pedals. The theory was that the girl was pulled bodily from the front seat; in the process of grabbing for anything to save herself from being dragged from the car, she had pulled the rubber cover off the clutch or brake pedal. This would explain her bruised and bleeding fingers. The other item found at the scene was a half-inch open-end wrench, with the trade name "Star" on it. Its significance was totally unknown. There was nothing on the body to indicate Mabel had been beaten with it. In any case there was no longer any doubt that Mabel Wickham had been murdered.

It was the most serious crime ever committed – or at least known to have been committed – in the whole history of Grandeur, Saskatchewan. It was also by far the most serious case I had ever been involved in. I knew what was expected of me. I was certainly heartened by the continuing response to the signs I had posted. Not only had they brought Neva to me, but after Mabel's death had been confirmed a twenty-one year old woman came forward with a useful story of her own. About a year before, she said, she had been stupid enough to get into a car driven by a man she didn't know. Almost immediately she had realized that something was very wrong about him. He had promised to take her into town, but at the next intersection he turned towards open country. Of course she protested, but he moved to grab her. A vicious struggle had ensued, so vicious, it seemed, that the driver decided to cut his losses. After again trying to put her neck in an arm lock, he brought the car to a screeching halt and literally kicked her out into a ditch. "I'll find you and kill you if you ever tell anyone about this!" were his parting words. Then his car disappeared in a cloud of dust. The girl had subsequently missed work for three days with a terribly sore neck, but otherwise there were no lasting effects, and the memory of the driver's last threat kept her from going to the police.

Her story almost exactly paralleled the experience of Neva Graham, without the rape. She had been extremely lucky, I thought. When I asked her if she had seen anything at all in the car that might help us identify her assailant, all that she could remember was a chrome or silver flask decorated with a cross, or possibly a swastika. Regardless, I could not help noticing a pattern: in all three incidents, Mabel, Neva, and now this anonymous young lady, the attacker seemed to have employed a brutal neck hold, although only in Mabel's case had it proven fatal.

Unfortunately, after the emergence of my second informant progress on the case ground to a halt. In desperation I felt I had no choice but to talk to Neva Graham again. She was not enthusiastic, but agreed. "I'm getting nowhere in the investigation," I explained to her over a cup of coffee. "I've got to ask you, was there anything distinctive about the man or the car that you can still remember?"

She sighed, and thought for a moment. "I think it was an older model car. It looked expensive, but I couldn't say what make it was. It was maybe dark blue."

"What about the man himself?"

"He wasn't tall, but he was well-built. I remember how strong his arms were."

"Were there bags or tools or any other equipment in the car?"

"No, none of that. The only thing that comes to mind is that the rum came out of a silver flask with a small triangle embedded in the side. It's almost silly, but since then I've wondered if it might have been a swastika."

I thanked Neva again and tried to assure her that her secret was still safe with me. Then she left. I stayed behind to make a few notes. I had the feeling that if only Mabel had still been capable of talking to me, she too would have described her assailant as having possessed a silver flask decorated with a swastika.

CHAPTER EIGHTEEN

Joan Driger

My meeting at the church was over earlier than I expected, but I didn't mind. It might give me a chance to have an extra beer with Kurt and his "gang." I was a little worried about Kurt. Recently he seemed to be drinking far more than he did when I first met him. I was no prude about him tying one on now and again. But it was getting to be more than that. On the previous Saturday night I had got a phone call from Rudy Schreiber asking me if I could come down to the bar and pick up my husband, because he was in no condition to drive himself home. When I got there I was shocked to see how far gone Kurt really was; a couple of his chums actually had to carry him out to my car. I could not understand why his drinking had taken this sudden turn for the worse. Was something bothering him? Or was it just the influence of that damn gang of his? Kurt and I had not quarreled, but he did seem very troubled.

The more I thought about it, and the more I got to hear about Kurt's friends, the more troubled I became. I knew all their names: Punch Stuka, Pete

Heider, Wolfgang and Russ Kessler, and Rudy and Anna Schreiber. They were all well-known characters in Grandeur. But I also noticed that Kurt's father John was close to all of them. I had no idea what they talked about all the nights they got together, but I could recognize the language. And it wasn't English. Fairly or not, the whole thing made me uneasy, even suspicious.

I reminded myself constantly that Kurt had never tried to hide his love of Germany, and I had known all about his crazy father when we got married, so I could hardly hold these facts against him now. But I couldn't shake my growing doubts. It had been one thing when it was just Kurt and John Driger reminiscing to each other about the lost glories of their homeland; it was quite another to see them spending more and more time with other people, other Germans, who gave every indication of feeling the same way. I was a proud Canadian. There were times when I felt like asking them where *they* were during the war. None of them, I knew, had joined the armed forces of Canada. Even Kurt had managed to stay home and live off the gravy train while so many brave boys went off to fight. By 1945, Canada had the third largest navy in the world. We had built thousands and thousands of Lancaster and Mosquito bombers, with our own squadrons flown by our own aircrews. Eighteen thousand Canadian airmen had died. Where was the patriotism of men like Russ Kessler or Punch Stuka or even my own Kurt? Unfortunately I knew the answer to that question.

Of course my own patriotism had not stopped me from marrying Kurt when he told me of his love for Nazi Germany. Love (or something very close to it) had overwhelmed every other thought or feeling I might have had. But real everyday life had now taken hold. So what was I going to do? I would never be able to support Kurt in his love for his homeland. Yet I did love him. And I was sure he loved me. Maybe, I thought, this was just another situation that could only be resolved by faith. If his love for me really was as strong as my love for him, then we would find a way out of this mess. There was probably no need to confront him. After all, the war was over, wasn't it? Who could possibly get hurt by half a dozen Germans crying over Hitler in their beer?

Then came word of Mabel Wickham's rape and murder. I felt more strongly than ever how lucky I was to have such a good and strong man like Kurt in my life. The thought of a murderer still being on the loose in Grandeur drove every other residual worry out of my mind. For a while, anyway.

CHAPTER NINETEEN

Judy Strome

About two months or more after the rape and murder of Mabel Wickham, I was making my way home. It was a hot, dry day and I turned into the pub for a cool beer. Sitting alone at the bar, in civilian clothes, was Corporal Tim Holden. I smiled at him as I sat on a neighbouring stool. "Do you mind, Tim?"

"No, not at all."

"What are you drinking?"

"Beer, of course. Can I buy you one, Judy?" He summoned the bartender.

We drank in silence for a minute or two. I was still suffering from the stifling heat. "You're more than likely one or two ahead of me," I finally told him. "Mind if I return the compliment and buy you another?"

"How can I refuse?" This Tim Holden was a charmer, just as I had thought.

We chatted on about nothing in particular, and lingered over our last glass of beer. "Have you had lunch, Tim? I make a pretty darn good sandwich, and I've got some home-baked apple pie left over from last night. If you're not going on duty, why don't you come back to my place with me?" I was as bold as ever, and the implication could hardly have been any clearer.

Tim was smooth. "You supply those perfect sandwiches, and I'll supply a half-dozen beer."

I was in the perfect mood to be with Tim. It didn't take long for proof that he was equally pleased to be with me. I had made up my mind that I would not say one word about the Wickham case. If things went as I hoped, I would have plenty of other opportunities to tap his brain. Tonight I wanted nothing more than his body. We consumed more beer, and shared sandwich-making duties. The pie came next, and we were well into a second beer. All the while the sexual tension grew more overpowering. Tim finished his pie first. "Finish mine, Tim," I told him. He opened his mouth, and I popped in the last spoonful off my plate. His lips held the spoon for longer than necessary, while our eyes locked. Then he took my hand and pulled me towards him. "You make great pie, Judy."

I didn't put up the slightest resistance. Rumour had it that Corporal Tim Holden was a sharp and efficient policeman. I was about to learn that he was equally efficient as a lover. I allowed my body to be maneuvered just as Tim wanted, and when his climax came I was right with him. We were both young and virile, and the opportunity for sex could not come along often enough. Each orgasm seemed to come with new intensity. When our sexual appetites had been satisfied, we turned back to other ones and consumed the last of the beer. At last, with night having fallen, it was time for Tim to go. "I'll walk with you to your boarding house, Tim." He offered no resistance, and I enjoyed the air. We kissed goodnight. "To be continued," were Tim's parting words.

Three weeks passed without further contact. I felt it was time to use my new friendship with Tim Holden to some advantage. I was haunted by the fate of Mabel. Why I was so affected I would never know for sure, but I could not resist trying to learn the true state of the investigation. I no longer trusted the gossip circulating through Grandeur about what had been found at the murder site. I phoned the RCMP and asked for Corporal Holden.

"Hi, Tim, it's Judy. Are you working this evening?"

"No. What did you have in mind?"

"You bought the last half-dozen beer, so I figure it's my turn. Ready to help me with it?"

He laughed. "You bet. I'll be there in an hour."

I was at my apartment with the beer when Tim arrived. We kissed hello, but I gently pulled away before matters went too far too quickly. "I'm in a chatty mood, Tim. Let's talk for a while first." He accepted this with good humour. While we consumed our beer we seemed to talk about everything under the sun. About halfway through our second beer I asked the question I had been dying to ask. "Why don't the police let us know the truth about the things that were found around Mabel's body?"

"Well, that would be pretty dumb. We wouldn't want the murderer to know how much we know about him."

I had to admit that made a lot of sense. But I pressed on. "One rumour I heard is that a woman came to the police and said she got into a car with some violent guy. Supposedly she saw a silver cigarette case on the seat with a funny cross embossed in it."

"Not a silver cigarette case, a silver flask with a swa..." Tim pulled himself up short. "No, never mind."

"No, go on, Tim. You were about to say a swastika, weren't you?" I felt suddenly cold. My mind snapped back to that bizarre final night with Punch, when he had been practically frothing at the mouth about the loss of his silver flask. But did his flask have a swastika? I thought so, but I wanted to kick myself for never having looked at it more closely.

Not knowing any of this, Tim was practically frantic. "Oh my God, Judy, the sergeant will kill me if he ever finds out what I just told you. Keep it to yourself, please!" I promised that I would, but then he conveniently remembered that he was due to go back on duty at nine o'clock. He dashed out the door. "Please, Judy, not a word to anyone!"

I was at a loss as to what I should do next. There was no chance of getting any more information out of Tim. Was it really possible that Punch was somehow mixed up in all of this? It could be just a coincidence that he had lost a flask that was similar to one owned by the chief suspect in Mabel's murder. But how many Grandeur men owned a flask with such a distinctive design? Coincidence or not, I had to tell the police. So, an hour or so later, I picked up the phone. "Tim? No, don't hang up. Please. There's something I think you should hear."

CHAPTER TWENTY

Tom Doyle

My small detachment continued to work tirelessly on the case of Mabel Wickham, but nothing would break in our favour. That all ended one evening with a single phone call. "It's Tim, Sergeant," said the familiar voice on the other end of the line. "I just wanted to make sure you were still at headquarters, because I've got to talk to you right away. I'll be there in five minutes. Please wait for me."

With a message like that I wasn't going anywhere, and Tim came barreling through the door in four minutes and thirty-five seconds. I could smell the beer on his breath, but he was off-duty, after all. In any case I could already sense that he was on a high, and that it had nothing to do with beer. "What's up, Corporal?"

He started talking very fast. "I've come across some startling information, sir. Now before I tell you, I want you to know that I realize I wasn't supposed to talk about the Wickham case with anyone, but in my own defense Judy sort of tricked me, although you'll see it was probably just as well, if you'll just listen to what I have to say…"

Tim was starting to babble, so I tried to calm him down. "Tim, relax, I'm sure you didn't mean any harm. Now tell me your news. Who is this Judy, by the way?"

She turned out to be Judy Strome. Tim rapidly recounted how she had loosened his lips about the silver flask, embossed with a swastika, which had been seen by both Neva and the other young lady informant. Judy had told Tim that her former boyfriend, Punch Stuka, had owned a flask which looked very much like the one described. But the really powerful piece of information was that on the very same night Mabel had been killed, Punch had come home in a drunken rage about having lost his flask. "Judy tells me she never saw Punch act so crazy as he did that night," Tim added.

All this was a potential bombshell that could blow the case wide open. But there was a slight problem: we had not actually found a silver, swastika-decorated flask anywhere near Mabel's body. Not yet, anyway. As soon as Tim finished his report, and I had put his mind at ease about his little breach of regulations, I knew what we had to do. We had to go back to the crime scene and scour the area all over again.

It seemed to take forever for morning to arrive, and I slept very little. At dawn Tim and I and every man I could spare drove out to the infamous spot. It was hard to believe the RCMP experts had missed anything, but not impossible. What really worried me was how much time had passed. I had ordered regular patrols of the area over the intervening period, hoping to catch the killer returning to relive the event. But I couldn't afford to have my officers there around the clock, not after the first few weeks. What if someone, maybe the killer, maybe someone else, had managed to disturb the scene? We would soon find out. It immediately became clear that the road leading to the grove of poplars off by Sandish Farm had seen considerable traffic since the murder. "What do you think?" I asked Tim grimly.

"Yeah, there's been a few amateur detectives wandering around out here, that's for sure. But that's always the case, as you know, sergeant. Let's face it: the odds are against us. There's no guarantee Punch lost his flask here. Or that his flask was the one those other girls saw when they were attacked in that car."

"Or, for that matter, that the guy who attacked those girls was the one who murdered Mabel," I completed Tim's train of thought. He had been a lot more optimistic the night before. But I still had a hunch. And I had learned over the years that a police officer had to trust his hunches.

I ordered my men to spread out. Not over the field where Mabel had been found; I figured the crime scene specialists would have found the flask if it were there. No, I was interested in the old dirt road that ran past it, about fifty feet away. We were already fairly certain that Mabel had struggled with her attacker in the car that had brought her to this remote area; I had a theory that the flask might have fallen out of the car during the struggle. So we slowly, painstakingly trudged up and down the track and along the verges. Every dusty pothole was checked. The morning sun was shining bright, and I prayed for some glint of light that would indicate an object made of metal. Then at last, after two increasingly frustrating hours, there was an excited yell from one of my officers. "Over here, sir!" He was crouched in an especially weed-infested stretch of ditch. And there, barely visible, was a silver flask. It was badly tarnished, and half-flattened as if it had been run over by a car and dragged for some distance. But even in its damaged state it still bore the symbol of Nazi Germany. I picked it up in my handkerchief and turned it over. I could read a tiny inscription identifying its owner: "To Punch. With regards, Martin."

None of us could believe our good fortune. Here was proof that Punch Stuka had been at this spot. It was also more than enough to go before a magistrate and get a warrant to search Punch's residence, and impound his car.

The next few hours were the kind that policemen dream about. The warrant was signed and the rooms that Punch Stuka rented were searched. We took a metal detector into the yard behind the rental house. It took a solid hour of scanning, but finally, success: after shifting an old barrel used as an incinerator, the detector began to beep like mad. Old nails and bottle caps were the first pieces of metal to be found, but even after they were removed, the detector went on beeping. We dug even deeper, and the signal became stronger. About a foot down, the shovel struck something hard and obviously metallic. The constable who was digging pushed hard, and turned the shovel sideways. Two chrome-plated wrenches appeared in the earth. I bent down and lifted them out of the hole. Brushing away the dirt, it was easy to read the word "Star" on each of them. "My God," I marveled, "I'd bet that these are mates to the wrench we found at the murder scene." I didn't say it out loud, but in my mind I thanked Judy Strome for getting us started.

The shovel continued to unearth unbelievable evidence: not only the balance of the wrench set but also a chrome door handle. I instructed Tim to take Constable Welsh with him, and to arrest Punch Stuka on suspicion of the murder of Mabel Wickham.

The corporal soon located Punch Stuka's car and had it towed into the RCMP compound. None of the door handles were missing, but it was obvious that the handle on the front passenger door had been replaced very recently. The broken handle we had found buried in the ground was identical to the other three door handles. The vehicle had a standard transmission. I pried off the clutch and brake pedal covers. Again, the brake pedal cover was much newer than the clutch pedal cover. Moreover, the raw metal face of the brake pedal was scarred by minute scratches, while the face of the clutch pedal was as smooth as the day it was painted at the factory. This suggested that the car had been driven for some distance without a cover on the break pedal. All of this fit the evidence recovered with Mabel's body.

The following day I had Punch Stuka brought from his jail cell into the interrogation room. He started out cocky, but sunk lower in his chair as each piece of evidence was put before him. In the end it did not take too much prodding for him to confess to the rape and murder of Mabel Wickham. It was a great relief that I did not have to bring in either of the two young ladies who had escaped from Punch to identify him in person. The confession put the case beyond all legal doubt. I felt like a new man. The detachment as a whole was reinvigorated. Success had evaded us for months but we had done our jobs and done justice to Mabel's memory.

In Grandeur we lacked the facilities to secure truly dangerous criminals for longer than a few days, so Punch Stuka was taken away to a more modern jail in Saskatoon before the week was out. I then took the time to make a few well-deserved calls of thanks and congratulations: to Neva Graham and the other woman who had responded to my initial plea for information; to Richard Drake; and most important of all, to Judy Strome.

CHAPTER TWENTY-ONE

Joan Driger

I was at yet another evening meeting of my church group when the news broke that Punch Stuka had confessed to the rape and murder of Mabel Wickham. It was all the ladies around me could talk about, but I was quiet, and inside I shuddered, because I knew Punch. I had met him when he worked on my husband's aircraft.

As usual I was due to pick up Kurt at the pub, so I had a good excuse to leave the meeting early. But Kurt was not at the pub. I stood by a table, unsure what to do. I had never seen the place like this. It was like a morgue. A familiar waiter walked over to me. He seemed somewhat hesitant, even nervous.

"Has my husband been in tonight?"

"No, Mrs. Driger, I haven't seen him. Could I bring you a beer?"

"Yes, I'll have one, please." He brought my beer without another word being spoken, but I had the uncomfortable feeling that he was remembering how friendly my Kurt was with Punch. I sipped and contemplated what this association with Punch would do to my reputation around town. It was shallow, I knew, but I couldn't help it. Then, as these thoughts were racing through my head, Kurt appeared. He gave me a kiss, signaled for a beer, and sat down.

Kurt did not have much to say at first. He looked as pale and tired as I had ever seen him. I could tell just by looking at him that he knew that I knew about Punch, a member of his own gang who had committed rape and murder. In the awkward silence I started thinking about the one occasion when I had actually sat beside Punch. The two of us had shared nothing but small talk until Kurt got him talking about a favorite topic they had in common, aircraft and all things related to flying. Punch started talking about high-speed stalls, and the effects of main rotor failure on a helicopter. Kurt was impressed by his knowledge. But even at the time I thought this was pretty morbid stuff, and it definitely he left me cold. There was something vaguely and unexplainably scary about Punch Stuka. Everybody had heard how Judy Strome had left him, and I began to understand why. It was a mystery to me how she could have stayed with him so long in the first place.

It seemed almost an eternity that Kurt and I sat sullen in the half-empty pub, but in reality it was only seconds. My left hand was resting on the table, Kurt reached over to take hold of it, and looked at me in a way that almost made me cry. He was very slow to speak, and his voice was somewhat broken, little more than a whisper. He told me that he had gone to see some of his friends to talk about Punch, but they claimed to have absolutely no knowledge of the murder. I didn't know how to respond, so I said nothing.

It was his next words, so softly spoken that I had to strain to hear them, that brought back the man I had married. "Joan," he began, "I just want you to know how much I hate what Punch has done. I won't give up my other German friends. I believe what they told me, that they are as disgusted and shocked as I am. But believe me, if I ever find out they're involved in something that could hurt someone, I won't let them get away with it." I looked in Kurt's eyes, and the tears streamed down my cheeks. I was crying for the man I loved. I understood now that his love for German and his loyalty to his German friends had definite limits.

We left the pub hand in hand, and talked no more about Punch Stuka. In a strange way the arrest of Punch Stuka reinvigorated our life together. I had given up hope of getting pregnant, but the renewed emotional bond between Kurt and me brought a new burst of activity in the bedroom as well. In due course I felt something had changed. I secretly went to my doctor for confirmation. I got it. It was only as I spread the amazing news that I realized what I had been missing, and how very much I wanted a baby. Everyone, Kurt, his parents, my Mum and Dad, and all my friends were thrilled.

I was in a mood to let go of a lot of old grievances. During one of the next socials held at the Flying Club, I had my first close encounter with Richard Drake for many years. The dance floor manager called a "Paul Jones," which required the ladies to form an inner circle, and the men an outer one: when the music stopped, you were expected to dance with whoever ended up opposite to you. I had always dreaded that one of these mixer dances would one day bring me and Richard face to face, and this night it finally happened. Without speaking, Richard calmly took my hand and swung me into the dance. Then the music stopped, Richard bowed, and we parted to rejoin our respective circles. And that was it. Like so many things we fear, it had not been nearly as bad as I thought. Maybe, I told myself, I really was over Richard Drake. I loved Kurt with all my heart and all my soul and we were having a baby. How could I regret how the past had unfolded if it had brought me to where I was?

The glorious spring gave way to summer. The farm was a busy place. After a heavy rain, Kurt's neighbor brought Richard Drake in to spray his field. Fortunately, while Richard worked nearby, Kurt happened to be in town picking up supplies; I knew that Kurt would let weeds infest his whole crop before he'd ever hire Richard Drake and his helicopter. But I found the sight fascinating. There was both a power line and a telephone line, running only a few yards apart, just next to our farm. From where I stood in our garden I could plainly see Richard sweep under the power line and then over the telephone line. He followed this with a climbing turn before diving back almost to the edge of the field. It was here, just as he reached the grain at the edge of the field, that the spray nozzle on the helicopter started to spew the mixture of water and weed killer. Richard flew unbelievably close to the ground, but I knew that he had sprayed thousands of acres in this manner with wonderful success. Compared to what he had done with his Lancaster bomber during the war, with anti-aircraft guns shooting all around him and German fighter planes stalking him at every turn, flying a helicopter like this was a piece of cake.

I was still watching Richard swoop back and forth when I heard the sound of Kurt's truck rumbling into the yard, and I hurried back into the house before he could notice what I had been doing. I might have made an unspoken peace with Richard, but Kurt was still a long way from feeling the same way. Richard Drake was still the one subject that could be guaranteed to put him in a foul mood.

CHAPTER TWENTY-TWO

Richard Drake

Purchasing the Hughes 300 helicopter added a new dimension to my life. Obviously I could not say it matched the flights I had made in my Lancaster bomber during the war, but there were similarities. The climbing and diving turns I would make at the end of a field I was spraying brought back the old rush of adrenalin and pride I had felt when I flew the mighty Lancaster. Going over and under telephone lines and power lines at high speed demanded all of my concentration.

In any case the helicopter provided an interesting and profitable sideline for Mavis and me. It was almost not even fair to call crop spraying a sideline, given how much of my time it absorbed. The real sideline was taking the helicopter out to sports days and country fairs. Helicopters were still an uncommon sight in rural Saskatchewan and so I had no problem getting customers for rides. We had a deal with the Royal Canadian Legion branch, whereby they sponsored our appearances, and we shared the take with them. Two years in a row Mavis and I spent a whole week at the

Saskatoon Fair, Mavis selling the tickets, me giving the rides. It was almost like a vacation for us.

Our life was not entirely carefree. We had both become aware that not everyone in Grandeur liked me. Every once in a while there would be whispers about some people badmouthing veterans in general and me in particular, but I figured this was just Russ Kessler spouting off with the rest of his Nazi-loving loser friends. Mavis was far more worried about it than I was. I joked to her that it was just another case of "heavy hangs the head that wears the crown." It was true: fortunately or otherwise, I knew that I wore a crown of sorts in Grandeur. I was arguably the most prominent veteran. I was a very successful businessman. I had started the Grandeur Flying Club. My helicopter had made me a minor celebrity for many miles around. I was a Justice of the Peace. I had a beautiful wife and a wonderful family. In other words, my life was very nearly ideal. This kind of success would always make some people jealous, even if they were not Nazi-lovers. I didn't care. I deserved what I had, I had no doubt about it.

Mavis and I seldom spoke of Joan Hanson, the girl who I was engaged to when I left for the war. Mavis knew all the details, but it was all history now. Both Joan and I had found our mates and were happily married. Even so, there were times when I had to wonder about Joan's choice of husband. I didn't know Kurt Driger very well at all, but I could sense his hostility towards me. I was certainly well aware of his father John's "unique" views. John Driger was not noted for keeping quiet, and of course it had caused him a number of embarrassing incidents during the war. On the other hand he was a hard-working farmer who had taught his son well. The Drigers farmed the kind of land that always seemed to produce grain, so there was never a time when they didn't make some money, even during the Dirty Thirties when many others had suffered. For as long as I could remember Kurt had always had spare cash and had always driven a nice car. To top it off, he was handsome, and he knew it. So it was not difficult to see why Joan had married him.

I never saw Kurt or Joan in my business place, but that was understandable. One day, when Mavis and I were working together in the office, we got talking about how many couples that had married near the end of the war had ended up with large families. It was all in good fun. "Well, we're not doing too badly," I told my wife. "We've got one child, at least so far. My old girlfriend Joan hasn't got any!"

"She'd have had a bunch if she'd married you, you horny bugger," was how Mavis replied. We laughed and the discussion ended. Mavis had no insecurities where Joan was concerned.

June was my busy month with the helicopter. Word had spread far and wide about the versatility of my machine, which ensured that I was always in demand. The only days that my helicopter sat idle during the spring season were those days when the wind blew so hard that the amine and ester spray would drift where it wasn't supposed to go. Neighbouring farmers, especially those with specialty crops, didn't necessarily appreciate such overspray, so when the wind blew, you didn't fly and you didn't spray.

One Thursday our first job was not far from the airport, so on Wednesday afternoon I asked Emma to back the trailer with the helicopter into the Grandeur Flying Club hangar and leave it there. Thursday morning turned out to be windy, so for a while Emma and I worked at Grandeur Ford. It was not until two o'clock that the wind slackened enough for Emma to phone Maggie, her helper, and for the three of us to head out to the job. On the way I made a detour to Mavis's office to let her know where I was going. Mavis wrote the information in her daybook and gave me a kiss goodbye. We could not go, of course, without hearing Mavis's standard parting words: "Be sure to fly low and slow." You had to have a bit of flying know-how to appreciate that flying low and slow was actually a no-no for any good pilot. We gave our usual giggle to the advice and were gone.

When we arrived at the hangar, the trailer had been moved outside. We checked to see that the clamps which held the helicopter securely to the trailer were in place. All was well; Rex waved from the hangar door, and off we went to kill some weeds.

We began by dropping Maggie off at one end of the mile-long field. Emma and I then moved to the other end of the field with the trailer. The target area, all of it seeded to wheat, was exactly one square mile. This meant that once we had moved a mile across the field, we would then have covered six hundred and forty acres. In farming lingo, this was known as a square section.

Emma had her normal duties. She was the one who prepared the amine mix, or the ester mix, or the grasshopper poison mix, or whatever else we happened to be spraying. Over the years she had become my right hand in the field, and Mavis's right hand in the office. "Why the hell doesn't she marry one of our staff?" I had asked Mavis more than once. "Then we could be sure that she'd be around to help us for the long haul."

Mavis always had a quick answer to this. "What the hell's the matter with your brother Clint? Why don't you talk to him? He's missing a good bet by not putting some heat on our gal Emma. I'd bet you a dollar Emma would go to bed with Clint in a heartbeat if he would only get off his ass and play a bit." I knew she was probably right. It was 1963, and the old standards of morality were breaking down everywhere.

Having finished with the spray mix, Emma hollered the all-clear. She pointed to the clamps and gave the thumbs up, which meant that the helicopter was now free to be lifted off the trailer. To avoid sucking up a lot of dirt that could be ingested by the engine, which would tend to shorten its life, I did my standard run-up and engine check while the helicopter remained on the trailer. As soon as I was sure my rotor speed was fine, I slowly raised the collective, countered with rudder, and lifted into the air. Emma had meanwhile moved to another position some distance from the edge of the field. I began my flight with maximum load, which meant maximum fuel and maximum spray. Everything seemed to be working beautifully. My first turn, I decided, would be slow and lazy. So I moved the cyclic forward, made the turn as planned, and headed for Emma's flag. As I was now approaching the edge of the field of grain, I flicked the switch that started the spray pump. I could see the ester beginning to spurt through the nozzles in the sprayer booms. And there was Emma, right where she was supposed to be, a hundred yards in front of me. Good old Emma, I thought. Keep your eye on her flag, Rich.

Then in an instant it all went wrong. The helicopter fell out of the sky. My last thought was of my wife. I love you, Mavis!

CHAPTER TWENTY-THREE

Emma Jones

Working with Mavis and Richard did not leave room for many dull moments. When Richard got the idea to buy the helicopter and start a new business, I entered a whole new world. I learned more than I ever wanted to know about crop sprays, about which mixture of chemicals was most effective against which weeds, and how to most effectively exterminate grasshoppers. The really exciting part was when Richard was out working with the helicopter, because I was always with him, mixing the weed spray at whatever strength the farmer requested, filling the spray tanks on the helicopter, and recording the details of the job in our log. I thoroughly enjoyed the shift to outdoor work. I felt that in many respects I was the luckiest girl in Grandeur. Best of all, I knew that I had Mavis and Richard's total confidence.

"You're doing a great job." I had not heard Clint walk up behind me. At the time I was lying on a creeper, half buried beneath a vehicle that was not running properly. Had anyone else in my department spoken to me in these circumstances, I would have taken it in my stride. To hear Clint's voice, though, made it very different. I was suddenly very conscious of how I looked, flat on my back and smeared with grime. I rolled myself out from under the vehicle. Clint reached out for my hand. "Want a pull?" he asked with a glint in his eye.

"What makes you think you're strong enough?" I was sure I blushed as I said it, but I couldn't help myself. What made me think I knew Clinton Drake well enough to speak to him in such a cocky fashion?

"You're not that heavy. Come on, give me your hand."

I gave it to him, let my heels grip the concrete, and let him pull me to my feet. I was flustered and I was sure it showed. More than once I had dreamed of going on a date with Clint. He was a handsome devil. As a chartered accountant, he worked for a company that did bookkeeping for a number of Grandeur businesses, including that of his brother Richard. Unfortunately the company offices were in Saskatoon, so I didn't get to see him too often. And usually he didn't have too much to say. Today was typical. "I'm impressed with the results I keep seeing from your department," Clint told me as I tried to brush myself off. "Keep up the wonderful work." Then he swung on his heels and was gone.

"Couldn't we have discussed it over coffee?" I muttered to myself. Oh well, no matter how spectacular my department's success, I probably didn't look so good rolling out from under a car on that blasted creeper. The shop coveralls didn't do much for my figure, either, notwithstanding Mavis's assurance that I looked quite sexy in them.

This business of being thirty-five and considered a spinster was starting to bug me. Was it Clinton Drake, or poor little me, that was shutting the door on such a simple little thing as going out for coffee? I wasn't going to do anything crazy, but I decided that my private life needed a big change. Talking to Mavis seemed like a good place to start. She had become the closest thing I had to a big sister, and I knew she was constantly on the lookout for the right man for me.

I wondered if my problem was that my standards were too high. But it was hard to avoid high expectations when you worked around the Flying Club as much as I did, and saw some of the great guys, generally married, who spent time there. There was Jim, the manager and flying instructor; Rex, the chief mechanic; Richard Drake, my boss and hero; and of course Clinton Drake. These guys had all risked their lives for Canada and made it through the war. None of them liked to brag about the fantastic contributions they'd made and the dangers they'd overcome, but I'd heard it all from their various wives, friends, and relatives. No challenge in peacetime could possibly compare to what they had faced at war. Imagine reaching for your parachute, as Richard had once done, and finding that shrapnel had pierced and burned it so badly that it was useless. But rather than panic, Richard had kept his Lancaster as stable as possible for as long as it took the other six members of his crew to bale out. Then he had managed a crash landing in a German field. What a man!

I thought of Rich's Grandeur fiancée, Joan Hanson, the girl he was engaged to marry when he left for overseas. On the surface Joan seemed to have done well for herself, having married an aggressive and successful farmer named Kurt Driger. I had heard the talk that Joan's marriage to Kurt was too sudden, that it was a classic case of a girl being on the rebound and doing something for no better reason than to show her old boyfriend that there were more fish in the ocean than he realized. Regardless, it was obvious that Kurt was not a run-of-the-mill farmer. He had bought an aircraft and taken lessons at the Grandeur Flying Club. There was also the fact that Kurt had not joined any of the armed forces, and was always being seen in the company of other wartime shirkers like Russ Kessler. Considering the notorious views of both their fathers, it was easy to see why so many people in Grandeur assumed that Kurt and Russ and the rest of their friends were Nazi sympathizers as well. Unlike their fathers, they did not shout it from the rooftops. But when they got too much beer under their belts, they tended to be less careful and hints would slip out.

Winter came and went, and even though I still had no luck on the man front, I found my days, weeks, and months as enjoyable as ever. Although according to my job description I was manager of the reconditioning department, I still seemed to spend most of my time in the garage with my hands dirty. I could not believe how much satisfaction I got from preparing, sanding, and then painting the cars and trucks that came in as trades. I even came up with new colour combinations, and it made me proud to see how readily these were accepted by the buying public.

Through all this work my good-natured banter with Mavis continued. "Look at your face, Emma," she would tell me. "You'll never catch a man if he can't tell if you're a man or a woman." It was funny, but it was also good advice. On other occasions she would say something like, "Emma, you do a nice job of filling out those coveralls. It must take quite a pull to get them over your backside and bust." In response I would make a menacing gesture with my sander. "I'll sand down some of your bumps, Mavis, if you don't stop cheeking me!"

Spring came, and the farmers were in the fields doing their thing. Spring in Grandeur was always a beautiful time, when the ice broke up on the South Saskatchewan River and the crocuses burst into bloom. Best of all, I knew that the crop-spraying season was nearly upon us, and that soon enough I would be following Richard out into the countryside with his helicopter. I did not have to wait long, and when the spraying started, we went at it nearly every day, from first light until dark. The only exception was when it was windy.

Wednesday, the fifteenth of June, 1963, was a great day. We covered a lot of ground and the equipment worked just like new. The next morning we were scheduled to be spraying a place out by the Flying Club, so Rich asked me to leave the trailer and helicopter in the hangar itself for the night. I did as requested, unhooked the service truck from the trailer, closed and locked the hangar doors, and went home for supper.

Thursday, the sixteenth of June dawned like most June days in Grandeur. It was clear and warm. The wind, unfortunately, was too strong to allow Richard to apply the fine spray he had intended. "I'll call you if the wind dies down," Rich told me, and I worked the rest of the morning in the garage. Then at two o'clock the wind died, and I got the call. On our way out to the hangar Richard made a quick stop at Mavis's office. "I'll be a bit late coming home for supper," he warned her, "but keep everything warm for me, including supper." He blew her a kiss as she shook her head in mock exasperation. "And don't forget to keep your distance from those horny farmers while I'm gone!" We were out the door before Mavis could get in her own parting shot.

Towing the helicopter trailer from the hangar to the farm where we would be working took only a few minutes. I filled the two spray tanks and the gasoline tank, and unhooked the tie-downs for both the main and the tail rotors. My marker assistant Maggie was already at the far end of the field. In the meantime Richard was busy checking all those things you check before you start a helicopter.

I walked to my flag position, stepped off the proper distance, and checked my watch. It was now four-fifteen p.m. I heard the engine start. Richard lifted off the trailer and flew to the end of the field, where I saw spray start to flow from the nozzles. I had seen the same sequence of events a hundred times. But when Richard had reached a point about seventy yards away from my flag there was a sharp snapping sound, loud enough to be heard even over the noise of the helicopter. Then there was a flash, and an explosion. The helicopter instantly flipped forward onto its main rotors in a mass of flames.

"Richard! Richard!" I screamed, and yet I knew my screams were futile. By now the tail boom and rotor had crumbled into the roaring inferno. I screamed again. I tried to lift my leaden feet to run forward, but they would not move, and I fell to the ground.

I finally struggled to my feet, driven by the intense heat. Tears streamed down my face. Richard, I knew, was dead. He wasn't my lover, he wasn't my brother, but that didn't matter. He was the finest, most forthright and honorable man I had ever known. All I could think about was how I was going to tell Mavis. Richard was her whole life. She would never be the same. But I had to get word to her as soon as possible. Through the smoke I could see Maggie, my helper, running towards me from the far end of the field as fast as she could.

Within a few minutes I realized that we had not been the only ones to see the crash. The farmer who had hired us rushed up in his truck, driving straight through the field regardless of roads or crops. He had been working some distance away, but even there he had seen the flash and smoke of the crash. He now discovered that all his rushing had been in vain. There was no one to save. As for me, I was in no condition to explain the details of what happened. I didn't understand what had happened.

"I saw it all," I cried to him. "Richard didn't have a chance. I've got to get word to his wife."

"I'll take you to my house and you can phone from there." The farmer helped me into his truck.

I needed help. What was I going to say to Mavis? I kept asking myself this question, not altogether silently, as we drove away. I tried to plan my phone call. No phone call in my life would ever match this one. I dialed the number, and Mavis answered. She was my boss, my dearest friend, but I still could not find words. No sound having come from my mouth, Mavis hung up the phone. I pulled myself together and dialed again. Mavis answered again, and this time I blurted out, "Mavis, it's Emma."

"Yes, Emma," Mavis answered, in a voice that already had a quiver in it.

"It's Richard, Mavis. He's ... crashed. It's very bad. I'm so sorry, but he didn't make it out."

There was just an awful quiet on the other end of the phone. "Mavis, can you hear me? Don't move! I'm coming as quick as I can!"

The farmer immediately drove me back to the service truck, where Maggie was waiting, her face buried in her hands, weeping uncontrollably. The sight of her helped me pull myself together. I thanked the farmer for all he had done and asked him to do two more things: to phone Rex Doncaster at the Grandeur Flying Club and ask him to phone Richard's brother, Clint; and to alert the RCMP. The farmer assured me that both calls would be made. Then Maggie and I raced back into town.

CHAPTER TWENTY-FOUR

Tom Doyle

It was just after four o'clock in the afternoon when my office phone rang. "Sergeant Doyle speaking," I answered crisply.
"This is Frank Beardon, Sergeant. I farm out by the Flying Club. Well, it's just horrible, but I've just seen Richard Drake's helicopter explode. It's a hell of a mess. His helper Emma saw the whole thing too, and she asked me to let you know." The man's voice shook as he gave me the exact location. I hung up my phone, and held on hard to the edge of my desk. I pulled myself up and stood frozen for a moment. It was unbelievable. Of all people, Richard Drake, killed in a crash? How could this have happened? I had known the man for years, I considered him a good friend. Could he really be dead? I wondered if his wife Mavis had heard, and how she was taking it. My first instinct was to rush over to the Drake house and console her. But I knew there were plenty of other people in Grandeur who could do that. My job was to be a policeman, to get to the crash site and get an investigation under way at once. That's what Richard would have expected of me.

I sprang into action. I called Winnipeg and let the Department of Transport know that there was a report of a downed helicopter just outside Grandeur. They would send their own investigative team as soon as it was confirmed. Then I radioed Corporal Tim Holden and asked him to return to the office, fast. I broke the news to him, and together we drove to the location that Frank Beardon had given me. An appalling sight greeted us. Richard Drake's helicopter had been reduced to a mass of twisted, blackened metal, still smoldering. The smell was dreadful. I summoned one of my constables to guard the area until I received instructions from Winnipeg, and returned to my office a very sad man.

It was soon arranged for the coroner to visit the crash scene and begin a preliminary examination in advance of the aircraft accident experts, who would arrive at noon tomorrow. I now had the time to pay my respects to Mavis, but it was a short visit. She was frankly beyond consolation, at least by me. All I could do was hug her and promise that I would get to the bottom of what had happened if it was the last thing I ever did. That evening I had one more important conversation. It was with Emma Jones. When I visited her at home, she seemed overcome by rage and guilt. She almost screamed, "Richard didn't have a chance! He died in a mass of flames right before my eyes. I helped get the machine ready. Oh God! Was it my fault? Did I forget to do something? Did I?" She burst into tears. "There was a bang, and the tail came up, and it all fell in a mass of flames."

"Don't say any more, Emma," I told her as soothingly as I could. "We'll talk tomorrow." Then I went home. I had a sleepless night.

CHAPTER TWENTY-FIVE

Clinton Drake

I could not remember exactly what time it was when the phone rang, maybe five-thirty or so. I recognized the voice of Rex Doncaster from the Grandeur Flying Club. "Clint, Emma asked that I call you. Richard is dead. His helicopter crashed a few hours ago." I struggled to understand what he was talking about. My mind would not accept what my ears had heard. I could not speak. "Clint, are you still there?" Rex sounded worried. "Yes, Rex, I heard," I stammered, "I'll be there as quick as I can."

I was in no condition to get into my plane, so I decided to drive instead. The road to Grandeur from Saskatoon was mostly unpaved and demanded my full attention at the best of times, so it was lucky that this day there was hardly any traffic, or I might never have finished the trip in one piece. Over and over again as I tore down the road I told myself, "Use your head, Clint, use your head." My first duty would be to comfort Mavis. It would be difficult, but she would need all the support I could give her. I could not imagine that I would ever encounter two other people more in love than Richard and Mavis.

I made it to Grandeur with my wits more or less intact. I drove straight to Richard and Mavis's house, but at first I did not have the nerve to park the car. So I drove around the block a second time, trying to compose myself. I set my mind in gear and drove into the driveway.

It felt like my worst moments during the war, as if I was about to fly my Spitfire into the middle of three Focke-Wulf 190 fighters. Actually I would gladly have done that again rather than face Mavis now. Yes, there was fear. I knew the depth of Mavis's love for Richard. I knew the look in her eyes when Rich would go to her with the words, "I'm in the mood." And now he'd died in his beloved helicopter, which he had jokingly named, "In the Mood."

I tapped lightly on the front door. A cowardly part of me hoped that Mavis wouldn't hear the noise, but in only seconds she was at the door. We stared at each other, speechless. I reached for her hands and held them gently. Gradually, ever so gradually, we began to talk. Our first words were basically meaningless. Our grief was beyond the power of words. I had occasionally had my differences with my twin brother, but I could not recall a day that I did not love, respect, and admire him. Mavis had told me many times that meeting Richard had taught her the meaning of love at first sight. He had a way about him that made her a new and different woman. She would have followed him to the end of the world, and now he was gone. I thought of my niece Melanie, and of the business that would now have to be run in his absence. I vowed to myself that whatever the cost I would not let Richard down.

As the minutes went by, our words started to take on more coherence. Our sentences were constantly punctuated with the question "Why?" We were both fully aware of the meticulous way that Richard handled almost every aspect of his life. We had flown with him more times than we cared to count. The process of spraying crops was in no way new to him; he had been well into his fourth year with the helicopter. And his flying skills were absolutely beyond dispute. For him to die like this just didn't make any sense. Little did Mavis and I know that Sergeant Tom Doyle was struggling with the same thoughts.

I hated the ideas that were swirling through my mind. I sat Mavis down and decided I had to talk to Emma. I got her on the phone and she was just as distraught as I expected. But even in her extreme grief she seemed to understand that she really needed to talk to someone. I asked all the obvious questions. She described how there had been a bang, and how she thought she had seen a small piece of something fly off the right side of the helicopter. Then the machine had instantly pitched forward, burst into flame, and crashed into the ground. It did not sound like any ordinary engine failure. If that had been all that it was, Richard should have been able to handle it. I had personally sat beside Richard in the helicopter as he demonstrated an auto rotation, the maneuver designed to deal with a sudden loss of power to the rotors. I had plenty of experience around flying machines, and something about what Emma said sounded very wrong. I would wait until the accident team from the Department of Transport had their say. Then I would have to talk with Emma again. One thing was certain. She was the only real witness, and knowing her as I did, I had no doubt that what she told me was the truth.

CHAPTER TWENTY-SIX

Mavis Drake

Thursday afternoon was like any other day at the dealership, until about five o'clock. There was no outstanding business, and I was just getting ready to head home. Then the phone rang. It was strange: when I picked it up, there was nothing but a gurgling sound before it went dead. Some prankster, I thought. But then it rang again. I felt suddenly and inexplicably afraid. "It's Emma, Mavis," the voice on the phone said. "The helicopter crashed. Richard is dead."

I collapsed in my chair. I felt faint. My heart was pounding and my vision was clouded by a strange mist. I pressed off the light switch and did my best to stifle the screams begging for release. I told myself it was not real. It couldn't be. I was in another world, a horrible world. I wanted out! I struck the desk with my fist, but there was no pain. I let my head fall hard on the desk, but still there was no pain. Melanie's face appeared in my mind. Melanie was safe with her grandparents, thank God. For a long time this was the only rational thought I could manage.

I remembered how the bombs of war had destroyed

our neighbour's house, and left our own falling around our ears. But the terror of that had been nothing like this. There had been fear then, but at this moment I felt only hopelessness. Rich was my whole life, and my life was gone. Dear God, I pleaded, let this be a nightmare. Could it all have been some kind of mistake? But Emma wouldn't make such a mistake, that much I knew. She would be here any minute. There would be terror in her face and then I would know that it was true. All at once I felt tiny, insignificant, utterly lost. I wanted to curl up and go to sleep and never wake up. But I knew I couldn't, because Melanie would need me. She would need me now more than ever.

The office door opened. In the half-light of the windowless office I recognized Emma. I half-stood, and Emma was beside me. We clung to each other, and then the tears came. Emma's tears and the convulsive tremors that went through my body somehow brought a measure of relief. Then out of exhaustion I pulled away and fell back into my chair. Emma pulled a seat up beside me. It seemed forever before words were spoken. At last Emma took my hand and told me exactly what had happened. None of it really made sense. Rich had been a pilot for twenty-three years. He had survived the most unfriendly skies imaginable. He had avoided the ack-ack guns. He had avoided the enemy fighters. He had fought off the Germans in every way he knew how. Apart from that, I knew he was a good helicopter pilot. What could have happened? I had been with him when he demonstrated the dead-engine landing, and he did it beautifully. So why not this time?

I asked Emma to drive me home. I did not feel I

would be safe at the wheel of my car. I was sure that Clinton would be along any minute. I was already planning to have Clint drive me over to his parents' house, where Melanie had been staying all afternoon. Melanie thought so much of her Uncle Clint, and this would be a good way to handle it. I could use all the help that I could get.

I had not been home very long when there was a soft tap at the door, and sure enough, there was Clint. In our grief we stood wordless for a moment, one grieving the loss of a much-loved husband, the other grieving the loss of a beoved brother. Rather than talk we held hands and cried. When we did begin to talk, there were no answers, only questions. Our thoughts were running in the same direction. There was something about this accident that did not ring true. Clint promised me he would not rest until every avenue had been explored. He called his office to let his bosses know that he would not be in for a while; if they really needed his assistance, he told them, then he could be reached at Grandeur Ford. But once he hung up the phone he suggested that we close the business for the rest of the week. This led to yet another phone call, to Emma, who promised to contact all the staff before she went to sleep, even if it meant going to homes and pinning notes to front doors.

I asked Clint if he would come with me to break the news to Melanie and his mother and father. Clint, being a bachelor, often stayed with his parents when he was in Grandeur, but they were not expecting him this night. We were barely out of the car when Melanie was beside me, laughing, oblivious to anything out of the ordinary. But Clint's sudden presence at my side, coupled with Richard's absence, triggered immediate tension in Jim and Edna Drake. I sensed it. It was Clint who broke the strained silence. "Something terrible has happened. Richard is dead." I could not control myself any longer. I hugged Melanie and cried out, "Baby, your daddy is dead."

It took another second for the impact of the news to strike home. Melanie, though still only eleven years old, was certainly old enough to understand, and she broke down. Seeing my sweet little girl in such pain served to snap me back into control of my own emotions. Melanie had lost her dad, the best dad in the world, and I now had an extra pair of shoes to fill. I had to pull myself together if for no other reason than to see her through this horrible grief. I had assumed that Edna and Jim Drake would be upset, but strong. The stress of the Dirty Thirties, the hazards of the business of farming, the trauma of watching two sons go off to war: such experiences had hardened them. But it had not hardened them enough. Edna Drake screamed and collapsed into Clinton's arms. Jim Drake sank into the nearest chair, his face turned grey, and he seemed drained of all emotion. Only Clinton found enough strength to take charge. He hugged Melanie, promising her that everyone in the room loved her very much and that she could count on him for anything she might need. After this, he saw both Melanie and I safely tucked in his car, and drove us home. No one said a word the whole way. Dropping us off, he was sensible as ever. "It will be tough, but we must get some sleep," he said. Then he returned to Jim and Edna for the night.

Before I could go to bed I had a visit from Sergeant

Doyle of the police, who had little to say except that he would spare no effort to discover what had happened. I did not take much comfort from this, and notwithstanding Clint's advice, I slept little that night. Emma contacted me in mid-morning and let me know that she had managed to talk to all of our employees. Everyone knew the business would be closed for at least three days. Though I thanked her, I didn't really care. I had got out of bed feeling so down, so depressed, so confused, that I didn't care if I lived or died. But then I heard Melanie's sweet little voice in the hall, calling for me, and I realized again as I had realized the night before that I did not have the luxury to wallow in my grief. I had a huge responsibility. On top of everything else, I was pregnant, and I was the only one who knew.

CHAPTER TWENTY-SEVEN

Emma Jones

My mind could not leave the scene of the accident. Richard Drake was in the helicopter coming straight for my outstretched marker flag. I was poised to move quickly to the left in order to avoid the spray. Then, after Richard's pass, I would have moved to the right, while my boss made a slow, one hundred and eighty degree descending turn to take a sight on Maggie's flag a mile down the field. The three of us had done all of this hundreds, maybe thousands of times. Yet it had all gone horribly awry. One minute Richard was sitting there inside the transparent bubble, his feet on the rudders, one hand on the cyclic, the other on the collective; and the next....

I shook my head. What could have happened? I went back again to the sharp snapping sound, followed by the strange muffled explosion, which seemed to set the disaster in motion. Richard died right before my eyes, but I had not seen him die. As the inferno enveloped the helicopter I had involuntarily shut my eyes, not against the heat, but the sight itself. Oh, if only he could have managed like he had always said he would do if an engine ever failed. But he had no time for that. The fire spread too fast. I would have fought the inferno with my bare hands to save him. But there was no time for that, either. It was all over before anyone could have done anything.

The next days were very difficult. Out of respect for Richard, and because no one could possibly think about work, Mavis and Clinton closed Grandeur Ford. I was especially relieved because I knew that had we stayed open, a lot of customers would have come in just to ask me what I had seen. I knew they loved Richard and ninety-nine percent of them were genuinely shocked, but I loved him too, and I could only stand to talk about his death so much before the grief became overwhelming again. Of course I had no problem talking to Mavis, or Clinton, or Sergeant Doyle, or to any of the investigators from the Department of Transport. I was seeing a whole new side of Clinton. I knew he was as sad as any of us, but it was amazing to see how he was able to keep his cool and help Mavis. I had made it as clear as I could to Mavis that I would be there for her and for Melanie in whatever way she might need me. Mavis did need me, and I found that helping her was also helping me. I felt like I was doing what Richard would have wanted, and that was a good feeling.

It was at night, when I was left alone with my memories, that my composure deserted me. I woke up screaming, tormented by the sight of a helicopter hurtling towards me. I thought of all the terrible situations Rich had been in during the war, and how he had lived through all of them. There was something so unfair about him dying now, before my eyes, in his hometown. I dreamed of Richard trapped in his helicopter, his hands and feet off the controls, pounding desperately on the canopy, while I yelled at him from across the field, "Put your hands and feet on the controls! Now! Now!" After such dreams returning to sleep was next to impossible. Or I dreamed of Richard looking at me through the helicopter canopy, begging for help, help I would have given him without reservation if only I had the chance. Then as I lay awake in bed, I couldn't stop thinking about what I might have done wrong. I was the last one to add grease to the specified grease points. I had put the last gasoline in the tank. What if I had forgotten to tighten the gas cap properly? I had done all these things so many times before, had I become sloppy? But even if that were true, how could Richard have missed it? I'd never known Richard to miss anything, ever. No, the blame had to lie elsewhere.

CHAPTER TWENTY-EIGHT

Joan Driger

On Wednesday evening Kurt and I were committed to go to a family gathering at his uncle's place, which was not far from the town of Watrous, around eighty miles due east of Grandeur. We had originally promised to stay overnight, but I begged off. We left Watrous very late, and it was after three a.m. when we finally saw the lights of Grandeur. The Grandeur Flying Club was off to our left, and I noticed a car leaving the club and heading for the highway. What a strange time for someone to be at the club, I thought. Even more bizarre, the car slowed down and actually stopped about a hundred yards or so short of the highway. As we passed it, I saw that the car was equipped with amber fog lights just under the bumper.

Kurt and I didn't speak a word during the trip home. I was very tired and I had feigned a deep sleep virtually the whole way. Within minutes of passing the mysterious car we were home, and because it was so late, we went straight to bed. I woke up just before eight a.m. to find that Kurt was already out of bed. I went downstairs to the kitchen, and looked out the window into the yard where Kurt always parked the tractor when it needed fuel or servicing. The tractor was there, but so was a gray car with white trim that I did not recognize. Kurt was nowhere to be seen. I'll never know what came over me, but I pulled on my dressing gown and walked outside. Even when I reached the tractor I still could not see anyone, but I could hear voices. How many voices, I couldn't quite tell. But one of the voices was instantly recognizable.

"Kurt, I recognized your car on the highway as I came out of the Flying Club." It was Wolfgang Kessler; his accent was unmistakable.

"Yeah, we were coming home from my uncle's place."

"Was your wife with you?"

"Yes, of course." Kurt sounded annoyed.

"Do you think she recognized me?"

"No, and what the hell difference does it make whether or not she recognized you? I suspected it was you, but you dumb bastards are forever partying, so I didn't give it much thought." The conversation went on, but the voices became progressively harder to follow. The last thing I heard was someone ask Kurt if they could throw some stuff on his junk pile.

I made my way back into the house to prepare breakfast, and it wasn't long before Kurt followed. He gave me a kiss, washed his hands, and sat down at the kitchen table. "Did you see that car out there?" Kurt asked.

"Yes," I replied. "Who does it belong to?"

"Oh, it was just old Wolf and a few others of the usual crew. Apparently they were out partying all night, and at one point on the highway they saw us coming home, as if it matters. I think they're still half-drunk. And can you believe the bastards had the nerve to dump their garbage here?" Kurt shook his head and munched his toast. "For some reason they wanted to know if you had recognized their car on the road last night."

Kurt seemed to think the whole business was a bit of a joke, but right away I was suspicious. Why would they care if someone else had seen their car, unless they had been up to no good? I had noticed that Kurt wasn't spending nearly as much time with the gang lately. I had put it down to the season. Weeds didn't stop growing in the grain just because you wanted time to go to a party, and with Kurt the farm always came first. But now I began to wonder if some kind of rift had developed between Kurt and his German friends.

"Well, I was asleep most of the way home," I reminded my husband. "I think I remember seeing some headlights out by the hangar, but I couldn't tell you who they belonged to."

"Don't worry about it, darling. I don't even know why we're wasting time talking about it." And with that Kurt swallowed the last of his breakfast and headed out into the fields.

We both had a busy day ahead of us. Assuming the weather cooperated, Kurt intended to lay down some weed-killer spray. Other farmers were inclined to hire Richard Drake and his helicopter to do this sort of spraying, but I knew better than to suggest this to Kurt. So after cleaning up in the kitchen I took the truck and went for water. After lunch the wind had died down enough to allow for spraying, and I helped Kurt top up the sprayer tank with the amine mixture he preferred to use. "Thanks, sweetheart." He kissed me, mounted the tractor, and was gone. I would have just enough time to get dinner ready before I had to get our other truck, the one with the big water tank, to the spot where Kurt would need to refill the sprayer tank. There was never a spare moment when Kurt was crop-spraying. On these occasions Kurt always drove the tractor. He was more flexible when it came to the summer fallowing. Then I would often drive the tractor, pulling a thirty-two foot cultivator behind me. Kurt liked to ride alongside me, and sometimes we would get silly spells, right out in the field, which had a very satisfying conclusion. There was nothing like hanky-panky on the warm ground beside a big tractor tire. I teased Kurt that there must have been something special about that tire, because it wasn't long after one of our outdoor trysts that I became pregnant.

Heading back to the house to make our dinner, I could hear the phone ringing. I lifted the receiver to hear a recorded message, the sort that the police sent out during an emergency. The message was short and simple. A helicopter had crashed nearby. Richard Drake was dead! I dropped the phone back into its cradle. Slowly, ever so slowly, my mind began to grasp what I had just heard. The man I had once planned to marry had just had his life snuffed out. Richard Drake was dead.

All I could think about in that moment was that I had to tell Kurt. I raced out to the tractor just as Kurt was stepping down. Something in my expression must have scared him. "What is it, Joan?"

"Richard Drake has been killed in a helicopter

crash," I said breathlessly.

Kurt closed the gap between us and took me in his arms. "Come on, let's get back to the house." He opened the passenger-side door and helped me in. His arm never left my shoulders as he drove us home. He did not speak, but I could feel his warmth and his sympathy. He was grieving for me. I leaned in so our cheeks touched. "Kurt," I whispered, "I love you so much."

Once indoors we began to talk. I could not believe how much Kurt seemed to understand my sense of loss. After all, the subject of Richard Drake had always been a touchy one between us. "Whatever problems I had with Richard Drake," he told me now, "I can't deny that in his own way he was a good man, and there was a time when you thought you loved him. That's all over now. All that matters is that I love you."

I had never felt such a strange mixture of grief and joy as I did for the rest of that afternoon. Richard was gone, and no matter how long I had tried to pretend it was otherwise, there was still a part of me that had gone on caring about him, maybe even loving him in some way. But Kurt's reaction to Richard's death was a revelation. Could there possibly be stronger proof of how much my husband loved me and the life we had built together?

The farm did not allow us the luxury of indulging our feelings for too long. In fact, after supper Kurt went out to finish up the work he had abandoned when I ran out to him with the news of Richard's death. I offered to help, but he smiled and told me to rest for once. So after I cleared away the dishes I went into our living room and plopped down on the chesterfield. I soon found myself dozing. Then, for the second time that day, the phone rang. I was jolted awake and instantly on edge. I was in no state for any long talks. I just wanted to sleep.

"Hello?" I answered weakly.

"This is Joan Driger?" demanded a raspy, unsteady, but oddly muffled voice.

"Yes."

"You like spying on other people, don't you, Joan? Hiding behind tractors, eavesdropping on their conversations, makes you feel clever, does it?"

"Who is this?"

"Never mind who this is. You just watch your step, lady. And keep your mouth shut. Or else that traitor husband of yours will be looking for a new wife." Click. The line went dead.

I staggered back, aghast.

"Joan, what's the matter?" Kurt had walked in just as I hung up the phone.

"I'm not sure, but I think someone just threatened to kill me."

All at once the colour drained from Kurt's face. "What?"

It took an immense effort, but I managed to describe the whole awful phone call. I also admitted what I had not told Kurt earlier, that I had gone out into the yard and listened to him talking to Wolf Kessler before breakfast. "I'm sorry, Kurt," I said. After all the consideration Kurt had shown me, I felt ashamed. But Kurt wasn't angry, at least not with me. "Those bastards!" he raged. He saw the same connection I did: the person who had threatened me was obviously one of the people who had come out to our place in the morning. But which one? I couldn't say.

And why was the person so worried that he would actually threaten me? It all seemed to go back to that damn car with the fog lamps that we had seen on our way home from Watrous.

Kurt was on the verge of storming over to Wolfgang Kessler's house and issuing a few threats of his own. This terrified me even more than the phone call had done, and I begged him not to do anything crazy. Whoever it was I had heard on the phone, it was definitely not Wolf; I could have recognized his thick accent anywhere. Several people had been sitting in Wolf's car that morning, and Kurt had not actually seen all of them when he was talking to Wolf in the yard. So we really couldn't be sure. We should let the police handle it, I urged.

Kurt looked more troubled than I had ever seen. His fury subsiding, he took both my hands and gazed into my eyes. Finally the words came. "Alright, Joan. Call Sergeant Doyle."

For the second time that day Kurt had proven his love for me beyond all doubt. I knew there was a part of him that would have preferred to handle this situation personally. I knew his feelings about the police, who he held responsible for unjustly persecuting his father for views which he himself shared. And I knew his loyalty to men like Wolfgang Kessler and the rest of the Grandeur Germans. But obviously something in Kurt had changed.

It was now very late, and I decided to wait until morning to talk to the police in Grandeur. With Kurt beside me I felt safe enough for the moment, and I was now so exhausted by everything that had happened that I just wanted to sleep. But first thing after breakfast, with Kurt standing protectively at my side, I picked up the phone and started to dial. My call to the RCMP was not without worry, since our telephone was on a party line that we shared with our neighbours. But they were decent people, and I thought there was little chance that they would intentionally listen in. In any case it was a risk I had to take. Sergeant Doyle proved to be very, very interested in what I had to say. When I mentioned the car and the fog lamps, there was a palpable change in his voice. He suggested that we should meet. He had many more questions for me.

CHAPTER TWENTY-NINE

Tom Doyle

So often in police work we begin an investigation with very little to go on, and the helicopter crash was no different. It was at first nothing more than a crash, shocking and tragic perhaps, but not necessarily evidence of a crime. It would take days, maybe weeks for the experts from Winnipeg to sift through what was left of the wreckage in the field. And for all I knew they would discover some accidental mechanical failure that would explain everything. In the meantime I had plenty of other routine work to occupy my time. The morning after Richard's death I was doing what I did every Friday morning, reviewing the various traffic-related tickets which had been served by my officers over the course of the week. I found one that had been made out to Wolfgang Kessler, father of the Russ Kessler who owned the General Motors dealership. The reason for the ticket was recorded as "turning onto the highway without due care and attention," although it also made mention of a set of amber fog lamps which the constable felt were mounted too low on the front of the car for safe driving. None of this was noteworthy at first glance, and my only concern was whether the constable was on solid legal ground when he instructed Mr. Kessler to have the lamps raised. But then I noticed the location where the ticket had been issued, the approach road to the Flying Club, and the time, three-fifteen a.m. on the sixteenth of June. This immediately struck me as suspicious: what was old Wolfgang Kessler doing on the road to the Flying Club so early in the morning of the same day that Richard Drake's helicopter crashed? I took note of the description of his car. It was a grey Chevrolet with white trim. My constable had not recorded the names of any occupants other than Wolfgang. But I knew exactly who the Kesslers tended to associate with. It was not a crowd that had earned much credit with me.

In most respects I could not put my finger on what it was that bothered me about the Kessler gang. Sure, there was the German connection, and the rumours about their Nazi sympathies. Russ Kessler wasn't exactly known as the most scrupulous businessman in town. And there was the terrible matter of Punch Stuka, which, fairly or not, reflected badly on all his friends. But with the notable exception of Punch, they were all solid enough citizens who had never caused me any grief. So why did they make me suspicious every time I saw them on the street or in the pub? I knew I wasn't the only one who felt this way. I remembered Mavis Drake telling me how she just didn't trust Rudy Schreiber. She couldn't understand why, because he was a hard worker and effective salesman. "But he just seems creepy," she had told me. I knew just what she meant.

I was still mulling over the Kessler ticket and what

it might mean when the phone rang on my desk. The caller was Joan Driger. I knew Joan through various Flying Club events, not to mention all the old gossip about her relationship with Richard Drake. The fact that her husband Kurt was one of the Kessler pals did nothing to commend him, or her, to me. On the other hand Joan seemed a very decent person in every other respect. This morning she was obviously in distress about something. She began to tell a bizarre and alarming tale, of a car with prominent fog lamps rushing away from the hangar at an ungodly hour, of old man Kessler and a car with grey paint and white trim in her farmyard the next morning, and of a chilling telephone threat last night before bed.

I had no doubt whatsoever that Joan was telling me the truth. She was very calm, but I could feel the strain in her voice which betrayed her fear. She did not want to be seen at the RCMP barracks, but I finally convinced her to meet me at a neutral location where we wouldn't attract as much attention. Her story remained consistent as we talked over coffee an hour later. Nothing I could tell her was much comfort. She did not want any police protection. She just wanted me to find out what the Kesslers were up to. She also made a point of telling me that her husband was totally supportive of her decision to come to me with the story. As she undoubtedly hoped, this last tidbit of information made me think of Kurt Driger in a much better light. Maybe he wasn't just another Nazi-lover after all.

Regardless, I was now fixated on the grey and white car with the fog lamps and the apparent Kessler connection. My instincts were screaming that there was far more here than met the eye. What did meet the eye was bad enough. A death threat made by someone in Wolf Kessler's car, against as sweet a lady as Joan Driger? This sort of thing just didn't happen in Grandeur. Or maybe it did. Punch Stuka had already proven that.

I now made a move that could only be called impulsive. There had long been rumours floating around town about the state of Russ Kessler's marriage. Like any good policeman I had filed these snippets of information away for possible use later, and the time had come. Without stopping to consider all of the potential ramifications, I placed a phone call to Sadie Kessler.

"Mrs. Kessler, this is Sergeant Tom Doyle of the RCMP. You may remember me, we met about two months back at the Flying Club. Anyway, I'd like to talk to you. Is it possible to meet without your husband knowing?

Sadie was very cool and collected. "Yes, I think I could manage that. You can come over to the house right now if you'd like."

I did as she suggested. The Kessler house was in the posh part of Grandeur, and when Sadie Kessler invited me into the living room I saw that she had laid out an impressive spread of tea and cookies on a small table. After exchanging the usual introductory chitchat I got serious. "Mrs. Kessler," I said between sips of tea, "I'm in a nasty position."

She looked me in the eye. "I imagine it's common knowledge that the only reason Russ Kessler still sleeps in this house is because of our daughters. Any love and respect I might have had for him disappeared a long time ago. Do you know what it's like to sleep in a locked bedroom, Sergeant? Well I do. It's the only way I can sleep safe when my husband comes home drunk, which is most nights. If I had an ounce of brains, I would have been in your office months ago. So what did you want to talk to me about?"

"Well, I need your help, Mrs. Kessler. One of the cases we're working on has us looking for a grey car with white trim and a big set of fog lamps below the front bumper. If this car ever shows up in your driveway, or if you ever see it anywhere else, please phone me."

"What's the case?" she asked.

"I can't tell you that. And you can't tell your husband anything about me being here, either." She got the message, vague as it was. I left her with a good deal of confidence that she would help if the opportunity arose. I wasn't even sure what I was expecting to come of it. I was just going with my instincts. If the Kesslers or their cronies were really up to no good, then Sadie could turn out to be their weak link.

She didn't disappoint me. After a few days had passed she phoned, saying that she wanted to see me, but not at her house or the station. We agreed on a spot near the school and I parked there in an unmarked car. As arranged between us I stepped out of the car only for a second, just long enough for her to recognize my uniform. Then Sadie strolled up to the passenger side and slid in through the unlocked door.

"I don't have any news about the car you mentioned," she said, "but there is something wrong, and whatever it is, it's got my father-in-law upset. Yesterday Wolf and Russ were arguing about something. I only caught the tail end of it, since I was upstairs with the twins and they were in the family room downstairs. But as I passed through the upstairs hall, I heard Wolf getting really angry, angrier than I've ever heard him, shouting about 'that bloody car with the fog lamps' and how they had to get rid of it. Then Russ started yelling, telling his father to hide it at the farm for a while if it was such a problem." Sadie shook her head and tapped the ash off the end of her cigarette through the window. "I don't see what any of this means, Sergeant. But something's definitely going on with those two. And they mentioned the fog lamps you warned me about."

With that, she was gone, having promised to keep me posted if she discovered anything else that might be useful.

I had no doubt that she had just given me a very important tip. I went back to the station and dug out a map of the district. Wolfgang Kessler's home was located in section thirty-three, two miles east of the highway, and four miles north. I needed to get a better look at his property, preferably from the air. I thought of calling Clint Drake for help, but then decided it might be better not to get Richard's family directly involved in the investigation. Instead I phoned Glenys Johnson at the Flying Club and asked for her husband Jim. He said he would have his plane ready in one hour. Once at the hangar I showed Jim exactly where on the map I wanted to go, and what I was looking for: a grey and white car. He knew better than to ask me too many questions. But he did suggest that we should probably stay above a thousand feet if I didn't want to attract too much attention from the Kesslers. Jim knew the farm and recommended starting at the southeast corner and heading northwest.

Along this path there were a series of drainage ponds surrounded by trees. This would be a good area for someone looking to hide a vehicle from passers-by.

In what seemed only seconds we were flying over the first grove of trees. In another thirty seconds, we had the third grove just off our left wing. There the trees were especially tall and thick. Jim and I both thought we saw something at the same instant. "Don't change course, Jim," I instructed him, trying to zero in on the object with my high-power binoculars. I could see it clearly now. Yes, it was a grey car with white trim.

"I'll fly straight ahead for a couple more miles, Sergeant, and then do a one-eighty, so we can get another look at it."

It was very well hidden in the trees, but through Jim's skill and a measure of good luck we were at exactly the right angle to see the grey car. I drew a mental map of how I might get to the vehicle on foot. Then we returned to the Flying Club, reasonably confident that no one on the ground had paid any attention to our little trip. I now had tangible proof of the mystery car. On the second pass over the site I had used the RCMP zoom camera and snapped several good shots. It was not yet enough for a warrant to search the property and seize the vehicle, but at least I now knew where it was. For the moment that was enough.

The following day brought further revelations, from a very surprising source. Judy Strome walked into the station and asked to see me. When the constable at the front desk asked her what it was about, she didn't hesitate. It was regarding the death of Richard Drake, she said. Even from the next room I could hear the determination in her voice. This was the same lady whose help had broken the case of Mabel Wickham wide open. I had the sudden overpowering feeling that she was about to solve another murder for us.

I invited Judy to sit down, and thanked her again for the role she had played in the arrest of Punch Stuka. She launched straight into her newest story. "Sergeant, I saw something the night before Richard Drake's death. I've gone over it in my mind over and over again, trying to decide what to do, and now I think you need to hear about it."

"Go on," I said.

"That night I was partying with Rex Doncaster, the mechanic at the Flying Club. We were around the back of the hangar in an area where there wasn't a lot of lighting. We drank rum and Coke for maybe an hour, did a bit of fooling around, but nothing serious. Then Rex got out of the car to dump what was left of his drink, or at least that's what he said he was doing. For whatever reason he walked all the way around the corner of the hangar. He was out of sight for a long time. I finally lost patience and went to find him. There's a small door with a window at the back of the hangar, and when I got there I could see Rex with a flashlight, looking at something on the helicopter. When he saw me at the door, he came out and told me that he was worried about the helicopter. He was responsible for all the service work that was done on the machine, it was his name on the service logs, and because Richard was scheduled to have the machine in the air in the morning, he just wanted to give it one more check-over. He said he just wanted to be sure that his assistant had done the work properly. When he came back to the car, he wasn't interested in another drink, even though I had one. So I asked him to take me home."

"Did Rex stay the rest of the night with you?" I had to ask, but Judy didn't seem to mind the question.

"Yes, he did. Sergeant, I don't want you to get the wrong idea about Rex. He's a good man. But he was acting very strangely, I thought, worrying about work in the middle of the night. While we're at it, there's something else I wanted to tell you as well. It goes back to when I was with Punch Stuka. It may not mean anything, but when Punch got drunk he would sometimes say strange things. There was a definite group of men he used to hang around with, you know who I'm talking about, all those German fellows, the Kesslers and the Drigers and a few others. Don't get me wrong, I don't have anything against people talking German, but it wasn't a coincidence that a guy like Punch was close to these guys. They are all bad news, more or less. Did you know that one of them worked for Richard Drake?"

"Rudy Schreiber." I knew the gang well.

Judy nodded. "That's the one. Anyway, from what Punch used to say when he was drunk, none of them liked Richard Drake. They really hated him, Sergeant. Of course Rex wasn't all that keen on him, either. I know that doesn't prove anything, but I wanted to make sure you knew."

"Judy, I appreciate everything you've told me. And believe me, what you've said confirms a lot of what I've already heard."

She got up to leave. "I know what people say about me, Sergeant Doyle. And it's true, I like to have fun, just like men have been doing since day one. If that makes me a loose woman, so be it. But I'm not just the woman you see at parties. I'm here for a good honest reason. Richard Drake was a wonderful man. It bothers me to think that someone might have deliberately hurt him."

She left me then, and I was left alone to consider my next step. So far all I had was a lot of hearsay, a peculiar traffic stop in the middle of the night, a distinctive grey car, and my suspicions. What I did not have was any sort of physical evidence that Richard's helicopter had been sabotaged. And without that evidence, there was still no crime for me to investigate.

CHAPTER THIRTY

Rex Doncaster

You don't live the kind of life I've lived without having the odd bad day. The day I received the phone call that reported the death of Richard Drake was a shock in more than one way. Obviously I had known Richard since we were kids, and though he had never been my favourite person, in recent years I had come to appreciate certain aspects of his character, especially those that kept me employed at the Flying Club. Beyond that, his death was a blow because I knew that there would be people who would think it was my fault. Who else could be responsible, they would say, but the man who was supposed to maintain the helicopter? I had an assistant, but it was true: it was my name that featured in the maintenance logs, so it was my reputation on the line every time Richard flew. Or crashed, as the case might be.

So I was hardly surprised when, a day after Richard's death, I received a phone call from an inspector with the Department of Transport. He explained that the investigation at the accident site would continue well into the evening, after which they expected me to meet them at the hangar, at eight p.m. He apologized for the late hour, but said it was unavoidable. Apparently there had been another aircraft accident that had claimed a life in Alberta, and he and his team would need to leave for that site early the next morning. In fact, the inspectors didn't get to the hangar until eight-thirty, which gave me an extra half an hour I didn't need to stew over what I might have done wrong. They got right down to business. They checked all the logbooks and noted the most recent inspections. I told them of Richard's three years of helicopter experience, in addition to all the time he had spent flying fixed-wing aircraft over twenty years of war and peace. The inspectors were tight-lipped. One of them did say something interesting, however. "The loud bang must have come from an overload and consequent rotor stall," he murmured to one of his partners. I pretended not to have heard, since this was clearly not meant for my ears. Yet I got the impression that it was the view of the inspection team as a whole.

What else could they do or say? All they had to go on at the accident site was a pile of molten metal. My logbooks didn't indicate anything amiss, and there was no physical evidence to contradict them. With another accident waiting for them in Alberta, the inspectors saw no point in wasting time on what they had already decided was a simple accident, most likely caused by pilot error. Richard had inadvertently overloaded his helicopter, causing the main rotor to stall. He did not have enough height to recover from the stall, so he crashed, and the helicopter burned.

I should have been relieved. No blame had been attached to me, officially or otherwise. Yet it all seemed a little too neat and tidy. Granted, I didn't have even a fraction of the investigative experience that the inspectors had. But I knew Richard Drake. As much as I disliked him, I had to admit that he knew his way around a cockpit. During the war he had flown Lancasters loaded well beyond what their designers had intended, off of runways that were often much shorter than they should have been. About forty or more times he had done this and lived to tell about it. I had talked to Emma just after the crash, and from what she said it seemed that Richard had not done anything he had not done hundreds of times before. His first (and last) turn was not especially steep, nor was there any reason it should have been, because it was the first pass on the field. He would have felt every beat of the main rotor as he made that turn, and would have known the distinctive slapping sound that was the hallmark of a happy rotor. I had no doubt that had he felt or heard anything different, he would not have attempted the turn at all.

I tried to visualize the scene. Richard had lifted his helicopter off the trailer, flew it to the end of the field, and made a lazy turn to line up with Emma's flag. The next turn, one mile down the field, would necessarily have involved a higher rotor-load. But there was nothing inherently dangerous about these maneuvers. Something in my mind told me that the crash had nothing to do with pilot error. The only explanation that even began to make sense was mechanical failure; but of what kind? It was here that my own reputation was at stake, whatever the inspectors might report.

The next day was difficult. I knew I ought to have

been getting excited about the impending return of Thelma and our children from their long trip to England, but the excitement would not come. The following day was no better. There was plenty of work to do at the Flying Club, and my new assistant Henry Hinkston and I had our hands full trying to keep up with it. It was probably a godsend that I was so busy, because it took my mind off the fact that no one seemed to want to talk to me. I had a feeling, though, that a lot of talk was going on behind my back. Even Jim Johnson, the club manager who was normally so friendly to everyone, was avoiding me. It was almost as if I had already been accused of Richard's accident, found guilty, and everyone was waiting to hear what the sentence was going to be.

Yet I had more than this to worry about. A few days earlier, that bastard Russ Kessler had walked in on me and Judy in a very compromising position. The episode kept tumbling through my mind. Judy and I had met at the Flying Club at eleven o'clock as agreed. We took a long drink of the rum and Coke which I had brought with me, and then set our glasses on the tail plane of one of the parked aircraft. There was a kind of unspoken contract between us. Without a word being spoken, we both knew exactly why we had come to the hangar and what was about to happen. It took only a few more seconds for our kisses to become passionate and our hands to start roaming freely over each other's bodies.

I whispered in Judy's ear, and we picked up our drinks and moved to the office end of the hangar. There was no stopping us now. I opened a door and guided Judy into the dimly lit room where the First

Aid supplies were kept. Our destination was the cot that lay against the far wall. Once there I undid the lower buttons of Judy's blouse. She positioned her arms so that her blouse dropped to the floor, while my hands moved behind her and unclipped her bra. It immediately joined the blouse on the floor. Judy moved my head so that my lips were exactly where she wanted them. In her pleasure her thighs had begun to undulate against me. I lowered my hands to her waist and with one smooth motion pulled her skirt and panties to the floor.

Judy was truly alive now. She removed my upper clothes, pulled me to my feet and took my place on the cot. She was in control; I did not resist. She turned me to face her and got to work on my slacks and underpants, which were soon at my ankles. Her hands were sweeping the inside of my thighs and her lips were on my stomach. Gradually she became more daring, her hands moving into more dangerous territory. It was a new experience for me, but Judy obviously knew what she was doing. At that moment I didn't have a wife. My common sense was gone. My penis was in heaven and my mind was close behind.

In my ecstasy one of my hands had become tangled in Judy's hair, holding her head hard against me. My other hand had her shoulders in a vice-like grip. Judy's head slid ever lower. I began to feel hot kisses in areas just vacated by her fingers. We had both been without sex for some time, and our desire knew no bounds. It was time. Judy pulled me down onto the cot with her. From here I needed no assistance. There was nothing that could hold back our frenzied passion. Our bodies crashed together again and again and again. Suddenly the heat of Judy's climax enveloped me, and I came with her. After that we lay completely spent, aware only of the nearness of the other and the fading glow of our orgasms. And then the First Aid door opened. There was Russ Kessler, silhouetted in the doorway. He wore a vicious grin. "I see you've found another one to add to your favourites, Judy," he snarled. Before we could do or say anything in reply Russ turned and walked out of sight, and I thought I heard him mumbling to himself in German as he left.

Judy and I were stunned. We frantically dressed and almost ran back to Judy's car. We agreed that Russ must have been in the hangar at the time we went into the First Aid room; how else could he have known where we were. What neither of us could understand was what he was doing in the hangar, alone, in the middle of the night. But that was a question for another day when my marriage was not at stake. The only question that really mattered to me in that instant was what Russ intended to do with the knowledge of what he had seen. Judy didn't sugarcoat our predicament. "I've snubbed Russ a number of times," she admitted, "and he hasn't taken it too well."

As for myself, I knew I'd been an idiot. I had betrayed the finest wife a man could find. It was not the first time by any means; as the old saying went, "a stiff penis has no conscience." But up to this point my sexual affairs had not caused me any grief. I had good reason to fear that it would be different this time. How far would Russ go to get even with Judy for repeatedly rejecting him? I recalled the dreadful look on his face as he stood in the doorway of the First

Aid room. He had never been my kind of a man, and I had delivered my fate into his hands. The thought sent shivers through my body.

If anything could have convinced me to smarten up and devote myself totally to Thelma, this experience should have been it. But Thelma was still not due back for several days yet, and a little voice inside me whispered that the damage had already been done. I reasoned that I had nothing to lose by seeing Judy at least one more time. Before Russ made his appearance she had made me feel so good. So I asked her to meet me again at the same place, on Wednesday night. She agreed, though not before asking me several times if I was sure I wanted to.

Of course the specter of Russ Kessler continued to haunt me. I could not shake the feeling of dread at what he might do to ruin my life–it even intruded on my second encounter with Judy. It was the reason that I had got out of the car in the middle of our date to make a brief inspection of Richard's helicopter; it had suddenly occurred to me that an easy way for Russ to hurt me would be to sabotage one of the aircraft I was responsible for maintaining. I didn't find anything wrong, but after the news of Richard's crash I began to wish I had not chosen to take Judy home at about one a.m. that night. I should have slept at the hangar.

Somehow or other I knew there were worse things yet to come. Although I could see the advantages of telling Thelma the whole story about me and Judy before Russ had his chance to torpedo my marriage, I could not bring myself to do so. The last time I had felt so helpless was during the war. My bomber crew and I were approaching our target for the night, a big factory complex in the Ruhr valley. The Ruhr valley was notorious. Countless Canadian bomber crews had been lost there, and the story was that there were more German fighters in this area than in any other corner of the Reich. So we were already even more on edge than usual when my tail gunner screamed over the intercom that two Focke-Wulf 190 fighters were coming straight at us from below. In the end we made it home. But I never really understood how we survived that mission. It was fitting that the memory of this particular incident should have come into my mind in the aftermath of Richard's death. On a bombing run, I could have been brought down by a German fighter, or by anti-aircraft fire, or even by the bombs from one of my own squadron inadvertently dropped on me from above. It was much the same now. People thought I was at fault for no other reason than that my tools were the last to touch Rich's helicopter. There was nothing I could do about it. All I could do was let the cards fall as they might.

Then the inevitable happened: Sergeant Tom Doyle wanted to see me. I thought I knew exactly what he was going to ask me, and I was nervous. Yet it was difficult not to like Sergeant Tom Doyle. He had a way of getting his work done as a policeman without sacrificing the respect of the community. In or out of uniform, he remained an ordinary Grandeur citizen. During the war I had spent years learning how to deal with men of authority. My flight commander had authority. My squadron commander had authority. And as a pilot, I had risen to a position of authority, too. So Sergeant Doyle's power did not frighten me as it might have frightened others. In fact we had a very pleasant chat, at least in the beginning. But a big part of me just wanted him to get on with asking what he had really come to ask.

In due course the talk took a serious turn. The sergeant stated that in various discussions with people regarding the death of Richard Drake, he had been told that I was seen in the vicinity of Richard's helicopter with a flashlight early in the morning before the crash. The witness, he said, was very definite about it, and had no obvious reason to lie.

The witness! I wanted to scream. It could have been no one else but Judy Strome herself. Why on earth had she felt the need to tell the police about me looking at the helicopter? "Yes," I told the sergeant as calmly as I could, "I was there, with Judy Strome, as I'm sure you know. We were partying. And I did take a minute to look at the helicopter. I had been servicing it earlier in the day, and I just wanted to double-check my work, since I knew Richard was going to be flying the next day. That is all I did. Then Judy got impatient, so we left. I spent the night at her apartment. I assume she told you that, too."

Tom did not ask me any further questions, other than to confirm the exact time I had been looking at the helicopter with my flashlight. After he left, I sat down and put my head in my hands. Why would Judy Strome have gone to the police? Did she truly believe that I had rigged the helicopter to crash? That I was capable of such a thing? How many other people felt the same way? In my anguish I began to second-guess my actions. Was it possible that I *had* made some kind of mistake when I was last servicing the aircraft?

CHAPTER THIRTY-ONE

Clinton Drake

I had a responsibility to learn the cause of Richard's death. It was a responsibility I bore not only as his brother, but also as Grandeur Ford and Farm Equipment's accountant. I knew that Richard's will was very clear: it named Mavis as the sole heir. One of my first tasks was to determine how the company's operation would be affected by the untimely demise of its owner.

Stated in these terms, it all sounded very clinical. But of course my feelings were involved. I never believed, not from the instant I heard the news, that the crash could possibly have anything to do with pilot error. Nor did I really believe in the theory of accidental mechanical failure. It was possible, but I had complete faith in Rex Doncaster as a mechanic. Which left only one other explanation: deliberate sabotage. Mavis and I both kept coming back to the possibility that someone harboured enough hatred to kill Richard. He was one of the most loved and respected men in Grandeur area. Yet such success also bred jealousy. Was there someone so jealous that it drove him (or her) to kill? Or was there some deeper motive? Both Richard and I had come to realize that there was an element, albeit very small in numbers, which resented our wartime service. Not everyone appreciates a hero. And as hard as it was for us to imagine, there were actually people who still believed in Hitler. For them a Canadian war hero represented only loss, failure, hatred, and persecution.

In the absence of any real evidence, it was easy for Mavis and I to come up with theories. Perhaps the person who tampered with the helicopter didn't expect to kill Richard; maybe the goal was to do no more than bring him down a peg or two. Perhaps someone had held a grudge for years, letting it fester, until the only solution seemed to be revenge. Could there be something in Richard's past that even Mavis and I didn't know? Was it possible that someone in Grandeur had lost a friend or relative in one of Richard's bombing raids? Names that might fit each of these scenarios came to mind, but unfortunately speculation was far from proof. I began to wonder if I was really doing poor Mavis any good by feeding into her suspicions. But that didn't change how I felt. We are all subject to gut feelings at various times in our lives. I had just lost a brother whom I loved and respected. My brother had left a widow, whom I had known from day one was the absolute cream of the crop. Now I was left with one of those strange gut feelings. It told me to be relentless in the search for the cause of my brother's death.

This was not the first time that my twin brother's death had weighed heavily on my shoulders. The first time had been during the war, when Richard's Lancaster had been shot down over Germany. The adjutant of his squadron, whom I had met on a previous occasion, bent the rules in order to let me know what had happened, and that Richard was missing. The following days were black indeed. I knew the statistics. The odds were that my brother was dead. But on the forty-second day, the adjutant called again. Richard was alive and back in England. Unfortunately the war would not let me get away to congratulate my brother on his amazing escape through Germany and France, at least not until after D-Day was safely behind us all. By then he was back with his squadron and flying again.

I decided to confide in Emma about my gut feelings. I could see how upset she remained in the aftermath of the crash, and I wanted her to know that I had no intention of just waiting for other so-called experts to tell us what had happened. I had only one question to ask her. She was the best and almost only witness to the crash, and I wanted to know whether she had heard any sudden change in the sound of the helicopter just before the crash. She answered without hesitation. "Yes, there was a change. There was a loud bang, and I saw tiny pieces fly off the right side of the machine." She went on to tell me other details, such as the precise direction of the flight. I wrote it all down.

Emma's comments only strengthened my resolve to carry on with my own private investigation, and carry on is exactly what I did. My next call was to Sergeant Doyle, but I did not take too much of Tom's time. I simply wanted him to know that I didn't accept the preliminary findings of the Transport experts. I decided to go to the accident site again. On the way, I picked up a rake from Richard and Mavis's garden shed. Then I went directly to the north side of the field.

I knew Richard's helicopter exceedingly well, having taken many trips in it with Richard and Mavis. Emma and I had both been passengers when Rich cut power at five hundred feet in order to demonstrate a perfect auto rotation. He had done it for me again some time later, and that time I had concentrated on Rich's hands. Just as it seemed we would have to hit the ground, Rich's hands on the cyclic moved smoothly backward, and the nose of the helicopter lifted. Almost simultaneously, Rich's other hand eased the collective up, and drawing on the inertia that had been maintained in the main rotor, the machine slid into a perfect landing on its skids. That day I knew I was watching a true artist in the cockpit. What I wanted to know was why he didn't (or couldn't) perform equally well the day of the crash.

The accident investigation people had released their authority over the scene, so I was free to pick up the pieces of material that I wanted and put them in my car. I got out my rake and began to comb the area north of where the helicopter had come down. I quickly found pieces of what I was sure was fiberglass, of the same green colour as Richard's helicopter. My mind raced as I continued to rake. I had served two tours of duty as a fighter pilot. I knew all about the principles of flight and airmanship. One of the investigators had used the term "main rotor stall." The main rotors of a helicopter are like the wings of an aircraft. They tend to stall if they move too slowly or are handled violently under load. Rich had finished his turn and had been flying straight and level towards Emma. The conditions simply were not right for a main rotor stall. Even as the thought of such a stall was troubling my mind, the rake flicked up a small round piece of wood. I picked it up and wiped off the dirt for closer inspection. It looked like a hardwood dowel, just under an inch in diameter, and about six and a half inches long. There were holes in each end about the width of a two-inch nail. There were black marks equally spaced on one side, and gouges equally spaced on the other.

My skin began to crawl. I desperately wanted to know the cause of those black marks on the hardwood dowel. Their spacing seemed alarmingly similar to the spacing of the engine belts in Rich's helicopter. Stowing my discovery in a pocket, I resumed my raking. I was excited now. A plan was already forming in my mind. Then I made one more find. My rake caught a piece of soft wire which was about the same diameter as a two-inch nail and about a foot and a half long. It could have served any number of purposes on a piece of farm machinery, but if it had been in the soil very long it would have shown some sign of rust, which it did not. The most intriguing aspect of the wire was the series of scratches and gouges which it exhibited. When the wire was cleaned with a tissue, the gouges were very shiny, which meant they were very fresh. In my mind's eye I visualized the drive mechanism of the helicopter. If someone were determined to put a monkey wrench in the works, somewhere in or around those eight drive belts would be the most effective place to do it. The person would need to be clever, or at least clever in mechanical ways, and surely he would need to know something about the particular drive mechanism of a Hughes

300 helicopter. But how did a wooden dowel and a piece of wire fit into this picture? I felt like I was beginning to get closer to the truth, but clearly I still had a long way to go.

It was time to get some help. I knew precisely who to call. Back in wartime days, when I was flying Spitfires, one of the best friends I had in my squadron was a pilot named Bob Ransom. After the war he had gone to university and studied various technical subjects that were frankly beyond me. Now Superintendent Ransom of the Royal Canadian Mounted Police, Bob was in charge of the RCMP crime lab in Regina. I had not talked to Bob in about two years. But I knew I could count on him for whatever help I might need, especially when the mystery involved a war hero like my brother. Before making the call to Regina, I took the precaution of telling Sergeant Doyle what I wanted to do. Tom had no objection; in fact he offered his own phone for the call. I got through to Bob at once, and after hearing about Richard's death, he told me that of course all of the resources of his lab were at my disposal.

Within half an hour Rex Doncaster had my aircraft full of gasoline and ready to go. I filed a flight plan from Tom's office after receiving a weather briefing, and Tom followed me to the airport so that he could place another call to the superintendent the minute I was airborne. Bob Ransom was as good as his word, and he was there waiting for me when I stepped down from my aircraft at Regina. Together we tied it down, closed my flight plan, and headed for the RCMP laboratory. The drive gave me a chance to elaborate on the reason for my visit. But Bob would have none of my apologies for bothering him. We had been through enough together during the war to have a good understanding of each other. As the old air force saying went, Bob had "covered my ass on a number of flying occasions," and those were the sort of experiences that inevitably bonded men together for the rest of their lives. One way or another, Bob would always be my wingman.

Bob led me into his office, and he called for a constable to catalogue the exhibits I had brought with me. For now this was all that could be done, and we headed off to his house for supper. I had met Bob's wife Kathy on a number of occasions and she had already been warned to expect me, so my welcome was warm. As we settled down on the couch, she referred to the days when Bob and I had flown together over Europe. "I'll keep quiet for a while," she joked, "while you two re-win the war. I'm sure I'll be able to smell the cordite and hear the Rolls Royce engines doing their thing within a minute or so."

"Never mind her," Bob laughed. "Sometimes she gets a little bit big for her boots, but I can always bring her down to earth again."

"Maybe she heard about that interview you and I did back in London. Has she, Bob?"

"What's this about, Clint?"

"You remember. We were on a forty-eight hour pass, and our Wing Commander gave us an extension so it covered Monday as well. But only on condition that we report to a London radio station."

"Oh, now I remember."

"Well anyhow, they knew we were coming in, and they set up an interview. The guy doing the interview says to me, 'Now, Flying Officer Ransom, I understand you had a close call just north of London last Wednesday. Could you tell us about it?' I felt a bit silly, but I didn't want to be rude, so I said, 'Yes, it was a very shaky do. I've never seen more German fighters at one time.' The interviewer asked me what they were doing. I told him about the two Junkers 88s coming at me on the port side, and the couple of Heinkels to starboard, and the two Fokkers straight ahead. It was a bit confusing, so the interviewer cut in on the story to explain, for the benefit of the audience, that a Fokker is a German fighter aircraft. And then Bob says, 'No no, these Fokkers were Messerschmitts.'"

Bob's wife came close to dropping the gravy bowl. "That's enough out of you two," she said, "get over to the table." The hospitality did not end with supper. Bob had a bed for me, and it was only after a great breakfast and a lot more talking that we headed back to Bob's office the next morning. Bob had some unrelated work to do, so I volunteered to wait in the reception area, where my mind soon began to wander. I was brought back to reality when a sergeant called my name. "We'll bring your exhibits out in an hour, sir. Would you like a cup of coffee in the meantime?"

I gratefully accepted the offer and asked if I might also use the phone. The coffee came, and I phoned the Regina airfield to have my aircraft made ready for departure, which I planned for eleven a.m. Well before then Bob had returned the exhibits to me and explained what the lab had learned. "The black marks on the hardwood dowel were rubber. The wire could only have been in the ground for no more than a day. And the tape on the pieces of fiberglass is what is known as bookbinding tape." As for how these various items might fit together, there was still no way to tell. I thanked him for all his efforts, and he urged me to send him any other clues that turned up. Then we went our separate ways again.

When I got back to Tom Doyle's office in the afternoon, I handed him the exhibits and repeated what Bob Ransom had said. I knew now that I was on to something. All my remaining doubts had been swept away by what I had found on my return from Regina: my car had been broken into and ransacked. I had never heard of such a thing happening in Grandeur. It was obvious that someone had been looking for clues as to where and why I was flying. I shuddered as a heartbreaking thought crossed my mind. Could it have been Rex Doncaster? He had been practically the only person at the hangar to see me board my plane the previous day, and the only one, other than Sergeant Doyle, who had seen the police bag marked "Exhibits" which I had carried with me. I had heard what so many people in Grandeur were saying about his supposed role in Richard's death. No, I told myself, it couldn't be true. In any case I left my car with the sergeant so it could be checked for fingerprints. Tom had one of his constables give me a ride to Grandeur Ford, where Mavis had insisted on returning to work.

As I expected, Mavis was not doing well. She had not eaten, and even after I insisted that a meal be brought in, she barely touched the food. But she assured me that Melanie was safe at Grandma and Grandpa Drake's place. I told Mavis everything I had learned in Regina and concluded with the news of what had been done to my car. There was no longer any question that we were dealing with murder. We stared at each other and I wondered what Mavis was really feeling. Would she rather deal with a death by accident or death by murder? But it didn't matter what we thought or what we wished. Richard had been murdered.

CHAPTER THIRTY-TWO

Emma Jones

It would take many, many days before the shock of Richard's death wore off. For now I was still torn with doubts. I kept having the same terrible dream. Each time Richard would lead me over to stand beside the helicopter with him. He never said a word. He would just point to "In the Mood," the name stenciled on the side of the helicopter, and burst into tears. I would wake up crying every time.

I had been on the fringe of discussions between Mavis and Clinton. I hadn't joined in, but from listening to them I knew that they had an uneasy feeling about the accident. It was not so much the crash but the explosion which troubled them. What could have caused the helicopter to burst into flames even before it hit the ground? There was gasoline, but it was in a good strong steel tank designed to withstand all but the most extreme stresses. The explanation had to lie elsewhere.

Clinton continued his constant vigil over Grandeur Ford and Farm Equipment. Mavis was the sole owner now, but there was no less work to be done that before. I heard about Clinton's sudden trip to Regina, but Mavis did not tell me many details. I had a strong suspicion, though, that the Regina trip had something to do with the investigation into Richard's death. "I'm going to need your help more than ever," Mavis confided to me one day. There were tears in her eyes. "I'm capable of selling anything we have to sell, and I can handle the staff. But I just can't seem to find the energy right now. My work ethic is just not with me. Emma, you've been so wonderful through everything that's happened. Please bear with me for a while longer. Clint has already advertised for a new sales manager. Rudy Schreiber's not going to like that, I know, but it has to be done. Whatever happens, Emma, you will always have a home here with us."

I took Mavis's hand in mine. "I love you, Mavis, and there isn't one of us here that wouldn't go the extra mile for you. I know that can't replace the love and respect you've lost in Richard, but you can lean on me as much as you need to. Grandeur Ford and Farm Equipment will not lose one customer. Not if I have anything to say about it."

Clinton kept me informed about business matters, but seemed hesitant to talk more about Richard's death. I asked him how long he could afford to be away from his job in Saskatoon. "Don't worry, Emma," he said. "I'm in contact with my office, and they understand what I'm going through here. I've got to see Mavis through these critical days as best I can. You have no idea what a relief it is for me to know that you're here to help me. I'm not sure if you knew this, but Richard talked of you on more than one occasion. And he had nothing but good to say."

As the days passed it became clear to me that

Clinton was pursuing his own investigation. He told me that he and the officer in charge of the RCMP lab in Regina had flown together in the same squadron of Spitfires during the war. But Clint asked me to keep the information to myself. If Richard's death really had been the work of a saboteur, then it was better that the person not realize that the police were on his trail—at least not yet.

The news that Clint brought back from Regina, though horrible, brought me some comfort. It definitely restored Richard's reputation as a careful pilot. It removed the worry that I might have been negligent when I prepared the helicopter just before it crashed. But the comfort was definitely limited. The idea that someone in Grandeur was capable of taking the life of such a wonderful man as Richard Drake was sickening.

In a strange way the death of Richard had brought Clint and me closer than we had ever been. It was not, however, nearly close enough. I couldn't count the number of times I had wished Clinton Drake would give me a second glance in years past. Everyone thought of him as a very eligible bachelor. If Mavis was right, I was rather eligible myself. I was pretty, clever, and earning very good money. So why wasn't I engaged, to Clinton or anyone else? The answer was much closer than I realized. I was so wrapped up in my work and my sports that there just wasn't time for men. Sure, I had my share of romantic dreams. So far that was all they had been: dreams. Perhaps Mavis was right and I needed to change my ways before it was too late. Or maybe Clinton would finally ask me out to coffee or dinner one day. But in the meantime I had to do something to get him out of my dreams.

The time came for Richard's funeral. The Grandeur Royal Canadian Legion was in charge of the service. Held at the Grandeur United Church, it seemed to draw most of the town. The church was full, the church hall was full, and there were two or three hundred people outside listening on the public address speaker. They came from hundreds of miles around and from all walks of life; RCAF people were especially in evidence. It was a true reflection of the community's love for Richard. "It's different from back in Wolverhampton," Mavis told me later, "where only the men go to funerals. I can't believe the number of people who spoke to me after Richard's funeral. I cried, but they were all so anxious to comfort me. So many dozens that I had never seen before. Dear God, Emma, if only Richard could see how much he was loved."

Mavis and I both realized that such love was not the whole story. I had lived long enough and was observant enough to know that there is such a thing as a personality problem, and that Richard, for all of his strong points, had made his share of enemies. It was interesting to note who was *not* at the funeral.

For me life slowly returned to normal. Mavis told me that Clinton had found someone he thought would make a good salesman. The fellow worked at a business in Saskatoon where Clinton had done some accounting, and the two of them already knew each other. So Clinton phoned him up and asked him if he might be interested in a new career in Grandeur. The fellow was very interested. He agreed to come out and meet Mavis. I was in the office when Clinton brought him in. He was introduced to me as Garth Pringle.

He was single, thirty-four years old, and moving to Grandeur would involve him taking a cut in pay, at least temporarily. But he made it plain that he had dreamed of a job like this, and that furthermore he had always wanted to live in a small town. He was already talking about buying a small piece of land just outside of town. The next day it was all decided. Mavis offered him the position, and he accepted.

I sighed as I walked back to my department after hearing the news, and then I laughed at myself. This Garth chap was very personable, and I wouldn't mind doing a little dreaming with him sometime. In any case it was certain that I would be working very closely with him. Cars and trucks were often brought in to me before they were taken in on trade, so that I could appraise the vehicle and assess the cost involved in making it ready for resale. Deals were often made, or not made, on the basis of the vehicle evaluation form which I completed. So there was inevitably a lot of interaction between the sales and reconditioning departments.

Mavis was still in no condition to focus on business, however. She was just starting to regain a little spirit when Sergeant Doyle, full of apologies, came by to show her a typed letter he had received. It was from a very sick person; that much was obvious from the contents. The writer stated that he knew that Mavis had paid someone to rig the helicopter so it would crash. To add further insult to injury, the writer insinuated that Richard had been having an affair with his old fiancée. Mavis was in tears as she told me about it. I did my level best to console her. "Please, Mavis, you know there's a sick person out there somewhere.

Richard's death already proved that. And now this same person is getting scared. He's just trying to cover his tracks. My guess would be that one day he's going to make one mistake too many."

Mavis hugged me tight. "Thank you, Emma."

There was more I felt I needed to tell her, if only so she knew that she was not alone in her continuing grief. "You know, I still have nightmares over all this," I admitted. "I can't begin to understand why someone should have hated Richard so much. But if someone did murder him, at least we know that what happened was beyond his control. Or our control. I try to take comfort from that. I can't tell you how often in the days right after the crash I worried that I might have done something wrong to the helicopter." Now tears started coming to my eyes, too.

Mavis took my hand. "Emma, my dear sweet friend, I'm so sorry. I'm afraid I haven't given much thought to other people's troubles lately, how they might be feeling. I never stopped to think about what you've been through. I knew you were the only witness, but how much guilt you felt is only now sinking in. You've been an amazing friend, and I've drawn on your strength so much."

We hugged again, and then both of us felt the need to change the subject. "What do you think of Garth Pringle?" she asked me. "I think he's got a lot of potential. The staff seem to like him, and so do the customers."

I told her that yes, he was doing well, and that in fact the two of us were already working on a new strategy that might cut down on a lot of the paperwork between our departments. "Garth has plenty of automobile and truck experience," I explained, "but he's in deeper water when it comes to costing out and reconditioning farm equipment. But I think it will all work out."

"That's wonderful news, Emma," Mavis said, and then with a twinkle in her eye, "just don't start reconditioning Garth."

I smiled at the comment, not only because it showed how well she knew me, but because it reminded me of the old Mavis. So I left her office with a much lighter step than the one that had carried me inside. And I began to consider that maybe my own life was about to turn in new and interesting directions.

CHAPTER THIRTY-THREE

Mavis Drake

I was talking to myself again. I had been doing a lot of that since Richard's death. Actually, to be more accurate, I was talking to Richard. I knew he was with me. I could feel his presence. His body might not be here, but he would be with me as long as I lived. I was carrying his baby. For the sake of the baby and for Melanie, I had to get strong again.

I struggled with the idea of asking Mum and Dad to come to Canada and stay with me for a while. I knew they wanted to be here, and would drop everything to make the trip given the slightest encouragement. Dad was a very solid man and Mum was only moderately weepy. I desperately wanted to see them again, to have them near me again, to let them share my grief. Although my little Melanie had been wonderful, how much could an eleven-year old girl really do to help her mother? She was at an age where she lived in a different world. I had cut back my time at the office, but whenever I was there it was hard to avoid the subject of my loss even when it was the last subject I wanted to discuss. So even when people were trying to be supportive,

I would often come home close to tears. But was bringing my parents halfway across the world the answer? Grandeur was a long way from Wolverhampton in more ways than one. In the end I overcame my doubts and had Emma draft a telegram. The answer came as quickly as I expected. They were on their way.

I knew all about Clinton's trip to the crime lab in Regina. Now he was almost certain that someone had rigged something deadly on the final flight of the helicopter. He asked me to dig out the Hughes 300 manual and find the names of the people in Oklahoma from whom Richard had bought the helicopter. These people proved to be even more helpful than either Clinton or I had hoped. Hearing his suspicions, they offered to set up a complete drive system of a Hughes 300 helicopter for Clinton to examine; they were positive that they could explain every clue that he chose to bring them. But for this he would actually have to go down to Oklahoma.

Richard had been dead for ten days when Joan and Dan Clifton arrived in Saskatoon. I was still not comfortable about driving, so Clinton took Melanie and me to the airport. As usual he was happy to help, especially since he had fond memories of my parents from my wedding day, not to mention all the occasions when he had stayed at our house in Wolverhampton during the war. Melanie was thrilled to see her grandma and grandpa, and they shared plenty of hugs and kisses in the first few minutes. Even so, it was a terribly difficult way to welcome them to my adopted homeland. Once Clint had gently pulled Melanie back, Mum and I shared a few moments of tears.

I really hoped that my parents would love Grandeur as much as I did. I knew I had a lovely home, and I knew they would be very impressed with the business that I was now managing more or less on my own. Still, they would feel Richard's absence terribly. I did my best to explain what I had been going through. I had not only lost my husband and soul mate, but the father of my children and the driving force in our business. I was up to my neck in unfamiliar responsibilities. Without Clinton and Emma Jones, I would never have been able to manage. All of our old customers had been unfailingly loyal and sympathetic. Clinton had just introduced me to a new sales manager, and he seemed to be working out fine. "So maybe the worst is behind us," I told Mum and Dad with more conviction that I really felt.

As we drove back to the house I had no idea of the welcome that was in store for my parents. Clinton and Emma had prepared a modest surprise party. My in-laws Jim and Edna were there, along with coffee and a hearty Saskatchewan lunch. When I saw the effort that had been made, I started to tear up again, but for the first time since Richard's death, they were tears of joy. Suddenly I knew what I wanted to do. When we were all seated, I asked for their attention.

"Mum and Dad, I know that you're sleeping on your feet, but there's something I need to say, something I've been keeping secret from all of you. The truth is that I'm pregnant. Richard and I are going to have another baby."

There was a stunned silence. Virtually every eye in the room got moist at the thought. In a very real way, Richard was about to live again. At the very least

Melanie would get the sister or brother she had always wanted. Then the room erupted in unrestrained delight, everyone crowding around me to give me a kiss or a hug. In the midst of it all I lowered my head and unashamedly thanked God for this moment. It was storybook stuff, a miracle. But then Richard's life had been full of miracles in war and in peace. Melanie asked Grandma Jean if she could stay in Grandeur until the baby was born. My mother said she would have to talk it over with Grandpa Dan first, but that yes, she would certainly like to stay. I could tell just by looking at him that Dad would have no objection. My only regret, and it was the obvious one, was that Richard would not be able to meet the tiny son or daughter which he had helped to create.

The next morning Melanie came bounding into my bedroom with great news. She was breathless. "Mom, Grandma and Grandpa might not go back to England until after the baby is born! Isn't that exciting?"

"Yes it is, sweetheart," I replied, and I meant it. But the glow of the previous day had faded for me. I had woken up with the same feeling of emptiness that I had become accustomed to. It was almost as though I felt a little bit ashamed that I had dared to feel a few moments of real happiness. After all, Richard was still dead. How could I ever be happy again? In the lonely space of our bed, the memories of all the pleasure we had shared were hard to suppress. Richard's face was forever in my sight. I yearned to take him by the hand, like I used to do when we strolled along the banks of the Saskatchewan River on warm summer evenings. Oh, how I missed those walks!

CHAPTER THIRTY-FOUR

Rex Doncaster

The stress was not easing, the rumours were not abating, and really, why should I have expected them to? I had been stupid enough to go into the hangar in the middle of the night before the crash, and there was a reliable witness to say that I had been looking hard at the helicopter. Only I knew for certain what I had been looking for, and what I had found, which was nothing out of the ordinary. For all the good I had done, I wished to God I had never gone near the damn machine.

It was all Russ Kessler's fault. If he had never caught Judy and me in the First Aid room, I would never have been so paranoid about what he might do to get back at me. Well, he had certainly got back at me: the whole town had decided I had done something wrong. Nevertheless, the question of what had gone wrong with the helicopter had not been answered. Was it possible that my instincts that night had been more correct than I realized at the time? I knew Russ was a mechanic and a good one. He definitely had the skill to cripple a helicopter.

I knew I had to go to the police and tell them the whole story. I had to tell them about the bed in the First Aid room where Judy and I had been discovered together by Russ Kessler two nights before the crash. I had to let them know the rage I had seen in Russ Kessler's eyes. Most important of all, the police had to hear that I had spent every hour of the night before Richard's death in Judy Strome's apartment. But before I told the police any of this, I needed to tell Clint first. I owed it to him, and I owed it to his brother.

The decision made, I wished again, with every fiber in my body, that I had stayed true to Thelma. So much trouble would have been avoided. This had not been the first bed-hopping of my life, but I promised myself again that it would be the last.

I went to see Glenys Johnson and booked off work, then I drove into town. My destination was Mavis Drake's office. Mavis let me know that Clint had phoned and would be there momentarily. She was perfectly polite: if she had heard the rumours about me and the helicopter she was showing remarkable self-control. I knew I could not count on Clint to show the same restraint if he believed the rumours. So I launched into my story as soon as he walked in. He listened without expression. But when I finished, he thanked me and agreed that I should go to the police right away. He made a call to Sergeant Doyle and we went into the station together. For a few hours I felt as if a heavy weight had lifted from my shoulders, even though what I had said was not enough on its own to prove my innocence to anyone. It was still possible that I would be charged with the murder of Richard Drake.

Over the days that followed my fears caught up

with me. I had expected to be called for further questioning by Tom Doyle, but no call came. The suspense really began to take a toll. Unable to concentrate on my work, I thought it best not to attempt any hands-on maintenance on aircraft at the Flying Club. I lost weight that I really didn't have to lose. My libido, which had always been very close to the surface, seemed to disappear altogether. For the first time in my married life, I had to apologize to Thelma and assure her that I still loved her. Thelma, being Thelma, was very understanding. I found myself spending a lot of time feeling sorry for myself. It was all quite predictable. You couldn't take an ordinary, hard-working Canadian guy like myself and put him in the sort of trouble I was facing, and expect him to take it lightly. Gone was the lighthearted banter that normally enlivened my conversations with people. There was a cloud over my head, and the weight was back on my shoulders with a vengeance. This time it was going to stay there until the murder of Richard Drake was solved and I was exonerated completely.

Surely, I told myself, there was someone who could shed some light on where the investigation was at. What did Clint know? He had only recently come to the airstrip and flown off to someplace or other. It had been more than a brief hop; wherever he had gone, he had not returned until the following afternoon. Of course it was possible he had just gone back to Saskatoon to check in at his office. I could have found out the truth easily enough by making a single phone call. But if anyone in Grandeur learned that I looked into Clint's flight plan, it would only make me look even more suspicious, and I knew it.

I finally pulled myself together. The fact of the matter was that I had done nothing wrong. I did not murder Richard Drake. My only crime was being stupid enough to have a bit of nookie with Judy Strome. I made another silent vow that if my penis stood up for a woman other than Thelma ever again, I would chop it off. As for the police, I realized that if they needed to talk to me, they would talk to me. If they never talked to me, it would mean one of two things: either they would have found the real murderer, or they could not find enough grounds to accuse me outright. Either way, I would be home-free. At the moment I was only a tiny fish in a much bigger pond of potential suspects, and the smaller I stayed, the happier I would be.

Not long after I had come to terms with my fate in this manner, Clint appeared at the Flying Club. I could sense his excitement, though I was wise enough not to ask him about it. "I want a few minutes flying," he said. "All of a sudden I have this burning need to get some good old Saskatchewan air under my ass. Maybe about five thousand feet of it." But before he could get in the air, Glenys called Clint back into the hangar to answer an urgent phone call. The next thing I knew, Clint was racing out of the parking lot in his car, leaving his plane cold on the tarmac.

It took a few more hours before I discovered what the rush had been all about. From across the hangar Glenys and Jim Johnson came running towards me. Glenys' Welsh accent came through the clearest. "They've solved the murder!" Glenys repeated it as if to make sure that I'd heard. "They've solved the murder of Richard Drake! That's all we know!"

In that instant I knew my ordeal was over. I had faced hell before, in my Halifax bomber over Germany, but it had been different in those days. I had been younger, the danger had been more immediate, and anyway I had been too busy keeping an eye out for Focke-Wulfe 190 fighters and keeping my plane in the air to think too deeply about what was happening. The days that had passed since Richard's murder were an altogether different kind of torment. It was the hell of uncertainty. I had been targeted as guilty, but the accusers were like ghosts. They were there, but they didn't confront me. Even now I knew that not one of the accusers would walk up and say he was sorry. But I didn't care. I had admitted over and over again that most of the blame for the trouble I'd endured lay with the guy I saw in the mirror. All I wanted to know now was who had actually murdered Richard Drake.

CHAPTER THIRTY-FIVE

Clinton Drake

I could not stop thinking about the trip I had taken to Alva, Oklahoma. It was obvious that the chief mechanic at Hughes had been listening very carefully when I spoke to him over the phone before I arrived. When I got there I found that he and his team had made up an exact replica of the number nine wire and the wooden dowel I had discovered at the crash site. They had dropped the ends of the wire into the holes that had been drilled in the ends of the dowel. Their next step was to fasten the contraption onto the inside of the fiberglass that covered the v-belts. The fastening was done, as I instructed, with simple bookbinding tape. This accomplished, the Hughes mechanics started the electric motor and slowly moved the lever, forcing the eight belts into the grooves of the idler.

Slowly the mechanism started to revolve. Since they were using only a very small electric motor, there was none of the load on the drive that would have been present in the operation of a real helicopter engine, nor was there a comparable buildup of heat or vibration. But at this point the Hughes mechanic flicked a switch. I could not believe what happened next. The simulation began to vibrate as if it were in a normal helicopter. A small amount of heat was applied to the outside of the fiberglass cover, at a point exactly where the bookbinding tape was holding the number nine wire. In less than a minute, there was a bang and the electric motor stopped dead. If this had been a two hundred and fifty horsepower engine, the whole mechanism would have been tangled with eight shredded belts. As it was the dowel was pinched between the belts and the lower pulley. Closer examination revealed distinct black marks along its length–just like on the dowel I had found. I knew beyond a shadow of a doubt that here was the contraption that killed my brother.

The chief mechanic at Hughes had not let it be widely known what was happening, nor did he invite anyone else to watch. I could understand why: it would not do to let the general public know how simple it was to destroy a Hughes 300 helicopter. Yet the chief mechanic was nevertheless impressed. I had one more surprise for him, which previously I had revealed only to Tom Doyle. I reached into my inner jacket pocket and took out a small locking device of the sort that holds the lever in place after the idler pulley engages. Like the wire and dowel, I had taken it from the burned-out wreck of Richard's helicopter. I held it alongside the comparable device on the mockup, which was still holding the lever in place. They were obviously of the same design, but mine had been broken open, presumably by the force unleashed when the dowel did its work on the drive system. The Hughes mechanic shook his head. "If you need further proof, there it is," he said sadly. Pictures of every step of the test had already been taken with both a Polaroid and a movie camera. Before I left, I made sure to take a picture of the damaged locking device displayed alongside the undamaged one.

I returned to Grandeur very proud of what I had accomplished. But I knew it wasn't enough. I still didn't know the identity of the bastards who had masterminded Richard's death. Oh, how I wished we still had the death penalty in Canada. I knew of more than one person in Grandeur who would have happily flicked the switch on the son-of-a-bitch who murdered my brother.

Unfortunately I had other responsibilities that could not be ignored forever. My bosses in Saskatoon had been very understanding of my absence, but it was time to head back to the city and see how things were going. Before I went, I dropped in to see Mavis and Melanie one more time. Mavis was beginning to look more like her old self. It was a slow process, but she had clearly benefited from the arrival of her parents from England, and I liked to think that maybe what I had found out in Oklahoma had helped as well. Both Mavis and Melanie were sorry to see me go, but I assured them I would be back in Grandeur the minute the baby was born. I had promised Mavis my help and I would keep my promise.

Two weeks passed. I received a call from Sergeant Doyle regarding some files which he wanted me to examine. So I headed back to Grandeur much sooner than I expected. Rather than make my way directly to the RCMP station, however, I made a quick stop to see Mavis. Naturally she asked the reason for my visit. Not having visited the sergeant yet, I wasn't entirely sure of my answer. So I decided to let her in on some older news. "Mavis, I've been keeping something from you, something I know you've been wondering about for a while. It's about Rex Doncaster. People in this town have been blaming Rex ever since the crash. I would have told you if I'd heard anything about him being charged, but there's a good reason why that never happened. It turns out Rex spent the whole night before the crash with Judy Strome. She's signed a statement that he was in her apartment from one a.m. until morning. Rex told us the same thing. There's very little chance he could have had enough time before one a.m. to sabotage the helicopter in the way I discovered during my trip to the States. In fact," and now I chuckled in spite of myself, "this may be the first time in history when getting some nookie actually got a guy out of trouble."

"The bastard." Mavis wasn't amused. Or at least she was trying hard not to be.

"Never mind, Mavis. Sometime soon I'll tell you the rest of that story."

It was the most lighthearted exchange I had had with Mavis since Richard's death, and I was very glad to see her loosening up at last. A few jokes might be the best therapy for her.

CHAPTER THIRTY-SIX

Emma Jones

As Garth and I worked together, we had plenty of time to chat. We soon learned that we had much in common. Both of us had been working non-stop since leaving high school. We both loved athletics, and Garth committed himself to come and play softball in my league. We agreed that whenever problems arose in the business, we would settle them over a meal. I smiled at the thought of quiet time with Garth Pringle. I began to wonder what sort of business problems I could drum up at short notice.

I was already beginning to hope that Garth might feel the same attraction to me that I felt for him. I had often joked to Mavis that the first eligible bachelor to come along would have to look out, and here he was. I could not have been more pleased when Garth asked me if I would like to go out one Saturday night and see a movie with him. I didn't even bother to check what was showing at the theatre before I agreed. Though I would never admit it to my friends, I was a little uncertain about the etiquette for going to a movie on the first date. How exactly was I supposed to act? If we each had popcorn, then that would take care of two hands, but what was expected of the other two? I decided to be bold: if Garth didn't make a move to hold my hand, then I'd make a move to hold his. As it turned out, Garth did make a move. He handled his popcorn with one hand and I did likewise. Our other hands did what came naturally to them, which was nothing too scandalous. The most we managed to do on our first date was hold hands. We were both nervous and for a while our conversation was all about the movie, which helped to hide the awkwardness. I began to think Garth was even worse at this dating business than I was. Once the movie was over, it seemed to take him forever to ask me if I'd like to go for an ice cream. But it also took me a ridiculous amount of time to say yes. When I realized this, I couldn't help laughing at myself. "Garth," I said after the giggles subsided, "you and I seem to relate better at work. I'm acting like a fifteen-year old girl on her first date."

Garth took my hand again. "I'm no better, Emma. But maybe on our second date I can do better. That is, if you're game to have another date."

We found a corner booth in the ice cream parlor. I had let his second date suggestion go unanswered, but not because I wasn't interested. I almost shocked myself by what I did next. I let go of his hand, moved mine to the far side of his neck, and pulled him gently towards me, kissing his cheek. "Just try me on that second date idea, Garth. There are lots of things that I might be game to try with you."

"I feel the same way," Garth replied with a grin.

The ice was broken. There would be no business

talk now. There was no longer any need for it. We talked about our lives, our backgrounds, and how each of us had let the workaday world dominate our time for far too many years. Sometimes, when I looked deep into Garth's eyes, I had the urge to take him in a passionate embrace and kiss him on the lips like there was no tomorrow. But I managed to control myself. Then in what seemed like no time I heard Garth's voice telling me, "They're putting things away, Emma. It's time to take you home." As we walked to the car, Garth's arm was around my waist and my arm was around his. Garth opened the car door for me and kissed my cheek as I slid into the passenger side.

We drove to my home more or less in silence. Garth parked, turned off the engine and turned towards me. His right arm crossed behind my neck, and his fingers touched a bare spot on my shoulders. A little shiver went through me. I could sense rather than see our faces drawing closer as he pulled me gently to him in the semi-darkness. There was still a slight uncertainty in his movements and I was afraid he would pull back. But I had nothing to worry about. We kissed, and then he pulled me tighter and we kissed again. In that moment my world gained a new meaning. Slowly I eased myself from Garth's arms, and making silly excuses I had him walk me to my door. "Thank you, Garth," I said, before we kissed goodnight.

Once Garth had left, I found myself in a daze. "What's happening to me?" I asked myself, half-aloud. What was this about? And more importantly, why had it taken me so many years to find out? I could not believe what I had been missing. I knew that if I wasn't careful, I'd start thinking that I was falling in love. Maybe, I thought, I won't bother trying to be careful.

The next morning I tried to get a grip on myself. At work I heard rumours of new developments in the murder of Richard Drake, that extra police were on their way to Grandeur, and a number of search warrants were being issued. Apparently fingerprint experts had gone over Judy Strome's apartment and Clinton Drake's car (which had been vandalized) but nothing was found. Some guys in the garage could not resist joking about how many fingerprints might be found in Judy Strome's place, in one room in particular. I laughed, but for reasons they did not know. Maybe I ought to have a talk with this Judy Strome, I thought. She might be able to give me a few pointers.

As always, working at Grandeur Ford left nothing to be desired, except in one very specific respect: Rudy Schreiber. There were many occasions when Rudy Schreiber would consult with me about a deal and I would come away with mixed feelings. His tendency was to want to leave his deals, whether they be for a car, truck, or piece of farm machinery, somewhat open ended. To me this seemed like an invitation to trickery. But I had never gone to Mavis with my concerns. Mixed feelings or not, I hated to say something bad about another employee which I could not prove.

Suddenly I felt like I was living a new life. I had never imagined that my priorities could change so dramatically. I was in love even if I did not really know what it meant. I had heard the expression, read the expression, and witnessed the expression come to life in the actions of at least one close friend. But when she had told me that she was in love with a man she was dating, I did not question her about how it actually felt to be in love. I also remembered a sixteen-year old classmate telling me that she was in love with a boy two grades ahead of us. At mid-term that girl was an above-average student, but by June she came close to failing the year. It was a sobering memory.

"I don't really need that kind of trouble," I muttered, but I knew it was already beyond my control. My whole personality was being affected. When Garth came to my department with a simple query about the cost of reconditioning a certain vehicle, I almost stammered. I yearned to see him and yet I was almost afraid to see him. I kept thinking about how handsome he was. I noticed how well he handled his customers, and how smartly he walked as he went about his work. There was something big going on inside me, there was no doubt about it. I loved the way I felt, and the newness of what I was feeling. There was no other answer. I had fallen in love with Garth Pringle.

With these thoughts still playing havoc with my mind, I went to see Garth with the reconditioning quote he had requested. At first we were all business, but as the conversation wound down, and I turned away to return to my department, Garth called me back. "Emma, I've got something else for you to consider. I'm not too bad a cook. How about this Saturday I do the steaks with vegetables and wine, and you bring the dessert?"

The implication of the request was clear as far as I was concerned. I didn't hesitate. "It's a deal. But for now, duty calls." Knowing he was watching me, and one part of me in particular, I found it difficult to get my legs to move normally as I walked away.

I had three solid days to think before Saturday rolled around. I had ample time to weigh the negatives. How was it possible, I demanded of myself, that at the age of thirty-five I had never been in a situation like this? I was old-fashioned to this extent: pregnancy out of wedlock was wrong and I didn't want any part of it. Up to this point it had been a moot point, since my peculiar lifestyle had kept me a virgin. Now I absolutely had to consider the dangers of what might be about to happen between Garth and me. But for the first time in my life, these were dangers I was prepared to risk. This was what meeting Garth had done to me.

I had not asked Garth what his favorite dessert was, so on Saturday night I opted for apple pie. When I arrived at his apartment, I was welcomed with a hug and a slightly more than casual kiss. Then Garth returned to his kitchen, for he was still working on supper. I had time for a good look around Garth's apartment. It was pretty much what I had expected. It was more of Garth, neat but not gaudy. He brought out a bottle of red wine, and apologized for neglecting to ask me which I preferred, white or red. I countered by saying, "I made apple pie without asking you what you liked for dessert. We're even now. But for future reference I do like red." Another quick kiss followed.

We shared the chore of setting the table, and decided that the sensible way of filling our plates would be to go to the stove where the food was all piping hot. Garth already had the wine uncorked, and in a moment or two we were sitting down to eat.

"Garth," I said after swallowing the last bite of my steak, "I hope it doesn't sound patronizing, but that was a wonderful meal. Now, shall we have my dessert?"

"Thank you for saying so," Garth replied. "And absolutely, let's have some of that pie. May I freshen up your wine?"

"Only if you have some more as well."

I proceeded to cut the pie and place a piece on each of our plates. We ate slowly and sipped our wine. The company, the good food, and the red wine were making for a very relaxed atmosphere. "This is lovely pie, Emma. Does your baking always turn out like this? Or did your mother make it?"

I reached over and twisted Garth's ear. "Hang around a bit, and maybe one day you'll know the answer to that question."

Garth stood up and took my hand. "Let's share this last bit of wine, and sit where it's more comfortable."

"You can pour my share, Garth, but I can't guarantee to drink it all."

"Don't worry, Emma, I'm not a big drinker, either. Still, there are times when I enjoy a drink. This is one of them."

We sat on the couch holding hands. Garth finished his wine before I did, and placed his glass on the coffee table in front of us. Instead of returning his arm to where it had been on his lap, he put it around my shoulder. I was taken somewhat by surprise, and felt a little uneasy: again I was very conscious of how little I knew about the basics of petting. I could not help but wonder about Garth's level of experience; or did these things just come naturally with men? But all this thinking didn't last long. A strange warmth swept over me. I leaned my head against Garth's and put my hands in his. Garth kissed my cheek before our hands parted so that we could embrace each other more fully. I had never felt such exhilaration. Each kiss seemed to demand further experimentation, but neither of us was yet prepared to take a step that would lead to greater passion. There came a point when we parted ever so slightly, and Garth said, "I'm sorry, Emma."

I put a finger on his lips. "You have nothing to be sorry about. To prove it, why don't we set up another date? I'd love to see you again."

Garth was relieved and enthusiastic. We arranged to meet the next Saturday night. I now had a natural opportunity to leave, but my mind was playing games with me. Was it the wine and the wonders of the evening that dared me to stay a while longer, or was it some female devilry suddenly surfacing? Whatever the reason, I turned to Garth again and placed a hand on each of his shoulders, boldly pulling him towards me, and then clasping my hands behind his neck. My whole body seemed to change, and I was able to kiss him freely. Time froze. It was only with extreme reluctance that I finally pulled back. I so wanted to say, "I love you, Garth," but I thought better of it. We were committed to another date; there would be plenty of time to express my feelings. "Can I help you with the dishes, Garth?" Somehow I knew that it was not the most fitting comment for the moment.

He gave me another quick kiss, and his mouth grazed my ear. "The dishes can wait. You're something else, and I don't want to waste a minute while you're still here."

"I feel the same way. Now, you better walk me to my car."

Over the following week my love for Garth actually began to bother me. My mind was far too strongly fixated on the man. At work I found myself going out of my way to walk near him. I could tell that Garth was making similarly feeble excuses to visit my department. I already had visions of taking him home to meet Mom and Dad, but I decided it was a bit too early in the relationship for that.

I frequently found myself hugging my pillow, reveling in these unfamiliar sensations. I was thirty-five years old and involved in my first love affair. It was almost ridiculous. By the age of thirty-five most other girls had been in and out of love a number of times. Yet I had not even had a case of puppy love, not even in my teenybopper years. It was also a bit worrying. Though it didn't bear thinking about, how would I handle a broken heart? My usual common sense kicked in, however, and reminded me of the old saying that nothing ventured, nothing gained. I was prepared to venture quite a lot with this fellow Garth.

For our third date we had agreed to eat out, and then go back to Garth's place for some wine and more of my pie. The wine was slowly working its way into every corner of my system. Garth poured a second glass, and we moved to the couch. Our minds and bodies were converging in more than the obvious ways. I moved willingly into Garth's arms, feeling his hand drop to my knee and creep under my dress. It slowly worked its way up my leg. It seemed charged with electricity. Then his fingers reached the edge of my panties. From far away I heard myself say, "Garth," and he replied, "Emma," and we kissed again.

Only the thickness of my panties kept his fingers

from touching my skin. I gasped and held his hand firmly, but I did not push it away. I felt no shame. I loved this man. One of his fingers shifted beneath my grip, touching a spot that took my breath away. I squeezed his hand even harder. I could have fallen back on the couch and let our love take its course. It would have been so easy. And a part of me was definitely urging me to do it. But another part said, "not now." Almost as if he had heard my thoughts, Garth's hand didn't go any further. Instead it gradually moved back from the wondrous places it had briefly reached and joined his other hand behind my back. We went on hugging and kissing until I was breathless, but we did not push our experimentation to its previous level. "I love you, Garth," I told him. "I love you, Emma," he replied.

My heart was no longer pounding, it was singing. If I had ever doubted that I was a normal woman, my doubts were now gone. I now understood how girls found themselves in bed with guys they barely knew. If neither the guy nor the girl had the willpower to stop the lovemaking before the pleasure became too great then the rest was predictable. Fortunately Garth and I had both managed to control ourselves. I felt a strange need to explain myself further. "Garth, I've never felt so wonderfully happy and yet so terribly inadequate at the same time."

Garth chuckled. "I know what you mean. It looks like we went to the same school. All I know is what I read in magazines a long time ago, the kind of cheap, trashy magazines that all boys sneaked into their rooms. Are you angry with me?"

"Of course I'm not angry."

"What we did felt so natural that I was almost afraid of myself," Garth continued.

"I feel exactly the same way. I wasn't sure I'd be able to control myself, that's how much I love you."

"Oh Emma, maybe what we went through tonight is trying to tell us something. I love you too much to do anything you don't want to do, but let's meet again soon."

"I'm so glad to hear you say that, Garth. Now you'd really better walk me to my car while I still have a clear head."

As I drove home I relived every moment of the evening. I could still feel the dampness left behind by my passion. I was looking forward to the day when I could unleash that passion totally with the man I loved. But it was a huge relief to know that Garth respected my desire to wait until marriage. When that day came, there would be no holding back.

Clinton Drake stopped by my department in the morning. When he shut my office door behind him, I realized that he had something big to say. "Emma, I wanted to say good-bye. I'm heading back to my office in Saskatoon for a little while. I can't stay away from work forever, I guess. If you need me, Mavis has all the contact information." He looked to make sure the door was really closed before going on. "But there's something else. I know I can trust you to keep this completely to yourself. You've heard all the talk about what Rex Doncaster might have done to Richard's helicopter, right? Well, I can't give you all the details quite yet, but I've learned enough to be able to say, without a shadow of a doubt, that Rex had nothing to do with it. Granted, he's brought a lot of the suspicion on himself by his own foolishness, but you can take my word for it, he's innocent of Richard's murder. But please, like I said, don't tell anyone, especially not Rex. If the real killer is out there, I don't want to tip him off to anything."

Having dropped this bombshell, Clint didn't even wait for my response. He looked at his watch and cursed the time, blew me a kiss, and was gone. He left me with much to think about, but for a few minutes all I could think about was Clinton himself. Old fantasies did not die easily, even though I was now in love with another man.

I smiled as I pondered the workings of fate. Clinton had not made a play for me, notwithstanding how often I had dreamed of him doing so. This had left me free to find Garth, the real man of my dreams. So who was Clinton destined to find? Many people would have thought I was crazy, but I thought of Mavis. God willing, she would feel her loneliness and eventually reach out to Clint. But how long this would take was anyone's guess. Of one thing I was absolutely certain. Mavis would have to be the one to reach out for anything to happen. It was no coincidence that Clint had lived for forty years without settling down with a woman. "Please God, slow him down," I prayed. "And when the pain has left Mavis, help her see Clint for the man he is." I decided at that moment to give God all the help he might need to make these things happen.

As my relationship with Garth blossomed, we talked more and more about our past and our future. Garth had dated other women, but none on a steady basis. He could hardly believe that I had never had a serious date. As for the future, both of us had been careful with our money and we were soon talking about buying a home together. We no longer had any qualms about expressing our love for each other. It got to the point where we were even talking about how many children we'd like to have together. I often felt like suggesting that we start practicing for the big event immediately. I knew that all I had to do was say the word and Garth would make it happen that very day. Each day and each week made waiting more difficult. But I was determined to hold on.

CHAPTER THIRTY-SEVEN

Tom Doyle

The investigation into the death of Richard Drake continued to frustrate me. Not because it wasn't progressing; it was. But as a good policeman it frustrated me that the heavy-lifting in digging out the truth was being done by someone else, who was not even a Mountie. Still, it was hard to be angry about it. Clinton Drake was a good man who loved his brother and only wanted to see justice done to his memory. Who was I to argue with that?

I had to admire Clinton's persistence. He had refused to accept the verdict of the Transport investigators, and sure enough, he had found clues at the crash site which they had missed. He had taken it upon himself, and at his own expense, to carry these clues off to Regina for closer examination by Superintendent Ransom and his lab team. Then it was off to Oklahoma, where he prevailed on the Hughes helicopter engineers to build a mock-up of the engine that had failed so catastrophically for Richard. He had returned with a bag full of photographs and film showing how the clues he had found in the field fit into the failure of the engine. I had never seen him so grim as he summarized his findings. "Can you imagine those eight belts tearing at the cyclic and the collective control rods that pass through the drive mechanism? One or both of those rods would have pierced the gas tank, and it would be all over in a matter of seconds. Emma was more right than she knew when she said that Richard never had a chance."

In the longer conversations with Clint that ensued, he made it clear that the person who devised such a murderous device would need more than just a casual knowledge of helicopter drive mechanics. If nothing else, the device would need to have been very well hidden since Richard obviously did not see it when he did his usual pre-flight inspection. All this made perfect sense as far as it went. But we were still a long way from finding the murderer. I knew that a court would need a much more specific picture of what had happened. Assuming we ever managed to zero in on a suspect, a smart lawyer would shoot down our theory as a cock-and-bull story about little things that happened to be found in a field. A piece of wire, a scrap of dowel, and the remnants of bookbinding tape would not carry much weight. My officers and I might interrogate people who had come close to uttering death threats, but we needed more than that to build a case; we had to have more to go on than what some person may or may not have said over a glass of beer. Richard Drake had been murdered, and from the events that had taken place since the murder, it was obvious that the murderer was close at hand. But who was it?

The obvious suspect, at first, was Rex Doncaster. I

had heard a lot about Rex over the years, and it was generally good. In his own way he was a war hero. He had completed a tour of duty flying Halifax bombers. After the war he had received extensive training on how to maintain aircraft engines. This, combined with previous experience in the air, made him a valuable asset to the Grandeur Flying Club. But his position there had made him uniquely responsible for the servicing of Richard's helicopter. It looked even worse for Rex when Judy Strome had informed us that she had seen him looking at the helicopter with a flashlight in the wee hours of the day that Richard died. But ultimately Rex had come in on his own initiative to explain what he had been doing that night, and how he had spent the rest of the night away at Judy's place. Judy having already confirmed that Rex was indeed in her bed until morning, it seemed very unlikely that Rex would have had enough time to do the sort of tampering which Clinton had uncovered. Maybe not impossible, but unlikely. Besides, I couldn't see what sort of motive he could have had to kill Richard. He had made a good living servicing Richard's various aircraft over the years. He owed his job at the Flying Club to Richard. For him to kill his benefactor in a way that made the whole town point the finger at him made no sense. I decided that unless some further incriminating information surfaced against Rex, I had to look elsewhere for the murderer.

My mind kept circling back to my initial visit with Joan Driger. I had never been able to shake the feeling that there had been something else on her mind that she did not tell me. It occurred to me that I might let her in on the results of my little aerial inspection of the Kessler farm, and my discovery of the infamous grey car hidden there in some trees. Telling this to Joan might be enough to loosen whatever it was that still had a grip on her tongue. I decided that a discrete note, delivered by one of my officers in plain clothes, was the best way to approach her with my request for another meeting.

It was with considerable relief that I watched Joan arrive at the place and at the time I had suggested in my note. She waved me into her car and we drove up a wooden trail to a secluded corner of the Driger farm. There was no small talk, but she nevertheless seemed slightly more at ease than during our last visit. She was at pains to make me understand how completely supportive her husband had been throughout her involvement with the police. But it was her feelings about the group she had come to know as Kurt's "Gang" that really interested me. The rape and murder committed by Punch Stuka had marked a turning point, both for her and her husband: for the first time, and for both of them, an element of fear had entered their relationship with the Grandeur Germans. The episode of the grey car was the final straw, she said.

Joan now began to give me precious details about the morning when Wolfgang paid his visit to Kurt. "I already told you most of what I heard between Kurt and Wolf, but what I didn't tell you was that I also heard someone else talking. I think this person must have been inside the car with the fog lamps. If I didn't tell you about it before, it's only because my husband couldn't hear it. His hearing is damaged, you see, after too many unmuffled engine noises, and at his age he's just too proud to go for a hearing aid. Anyway, one of the things I heard and Kurt didn't was the name Punch Stuka. That was enough to get me to listen closer, let me tell you. I can't be absolutely sure, but I think I heard the voice say 'Punch may be in jail, but he left a great gift for one of our heroes.' And the way he said 'heroes' was definitely sarcastic. I have no idea what this means exactly, but I do know that when I first repeated it to my Kurt, he went pale and took hold of my hands. He did not speak, but for the first time in all the years we've been married there were tears in his eyes. He was thinking very hard, I could tell. Sergeant, I know you have your doubts, but I married an honourable man. Kurt knows that I'm here with you and he asked me to tell you everything. His only concern is that if I must put it all in writing, he wants as much protection for our name as possible."

Joan Driger had nothing more to say, at least for the moment. She drove me back to my unmarked car and left me there to ponder all that she had said. In truth my mind was in a complete uproar. I sat motionless while my thoughts settled. If she could be believed, it seemed that Punch Stuka had left another murderous plan unfinished when he was taken off to jail for the murder of Mabel Wickham. His target was evidently a man worthy of being called a hero, which to my mind meant a war veteran. That would obviously describe Richard Drake.

I already knew that Punch had the technical know-how to design the sort of device that had brought down the helicopter. During the Wickham investigation I had come across many people, especially those who had seen him at work on aircraft, who described

Punch as brilliant. I remembered that all of his books and papers were still in boxes down at the station. It was time that Clinton Drake took a look at them. I had no doubt that he would be willing to do so, although I would refrain from bringing up Joan's name when I asked him.

While Clint was sifting through Punch's notes, I decided to take another gamble. I started work on a series of affidavits to take before a judge: I wanted a warrant to search the Kessler farm and to seize the car I had seen from the air. It would be a major operation. I intended to use every officer I could muster, so that we could swarm over as much of the Kessler property as possible in a very short time. Every metal detector we owned would be pressed into service, sweeping the yards and all the roadways for buried treasure. It was admittedly a long shot. I wasn't even sure what I expected to find in the ground, but experience had taught me that people who were running scared tended to hide things in the most unlikely places. Maybe we would find the saw that was used to cut the dowel; or maybe a roll of the same wire which Clinton had found along with the dowel. I told my men to be especially on the lookout for any piece of wood similar in diameter to that dowel, and any roll of silver-coloured bookbinding tape. But we would seize anything which offered even the remotest chance of furthering the investigation.

The preparations to go before a judge were still not finished when Clinton Drake rushed into my office with something extraordinary. There in his hand, taken from one of Punch Stuka's files, was a sketch of the very device which had been attached to Richard's helicopter in order to destroy it. There was no question about it: it matched what Clint had reconstructed from the fragments and which he had tested in Oklahoma to such devastating effect. With the discovery of this sketch, I realized that the search warrant I had envisaged was too limited. What I really needed was the authority to remove every last scrap of paper from every room and every desk in all of the homes my officers were about to search. Fortunately the lady I had hired to do all the typing of the affidavits was still in the office and she quickly made the amendments to the request I was about to submit to the judge.

All I needed now was a signature. The Justice viewed my affidavits in silence. I could sense his surprise at the severity and breadth of the warrants I was seeking. He spent a long time reading and re-reading the documents. But within an hour I had what I had come for.

CHAPTER THIRTY-EIGHT

Clinton Drake

At first I could not believe the stack of papers that Sergeant Doyle dumped in front of me. When I had agreed to look at them, I had no notion there would be so many. But the fact that they all belonged to Punch Stuka made me forget any irritation. Without giving me too many details, Tom made it clear that he had just learned something that tended to implicate Stuka in Richard's death. He wanted me to look for anything in Punch's personal papers that might confirm his involvement. It was an interesting change of pace for me. Up to that point I had only been involved in the mechanical, nuts-and-bolts part of the investigation; now I had a chance to start considering the human element of the whole mess.

The amount of dust kicked up when I opened the box made it obvious that Punch's files had not been touched since they were seized from his apartment. I guessed that no one had been willing to waste any time on them after Punch was arrested for Mabel Wickham's murder. The other evidence against him had been overwhelming, so much so that he had thrown up his hands and confessed. The first thing I noticed about the books and notes was how neat and orderly they were. Punch's handwriting was almost feminine in appearance, and his drawings were always precise. But the content was impressive; it was clear that Punch Stuka was indeed a master of mechanics. A chill went down my spine when I saw that he had owned a copy of the service manual for the Hughes 300 helicopter. I flipped hastily to the pages dealing with drive belt assembly, thinking he might have made some sort of incriminating note. But there was nothing there to excite me. Setting the manual aside, I picked up a large multi-compartment folder. I emptied the whole thing onto the desk and started sifting through a bewildering mass of letters, scrap paper, and random sketches. I set aside anything that had no obvious relevance, which was practically everything. Then I came upon a very strange diagram. Most people would not have given it a second look. But I immediately recognized it as the fiberglass cover that went over the eight drive belts in a helicopter engine. Along with this was an image of what was unmistakably a wire harness holding a piece of dowel. I froze. My eyes would not leave the drawing. Here was proof that Punch Stuka had devised the mechanism that killed my brother. But Punch was in prison. Someone else had to have installed it for him.

As soon as the shock wore off I raced away to find Sergeant Doyle. I knew he was already busy preparing his submission for search warrants, but what I had found in Punch's file suggested that he needed to widen his net and seek a warrant to search the homes and offices of every one of Punch's known associates.

I heard the sergeant's voice behind his office door. I burst in after only the most perfunctory of knocks. "My God," he exclaimed after seeing what was in my hand, "that bastard Stuka masterminded the whole murder. But who actually did the deed?" I had never seen anyone look so elated and frustrated at the same time as Tom Doyle did at that instant.

Tom rushed off to get his affidavits amended, and I busied myself putting the Punch Stuka material back the way I had found it. I had done all I could for now. It was time to leave the rest to the police. As I put the lid back on the box, I felt suddenly depressed. All the fatigue I had been holding back for so many weeks seemed to flood over me. How many times since Richard's death had I gone back and forth between Grandeur and Saskatoon, not to mention Regina, and even Oklahoma. When would it stop? My own career was being neglected. I had grown accustomed to spending lots of time with my parents, with little Melanie, and with Mavis. I felt glad to have helped them all through their grief. Especially Mavis. But once Richard's murderer was caught, would Mavis still be so anxious to have me around? She had thanked me often enough, but in my exhaustion I could not stop myself thinking that words were cheap. I cursed myself. I had spent my life in the shadow of my brother, and his death had not changed a damn thing. Even in death he was still lording it over me, mastering me, bossing me around. I was still in his shadow.

I had no sooner let loose my jealousy than I recoiled from it in shame. What was wrong with me? My brother was dead. Whatever problems I had in life were my own fault. And there was definitely something wrong with my life. I tried to remember how long it had been since I had gone on a simple date. I was a captive of my responsibilities and my promises, to my employer, to Tom Doyle, to my family, and yes, to Mavis. I knew it was not in my nature to quit. So where did that leave me? Mavis had made noises about a more permanent partnership. Melanie certainly needed me a little while longer. In my mental turmoil a host of long-forbidden questions began popping into my mind. Was it possible that Mavis saw more in me than just a business partner? Did she want to take me to bed? Could I take my brother's widow to bed? I didn't know a damn thing about love, and even less about sex.

If only I hadn't been so bloody busy all my life. That little girl in Swansea would have taken me to bed, but I had to stay up there on my high horse, didn't I? My chums at the time were all getting as much hanky-panky as they wanted just by using the classic line, "you'll be sorry if you don't say yes and I get shot down tomorrow." But I just couldn't love a girl and leave her.

In happier times, when Richard was still alive, Mavis had often chided me about Emma. But there again I had wasted my opportunity, and now Emma had found Garth. Which brought me back to Mavis. Maybe, I told myself, I should give her a shot of her own advice and see how she handles it. If you're going to test your luck, why not start at the top? Mavis was definitely one smart-looking gal. And with her experience, she could get me up to speed in record time. The more I thought about the idea, the more I began to like it.

A part of me knew that Mavis was the reason that I had not made a play for Emma. While Richard was alive I had done a good job of suppressing my feelings, but Mavis was always somewhere in the back of my mind. She was the last person who should have been urging me to go after any other woman. No one, not even Emma, could compare to her. She had never worn slacks since the day she came to Canada; it was always skirts for her, and their length followed the style of the day, sometimes even shorter. Yes, I had looked. She was my brother's wife, but still I had looked. Only a blind man could have failed to appreciate her beautiful legs, her bust, and her bum.

I shook my head as if doing so could fling away all these bizarre thoughts and give me my peace back. I just needed a rest, some time away from the merry-go-round of work and stress I had been on. "Take a vacation, Clint," I murmured. "Yes, as soon as Richard's killer is caught, take off. Clear your mind and go."

CHAPTER THIRTY-NINE

Mavis Drake

I hadn't seen as much of Clint since my folks arrived from England but I knew exactly what had been occupying his time. He was still working very hard to find out what had happened to Richard. He had paid me a brief visit earlier in the day on his way to yet another meeting with Sergeant Doyle, and by evening he was back. I had just finished putting Melanie to bed, so I thought Clint and I would be able to have a good long chat. But at the sound of the front door closing Melanie appeared on the scene and ran over to Clint. "I heard your voice from my bedroom," she said, leaning up against Clint in his chair.

My mother-in-law came to the rescue. "Off to bed, young lady," Joan Clifton said. Melanie gave each of us a little kiss, wasted as much time as she could, and finally went back to bed.

Then Grandma disappeared into the kitchen, leaving Clint and me alone. He seemed different, somehow. I put it down to fatigue. He let me know about the search warrants which had been just been issued, and hinted that some very interesting discoveries had already been made. Other than that, though, he said little. I got the sense that more had happened than he was letting on.

The following morning I had one of the most curious experiences of my life. I was alone in my office and there was a light tap on the door. I looked up to see Joan Driger. She didn't say anything right away, and it took me a while to overcome my surprise and invite her to come in and close the door behind her. There was another long pause before Joan found her voice. As she began to speak, tears appeared in her eyes.

"I know you must be a lovely lady, or Richard wouldn't have married you. I'm sure you've heard that I once loved Richard. Actually I took his marriage to you very badly. I was shocked when Richard died. But not for the reason you might think. You see, something had happened to me just before Richard's death, something terrible, and I didn't think it was a coincidence. The police know all about it. That's not why I'm here. I wanted to talk to you about the anonymous letter against you, the one that mentioned my name."

"Yes, Sergeant Doyle showed it to me."

"I told Corporal Holden that the person who wrote it was sick. When Richard died, I thought of you, and how horrible it must have been for you to lose him. I'm not blind, I've seen the two of you at Flying Club dances. The love that you had for each other was as obvious as that picture on the wall. You may not believe this, but whenever I saw you with Richard, I was always glad that if I had to lose Richard, it was to a person like you. It's true. So you see, I'm not a bad person, Mavis. May I call you Mavis?"

"Of course you can, Joan. And I believe you." In

spite of myself I started to cry. "Please forgive me. It's just that I miss Richard so much. He was such a wonderful man. I still can't understand why anyone would want him dead. I know there's a German element here that detests every aspect of the war, especially war veterans like my Richard." I was tempted to bring up the subject of her father-in-law, who had always been a vocal Nazi supporter. But I didn't. Joan, I was sure, knew all about John Driger.

We lapsed back into an uncomfortable silence, both of us preoccupied by our own thoughts. "Mavis," Joan finally said, "I don't really know if I should tell you this, it's very personal, but on the night that Richard left for the war, I offered myself to him. I was a virgin, but I was prepared to sacrifice my good name because I loved him so much. I was so hurt when he refused me. But I realize now that he was just doing what he thought was right. He didn't want to risk leaving me pregnant and alone."

I was strangely touched by her need to unburden herself to me, but I wasn't sure how to respond. "Yes, that's just who Richard was. Of course in those days a lot of people felt the same way. Richard and I were both still virgins on the night of our marriage. I don't think you'd find many young couples who would wait that long today. It's a different world, I'm afraid."

"It certainly is," Joan agreed sadly. After another pause she stood up and slowly moved to the office door. But before she could leave I reached over to give her a hug. "Thank you, Joan, for coming here and talking to me like this. You're a very strong woman. And I want you to know that however much that anonymous letter hurt me, I never believed you had anything to do with it. Not for a minute. Richard would never have cared about a woman who could do something like that, and I know that he never stopped caring about you."

This was too much for Joan. She started sobbing again. But as she walked away I could tell that they were now tears of happiness as well as sadness.

Clint often took the time to phone Melanie, and much of what I knew about his whereabouts from day to day I owed to my daughter. I had just recovered from talking to Joan Driger and was wondering whether Clint was still in town when who should walk through the office door but my brother-in-law, with my little girl beside him. Apparently he had just returned from another quick visit to Saskatoon, and realizing Melanie would be getting out of school within a few minutes, he went off to pick her up. I was thrilled to see them both. Melanie hugged me and then ran off. "I'm going to find Emma," she explained.

I looked at Clint and smiled. "If you found a woman who loved you as much as you love my little daughter, you'd be a married man by now."

"I guess you're right. But not to worry, there's still time. Remember, I'm only a tiny bit older than you, and since you're young enough to be having another baby, surely I can't be ready for the scrap heap just yet."

"No, I have to admit, you're still quite a catch. I'm sure there are plenty of women who'd love to get a hold of you."

I had become accustomed to this sort of banter with Clint. And it began to dawn on me that the pain of Richard's death would ease off a bit whenever Clint was around. I'd always known that here was a man who deserved a great deal of respect; but somehow it was different now. I found myself recalling how Richard had told me that his twin brother thought that I was "quite a gal."

It had often crossed my mind that without Clinton it was likely that Richard's death would have been written off as an accident. The police could not be faulted for that, and neither could the men at the Department of Transport; the accident experts had seen so many crashes caused by pilot error that it was the obvious conclusion. But Clint, God bless him, had refused to accept the obvious conclusion. It was lucky that a portion of Clint's air force service had involved him in aircraft accident investigations, and also that he had spent so much time around Richard and the helicopter. All this made him the perfect person to uncover the mechanics of the crash. Richard's murderer was not yet identified, let alone convicted. Yet Clinton, and my garden rake, had already tipped the scales in favor of justice. I would never forget what Clinton had done to preserve my Richard's good name. Whatever happened, the world would know that Richard was not at fault when he flew his helicopter that day.

The people of Grandeur had been wonderful to me in my grief. Having so many people sharing my grief seemed to lessen the pain. That made some sense, I thought: the more people to share the load, the less the load for each person. But there was more to it than that. Especially in the weeks before my parents had arrived from England, my friends and neighbours had made my life easier when I would otherwise have had trouble coping. When I was in no condition to cook, members of my church had almost buried me with food.

My work was also great therapy. Richard, who had always been the linchpin of the whole operation at Grandeur Ford, was gone. Garth was doing well as sales manager, but he was new and needed my help. I literally could not afford to take my eye off the business. And when you concentrate on business, grief takes second place, at least for a little while.

Life was full of irony. A terrible war that had caused so much suffering had also found me the love of my life. Richard had survived the war only to be killed in one of the most peaceful corners of the earth. And losing Richard had forced me to consider possibilities that might actually make my life more fulfilling in some ways. There were so many more opportunities open to women than there had been before the war. Very few women had gone to university when I was a girl; now the universities were full of them. The banks were staffed exclusively by men when I was a girl; now most of their employees were women. Just as women had stepped up to take the place of men in every type of workplace during the war, so I was stepping into Richard's shoes now that he was gone. I wondered what other big changes I could look forward to in the years ahead. But I was no longer afraid. Richard was gone, but I would survive.

CHAPTER FORTY

Joan Driger

Ever since that morning when I hid behind Kurt's big tractor and heard the snarled and drunken questions thrown at Kurt, I had been trying to figure out whose voice it was that I had heard coming from inside the grey car. It seemed familiar, but for a long time I couldn't place it. Then one day Kurt and I stopped in at the pub for a beer and my mind went back to another time I had been there, when Kurt had been surrounded by all the members of the Gang. This was when I realized that the voice in the car belonged to Rudy Schreiber. I also began to think that it was his voice I had heard warning me over the phone to "watch my step." I could not be absolutely sure about it, at least not sure enough to swear to it in a court of law. Whoever had made the threatening phone call had muffled his voice just enough to make certainty impossible. But in my heart I believed that it was Rudy Schreiber.

Kurt came in for supper. He had finished all the weed-killing without a single mechanical breakdown and was very pleased with himself. As usual he gave all the credit to a contraption he had devised to raise and lower the sprayer booms. I had heard his description of how it worked many times, and he was always rather amazed that I could understand the technical details so thoroughly. He liked to speak about the "law of the lever." When I proceeded to explain what that meant, he shook his head and suggested that maybe it was time to teach me how to weld; that way he could be sure that the farm equipment would never break down! I had a quick response to this. "Anything you can do to get me out of the kitchen suits me fine. But don't you think my baby bump would get in the way?" Kurt gave me one of his wonderfully impish grins and pretended to be shocked. "Joan, what are you talking about? You're pregnant? We've been sleeping together for years, and you never got pregnant before. Who's the lucky guy?" I stuck my tongue out at him and made a fist in front of his nose. This earned me a hug and a kiss, and another impish grin. The exchange ended with me sitting on his knee. "Joan, you are the finest thing that ever happened to me, and I love you very much. Don't ever doubt that."

After a brief pause Kurt started to talk again, only now his words were very serious. "I want you to know that there is nothing I wouldn't do to protect you. I don't ever want you to keep anything from me just because it may reflect badly on my old buddies. Do you understand me? If you're keeping something from me, or from the police, stop doing it. Your safety is everything."

It was time to tell Kurt exactly what I thought about the voice coming out of the car and the voice on the phone. My husband did not flinch at the name

Rudy Schreiber. He had not seen Rudy in the car that morning, but he had not really looked into the back-seat, which was hidden in the shadows anyway. The bigger question was what we were going to do about all this. The fact that one of Wolf's friends had been throwing around Punch Stuka's name that morning was far from proof of anything. A good lawyer would explain it away as a symptom of nothing more sinister than drunkenness. Suddenly a new idea came to me. They had asked Kurt if he would throw a bag of theirs on his junk pile. "Did you ever see what was inside it, Kurt?" I asked.

"Actually, no, I didn't." He was lost in thought for a moment. "I wonder what the hell that was about? I've been too busy to even think about it. Let's go and check it out. It should still be under the fuel tank, that's where I threw it."

The black plastic bag was not there, however. Kurt and I looked at each other, and we were both very troubled. Someone had come onto our property while we were asleep, or away, and taken the bag. It was something that someone had suddenly decided we shouldn't have a chance to see. "Sweetheart," Kurt said, his voice shaking, "this is too much. We've got to go to the police."

I didn't even have a chance to agree. Kurt had no sooner spoken than a car, which I recognized as an unmarked RCMP vehicle, drove into our yard. A plainclothes policeman got out and handed me a sealed letter. He said he would wait in the car while I decided on a reply. Kurt watched over my shoulder as I ripped open the envelope. The note turned out to be very short. Sergeant Doyle simply wanted me to know that he had new information about the death of Richard Drake, and wanted to talk to me about it. All I had to do was name the time and place.

I turned to Kurt. He took my hand. "It's too late to turn back now. So go and give him a time and place."

It was quickly organized, and within an hour and a half Sergeant Doyle was sitting in my car. I told him about the voice in the car and the sarcastic crack about the "gift for one of our heroes." I also told him about the so-called junk dropped off by Wolfgang Kessler, and how someone had found a way of taking it from our yard undetected. Considering that Wolf had brought the junk bag to us in a grey car with white trim and fog lamps–the same car which had been on the road to the Flying Club at around three o'clock in the morning before Richard's helicopter crashed, and from which I heard someone suggestively refer to Punch Stuka, a proven murderer–I knew that the Sergeant was wondering if the bag had anything to do with the destruction of the helicopter.

Before driving Sergeant Doyle back to his car I asked him one last question. What did he think was meant by the "gift" left by Punch Stuka? He told me there could be any number of threats hidden in that word. But if he had to guess, it sounded like something else Punch had planned to do to a male or female war veteran after he murdered Mabel Wickham.

As he said it, the Sergeant's manner was more intense than I had ever seen in any of my earlier dealings with him. Then he seemed to become uneasy, as if he felt he had said more than he should. He hurried off with the explanation that he had another appointment waiting.

CHAPTER FORTY-ONE

Sergeant Tom Doyle

My search teams fanned out across Grandeur. We had seven separate targets: Russ Kessler's residence, Russ Kessler's dealership; Wolfgang Kessler's farm; Pete Heider's residence; the residence of Rudy and Anna Schreiber; Rudy Schreiber's office at Grandeur Ford; and of course the Flying Club itself. At the last minute I decided to send another, much smaller team out to the Driger farm as well. I had no reason whatsoever to suspect Joan or even Kurt, given how great a role they had placed in advancing the investigation to this point. But I was concerned that the other members of Kurt's old "Gang" might seek revenge against him if it seemed that they had all been targeted and he had not. It was safer for the Drigers, and it was better for the investigation, if the other targets of the searches went on believing that Kurt was still loyal to them. I warned Joan about my plan, and she and Kurt raised no objections. Then I went off to focus on the real searches.

Ordinarily I disliked barging into the houses of private citizens, even Nazi-lovers like Wolfgang and Russ Kessler. I sympathized with the law of the land that protected Canadians from frivolous searches; in a free society there had to be some rock-solid rights, and the sanctity of a person's home was one of the most important of all. It was only fair that a police officer should have to present his reasons to an impartial judge before invading a homeowner's privacy and rifling though his personal belongings. Yet in this case what my men and I were going to do didn't cost me the slightest bit of sleep. I felt as though the bad guys had held all the good cards since the day of the murder. Now I had finally been dealt a decent hand. I was about to get back in the game.

It was a hectic day, and not everything went exactly as planned. Wolfgang Kessler turned out to be out on some sort of farm business, and when old Mrs. Kessler met us at the door to the farmhouse she pretended not to understand the concept of the warrant. The resulting dispute took more time than I would have liked. But while Mrs. Kessler was blocking her door and consulting her lawyer I instructed some of my men to head off into the fields with the map I had drawn for them. Not only were they to retrieve the grey car I had seen from the air, they were also to search for the "junk bag" which had been dumped at the Driger place before it disappeared.

I had no sooner got off the radio with my deputy out at the Kessler farm than I received an irritated call from another one of my teams, which was tasked with the search of the Schreiber household. Rudy was at work; I was sure of this because I had already spoken to Mavis to give her a heads-up about my intention to search Rudy's office at the dealership. But Anna was at home and she objected furiously to the sight of police officers at her front door. I warned my men to be as polite as possible, but to make her understand that one way or another, we were going into her house. The implied threat was finally enough to get her out of the doorway, but she hovered around the search team the whole time they were attempting to do their business, no matter how often they asked her to wait outside.

Throughout the morning and afternoon RCMP vehicles shuttled back and forth between the various search sites and the station in Grandeur, bringing with them a vast and varied array of seized items to be examined more closely in a controlled environment. Our first real break came when one of the RCMP technicians, an expert on typewriters who I had borrowed from Regina, identified one of the typewriters we had seized as the machine that had typed the anonymous slur against Mavis Drake. There was a problem, however, and it was a big one. We had picked up a total of four typewriters during our searches of various properties, and in accordance with procedure, they should each have been tagged with a record of where they came from. But in the haste of the search, one typewriter had been sloppily identified, and the police tag somehow disappeared before it reached the station. None of the officers I asked about it could remember the origins of the typewriter in question. Such a colossal screw-up might have been bearable if the machine had turned out to be of no evidentiary value. Unfortunately, it so happened that this was the very same machine the expert had pointed to. So we desperately needed to know who owned that typewriter.

But trying to identify this typewriter was hardly our only problem. In various rooms of the station, in addition to the two garages next door where we normally stored our police cruisers, teams of RCMP men were soon pouring over everything else we had taken from the six search sites. I tried to coordinate the effort as well as I could, directing those who had finished with their own mounds of paper to assist other teams who were not so speedy. As the hours dragged on without further result, I kept telling myself that such a large group of dedicated men was bound to come up with something useful. But with all the searching and all the papers, I was still seeing nothing but blank looks and empty hands.

Unable to sit at my desk any longer, I took to wandering from room to room and desk to desk, and I could feel the mounting frustration everywhere I went. There were a lot of unfamiliar faces; the scale of the operation had forced me to borrow men from many other detachments in the general vicinity of Grandeur. I came upon the team that was studying Rudy Schreiber's stuff. I originally had high hopes for what this might yield, but the team had finished examining his papers and reported that nothing useful was among them. I swore. Then the corporal leading the team, another officer-on-loan from Regina, spoke up. "Sergeant, I'm sure you don't want to hear this right now, but that Anna whatever-her-real-name-is has been pestering us all day about getting her stuff back, especially her typewriter. What should we tell her?"

"What typewriter? I didn't know you got a typewriter from the Schreiber place."

"Yes, I'm sure we did, sir. I remember it well because she claimed that she couldn't find the case for it, and I had to tie the ID tag to the shift key with a piece of wire. It was a miserable bloody thing to carry, let me tell you."

Suddenly the day seemed to be looking up. I excused myself from the room and went to where the fingerprint technicians were still painstakingly going over the unidentified typewriter. They had still not found any usable prints, but that was not what interested me. I took a close look at the shift keys. One of them was completely out of alignment, as if it had been yanked back from the mechanism beneath. I guessed that Anna had found a way of getting to the typewriter after it was tagged but before it was removed from her house, and in her successful attempt to tear the tag off, she broke the shift key to which it had been tied. It was a stupid thing to do, something we were bound to figure out eventually. It had been even more stupid for Anna to make such a big fuss about getting her typewriter back. But frightened people often acted stupidly. In any case we could now link one or both of the Schreibers to the horrible letter which had attempted to throw the blame for Richard's murder onto Mavis. It remained to be seen, though, if the Schreibers had done anything worse. I decided that the Schreiber papers ought to be examined all over again and brought in a different group of officers to do the job, not because I blamed the previous group for not having found anything, but because I thought fresh sets of eyes might have better luck.

There was something that still disturbed me very much, however. It was mid-afternoon. All the sites had been thoroughly searched, the grey car had been found at the Kessler farm and towed into Grandeur, and we were knee-deep in all sorts of seized correspondence.

But the one piece of evidence I was most anxious to find was still missing: the notorious bag of junk that had been so suspiciously dumped at the Driger farm by Wolf and his cronies the morning before Richard crashed, and then even more suspiciously went missing again before Kurt or Joan had a chance to look at it. Where in the hell could it be? When the day began I had assumed that if it were to be found anywhere, it would be near the other big and hidden piece of evidence, the grey car. But the car had been searched, and it wasn't anywhere inside. I questioned those of my men who had retrieved the car from the Kessler farm; they reported that even after using the metal detector over a wide area around the car, there was no sign of any bag. I still wasn't convinced. My gut told me that they had missed something, somehow. I wanted to take another look at the Kessler farm, and in particular at the remote spot in the trees where the car had been hidden.

After another quick visit to the judge to have the time-limit on our warrant extended, I summoned Corporal Tim Holden to accompany me back out to the Kessler property. This time it would be just the two of us. Mrs. Kessler was no more enthusiastic than the first time my men had showed her a warrant, but since I had no interest in going inside the house again, she did not bother to argue. Armed with metal detectors and shovels, Tim and I trudged off into the fields. It was about a quarter-mile walk to the trees and the slough where the car had been hidden. Once there, it was not difficult to see exactly where it had sat before being towed away: the four wheels had left definite indentations in the ground. Once there, however, I began to ask myself what the hell I had gotten myself into. There was no obvious place to start searching in this God-forsaken spot, at least not one that my men had not already swept with their own metal detectors. I could tell by the look on his face that Tim felt the same way.

I needed time to think. I turned to the corporal and asked him to pretend that we had a plastic bag to hide. Where would be the least obvious place in this area for us to put it? The obvious answer was to bury it in the trees, but there was no sign of disturbed ground, and in any case the earth was so old and root bound that even a shovel would have been hard-pressed to penetrate it. Half an hour of searching in the trees and the surrounding grass turned up nothing. So we turned to the slough. It had tall grass all around its edges, and it encompassed quite a few large rocks, some completely exposed, some partially so, and some fully submerged. Tim suggested that a partially exposed rock would make a handy hiding-place for someone without tools. I immediately saw his point: the person might gamble on a prairie cloudburst to come along and replenish the pond, thereby covering the partially submerged rock and the junk bag with it.

It was not easy work. Wading into the slough was damned tough on our standard-issue police boots. Our shovels were good enough to dislodge the rocks, but only brute strength could actually move them. After an hour of dirty work that left us wet and disheartened, we took a brief rest. We were two-thirds of the way around the slough, and were determined to finish the circuit, come hell or high water. So back into the muddy water we went, tackling three more rocks with as little success as before. Then came a fourth, and Tim noticed that it seemed to have been disturbed once already. "It doesn't quite fit the earth in the part that's out of the water." I could see what he meant. The rock in question was obviously not in its original resting place. It still required all of our combined strength to tip it over, but doing so exposed a black plastic bag, partially buried in mud.

Tim spread a newspaper on the grass and I dumped the contents of the bag on top of it. There was only one item that I really needed to see, and it was there: a long wooden dowel from which a piece had obviously been cut. There was also a roll of alloy wire, another roll of what looked like book-binding tape, some cardboard with a finish that looked like it would resist water, and various scraps of green fiberglass that might have been punched out of a helicopter engine cover. Even more exciting than the objects themselves was what they displayed: a whole series of magnificently greasy fingerprints.

Tim and I gathered up everything we had found and raced back to the station. There was quite a stir among the assembled officers when the two of us burst though the door, clutching a black plastic bag, our uniforms covered in mud. Yet I had no time for niceties. All I wanted was to get to the phone as quickly as possible. I hated to bother Clinton Drake again, especially after all the hours he had already spent on the case, but it had to be done. My trusty gut was screaming at me that we had reached the crucial point in the case, and I knew that Clint would want to take these items through to the crime lab in Regina for comparison to what he had found at the crash site.

And so it proved. When I told him about the new discoveries, he phoned the Flying Club and, for what seemed like the umpteenth time since his brother's death, had Rex Doncaster gas up his plane. Fortunately the weather was fine for a quick departure. Superintendent Bob Ransom was alerted and Clint was away before dusk.

After a quick trip home to clean myself up I returned to the station, which had been completely reinvigorated by the discovery of the junk bag. This was just as well, because there was still a vast amount of work to be done. We could not yet assume that the examination of the "junk" from the slough would prove decisive. However many tedious hours it might take, we needed to go on sifting through the rest of the material we had acquired by the search warrants before we would have a hope of drawing any conclusions. So all of us worked long into the night before calling a halt.

There were no messages waiting for me when I got into the station early the next morning, but within an hour Superintendent Ransom phoned to let me know that Clinton Drake was already on his way back from Regina. I could expect him at about twelve-thirty. "I have good news for you, Sergeant Doyle," the superintendent said. "The exhibits you found in that bag are an exact match to what was found at the crash site."

I was elated. "Thank God, and thank you sir, for letting me know."

"Don't thank me, Tom. Clint deserves most of the credit, as I'm sure you realize. He's a hell of a guy. I've always known it, ever since he saved my life during the war. Maybe one day, when you have time, I'll tell you that story."

"I'd like that, sir."

"Anyway, good luck with the rest of your investigation."

Clinton Drake arrived within ten minutes of his suggested ETA. He handed me the precious package he had carried to Regina and back, which I immediately handed over to the fingerprint experts I had on site. Now that we knew for certain that these items had been involved in the sabotage of Richard's helicopter, it was time to find out who had handled them.

While the experts set about doing their work, I invited Clint over to my house for a quick sandwich. I filled him in on all that had happened during his brief absence, which was not very much. I had hardly finished the words when a corporal I did not immediately recognize was knocking on my door. He was yet another of the extra men I had siphoned from a neighbouring detachment to execute all the search warrants. "I'm sorry, I'm afraid I don't know your name, Corporal," I said apologetically, "but come on in."

"I'm Corporal Benson, Sergeant. I was assigned to go through various personal papers." He looked nervously at Clinton. "Can I talk freely, sir?"

"Go ahead, Corporal. This is Clinton Drake, the brother of the murdered man. He has been very much involved in the investigation, and can be trusted to hear anything you have to say. Now what is it?"

"Well, sir, I was going through the files, like you instructed, looking for anything that might resemble the copy that you showed us." He was referring to the damning diagram that Clinton had uncovered in Punch Stuka's papers. "Well, I came across an unsealed and unaddressed envelope, containing a single sheet of standard-size writing paper. The paper is pretty wrinkled and has some clear fingerprints on it. But the important thing is that it shows a series of small sketches, and one of them looks exactly like the one you included in the background to our search warrants."

Clinton and I were not merely speechless, for a long moment we were actually breathless.

"Corporal Benson," I said when at last I had regained my composure, "guard that paper with your life. You may have just solved this case. What we need to do now is take a closer look at those fingerprints."

CHAPTER FORTY-TWO

Joan Driger

My life could have been hell. I knew, way down deep, that I had married on the rebound, and many marriages that started in that way ended in disaster. But my husband Kurt had turned out to be a truly honourable and loving man. Which is not of course to say that there had not been many occasions in the past when I had my doubts. Kurt had laid his love of Germany on the line before we even set our wedding date, and as hard as I tried to overlook it, to pretend that it did not matter, it had coloured our relationship for a long time. I trusted Kurt, but I didn't trust that damned gang of his. I had always worried that the other Grandeur Germans would get him into trouble in spite of himself. The fact that this had not happened spoke volumes about how much he loved me.

Even in the days when Kurt was still close to the Gang, I had kept my distance from it. The closest I ever got to associating with people like the Kesslers or Punch Stuka was when I would come by after one of my church meetings to have a beer or two with my husband in the company of his friends. It's fair to say that the tone of the conversation would change the instant I walked up to their table in the pub. I could tell that shins were being kicked under the table as a signal to be careful about what was said in my presence. It was not because I was a woman. After all, they welcomed Anna Schreiber, Rudy's wife, with open arms, and she seemed to participate fully in their meetings. But then Anna was a German, too.

I was curious about Anna from the first time I met her. Usually she wasn't inclined to say much to me, although sometimes we did exchange some small talk over our beer. For a long time all I knew about her was what little I could squeeze out of Kurt: that she was essentially a refugee, a German citizen who had been caught by surprise by the outbreak of war in 1939, and who had never made it home.

There was one occasion, however, when I found Anna chattier than usual, and her tongue a little looser. Well into her beer, she got to talking about her husband Rudy and his experience working for Mavis Drake at Grandeur Ford. Apparently Rudy had told her that it was his German background that was keeping him from the promotion he deserved. Mavis had just hired another salesman and moved him in as Rudy's boss. This did not sit well with Rudy, or with Anna. "And after all the things he had done for those damn Drakes, that he never got paid for!" Anna exclaimed. She added that Rudy was thinking of telling Mavis to find herself another "boy," because he didn't like being treated that way. I assumed there was more to the story than she was telling me. Kurt never took our vehicles to any place other than Russ Kessler's garage, but Grandeur Ford had a good reputation–certainly in comparison to Russ.

I was looking forward to a future where Kurt would have nothing more to do with these people. Russ and Wolfgang Kessler, Punch Stuka, Pete Heider, Rudy and Anna Schreiber, even my father-in-law John Driger: they had been like a cancer eating away at my town and my marriage as well. One of them had already gone to prison for committing a truly heinous crime, and it seemed likely that at least one more of them was about to go the same way for what had been done to Richard. And when that happened my Kurt and I would finally and totally be free of the lot of them, once and for all. I had only a few nagging doubts left. I wondered what Wolfgang Kessler thought he would accomplish by driving the car with the strange fog lamps to our yard that morning. And why were we the ones trusted, at least initially, with the bag of so-called "junk"?

But of all my remaining doubts, there was only one that really worried me. So far our involvement in the investigation into Richard Drake's murder had been under the radar. Kurt had supported me going to the police with my information, but this had been more or less in secret. Sergeant Doyle had even gone so far as to arrange a search of our house to preserve the illusion, for anyone who might be paying attention, that Kurt was as much under suspicion as the rest of his German friends. But how would Kurt react if the RCMP asked us to make what we had seen and heard a matter of public record?

The answer to this question was not long in coming.

CHAPTER FORTY-THREE

Clinton Drake

Mavis had told me more than once how happy she was with her new sales manager, whom I had found for her in the aftermath of Richard's death. It was not long before she noticed that Garth was proving himself in other ways. "If you ever toyed with making a play for Emma, Clint, you can forget it, at least for now," she told me. "From where I sit it looks like Emma and Garth have got something going. I believe they're very serious."

Of course I already knew all about this. "Wouldn't you know it, Mavis, but when you mentioned Emma's name a few weeks ago, it actually did cross my mind to ask her out for coffee or something. I guess it's true what you've always said about me. Sleeping at the switch seems to be a real problem of mine where women are concerned. All I can say is that the next time you give me advice about pretty, intelligent, and sexy girls, I'll try to do something about it. I promise. But for now, Mavis, I'm in the mood to take a little hop. I'm going to get in my plane and fly south along the river for a while."

For the first time in a long time, I felt truly carefree as I drove to the airfield. I rolled the window all the way down and enjoyed feeling the wind rushing at my face at thirty miles an hour. I knew in my heart, my mind, and my body that the mystery of my brother's murder was unwinding and that it was only a matter of time before the culprit was caught. It seemed safe to try to start enjoying my own life again.

At the Flying Club I greeted Rex Doncaster and told him I was in the mood for some fresh air if he could get my plane out of the hangar for me. I had seen a lot of Rex lately; how many times had I asked him to gas up my plane over the last few weeks? As he hurried off to do as I requested, I thought about how worn out he looked. It was sad. Mavis had called him a "bastard," and no doubt he had betrayed his wife Thelma; but he had been such a wonderful bastard during the war. He had given himself over totally to his country. How much of his innate common sense had been worn away during those nights in his bomber over Germany? There were only a handful of Canadians who knew what it was like to push the four throttles forward on a bomber loaded with twelve thousand pounds of bombs. Unless you had actually had your hands on those throttles, you could not know how fine was the line separating lift-off from death. If you dropped two hundred and fifty revs on one of those Rolls-Royce engines, you and your crew were dead. And then, if you managed to get off the ground, your ordeal was only beginning. You could look forward to swarms of German night fighters. You could look forward to mammoth searchlights that would envelope you and reveal your position to every enemy gunner for miles around. You could look forward to being targeted by radar-controlled anti-aircraft batteries that would blow you out of the sky without the slightest warning. Did Mavis know any of this? Did Richard ever tell her about the mind-boggling stresses? I wondered. Knowing what I knew, it was not so hard for me to imagine that Rex could have been susceptible to Judy Strome's mind games, which offered him a spectacular distraction from all the memories that still haunted him. Maybe if Thelma had not been away, Judy would not have had a chance. I couldn't condone it, but I could understand what Rex had done. In any case, he had suffered enough. If he ever asked me for forgiveness, I would certainly give it to him.

My aircraft was barely out of the hangar when I heard Glenys Johnson's voice calling me urgently back to the office. "Mavis is on the phone!" she yelled. "She wants you back at the dealership right away! Sergeant Doyle is there, and has something huge to tell you!"

The next hour was a blur. I found the sergeant and the efficient Corporal Tim waiting for me in Mavis's office, along with Mavis herself and Emma. I could feel their excitement before a single word was spoken. But Tom stayed as calm as ever, and as he spoke, the full wonder of his news became clear. The search for my brother's murderer was over.

In that moment I was so happy, and so proud, that I thought I might float away. I had lived and breathed the mechanics of Richard's crash for so long. I had worked my butt off to prove that my twin brother had not been responsible for his own death. I had practically made it my life's work to prove that he had been a safe pilot to the very end. My efforts had paid off.

Tom Doyle was extremely gracious, making it clear how great a debt he and the whole of Grandeur owed me for the success of the investigation. But I was not interested in taking credit. I had merely done what I had to do for Richard. He was the real hero. He had survived the worst war in the history of the world, only to be struck down by a murder that came later.

CHAPTER FORTY-FOUR

Tom Doyle

The fingerprint results were in. They were certainly persuasive, and confirmed my own guess about who had committed the crime. But I was not satisfied. This case was too important to leave to even the slightest chance. I did not merely want a conviction, I wanted a confession, which would not only spare the taxpayer the cost of a trial but also put the result beyond dispute. Juries, after all, had been known to do funny things. But before I dared confront the murderer I wanted to nail down every last piece of evidence, so that the murderer could be sure that I was not bluffing and that his fate was sealed. This was how a good policeman got a confession and closed a case for good.

Up to this point I had done everything in my power to keep Joan and Kurt Driger's name out of the official investigation, going so far as to arrange a phony search of their house. I knew that once the general public learned of all the help they had given me, their lives would never be the same, for better or worse. The murderer's friends were not all going to disappear into prison, and it was impossible to know if they would seek revenge. Yet I could not allow this consideration to influence my actions indefinitely. Taking a murderer off the streets of Grandeur was ultimately the only thing that mattered. And for that to happen, I had to disclose *everything* the Drigers had told me.

On my instructions Corporal Holden changed into sports clothes and drove me out to the Driger farm in an unmarked car. Kurt was at the machine shed and came over to the car at once. I held out my hand to him. Kurt smiled. "Are you sure you really want to shake a hand as greasy as mine?" I smiled back, and shook it anyway. I felt we were off to a good start. But now came the hard part.

We made our way across the yard to the house. Kurt seemed remarkably calm. "Joan and I have been expecting you, Sergeant."

"So you understand why I'm here."

"I do." We had reached the kitchen door. Joan was standing there, waiting for us. Clearly there was no sense in trying to soften the blow with any introductory small talk. So once inside the house I came rapidly to the point.

"I want you both to know that this isn't an easy decision for me," I explained, "but I can't put this off any longer. You've already been an enormous help to the investigation. But it's not enough. Believe me, I realize it won't be easy for you to assist me openly. Yet I have to weigh that against the possibility of a murderer going free, and that could easily happen if I allowed you to stay in the background."

They sat quietly as I reminded them that someone in the notorious grey-and-white car had already called Joan by name and made a threatening phone call to her home. So clearly they were already in someone's crosshairs on account of what they knew. They were the first people to make the connection between the grey car and the sinister events at the Flying Club before Richard's crash, having witnessed the car speeding away from the hangar even before one of my officers stopped it to issue a ticket for dangerous driving. Beyond that, only they could connect the "bag of junk" to the grey car and the people who were in it on the morning of Richard's death.

"Joan," I turned to her directly, "I'm sure you haven't forgotten the words of one of the people in the car that morning. 'Punch Stuka left us a present,' the man said. Well, we now know for sure what that present was. It was the device inserted into the engine of Richard's helicopter to destroy it. Punch left a drawing of it. And we found a virtually identical sketch in the possession of one of his acquaintances. This same man's fingerprints have been found all over items recovered from the bag of junk you warned us about, items that are an exact match to fragments of the device that destroyed Richard's helicopter. So we now know, without a shadow of a doubt, the way in which Richard was killed, who planned it, and who carried it out. It's time to lock him up. But I want to have as much evidence to throw at him as I can. And that means I want you to swear out an official statement about what you have seen and heard."

Before I could say any more, Kurt put up his hand for silence. "I think Joan and I need to take a little walk to talk this over, Sergeant Doyle. You can wait here, we won't be long." He took an unresisting Joan by the hand and led her out of the house.

They did not actually walk very far. Through the kitchen window I could see them meandering among the farm buildings, obviously deep in conversation, but totally out of earshot. Then Kurt gave Joan a tight hug, they turned, and together made their way back to the house. Kurt spoke first, and decisively. "We've made our decision. We both feel that it would be wrong not to cooperate. We've come this far. It's time to finish it. My wife will do anything you ask." Kurt hesitated for just an instant before going on. "And so will I."

We arranged a time for the two of them to come down to the station and take care of the formalities that very day. Corporal Holden and I had every reason to drive away from the Driger farm in the highest of spirits. It was without a doubt the biggest case I had ever solved. I had only one regret. I knew full well that there had been more than one bad bastard in that grey-and-white car the night when it carried the murderer to the Flying Club. In my mind these people were as guilty as the fellow who had sabotaged Richard's helicopter. But I was in no position to charge anyone else. The fingerprints pointed to one man alone, and trying to squeeze more convictions out of the available evidence might only weaken the case against the murderer himself.

And of course I still had work to do. I wanted a confession.

CHAPTER FORTY-FIVE

Joan Driger

So much had happened, there were times when I thought my head could hold no more. At every turn my Kurt continued to amaze me. When Sergeant Doyle had made his last visit to our farm, and we had walked off alone to discuss his request, Kurt had not wrung his hands or cursed the fate that had put us in the middle of a murder investigation. He just asked me what I wanted to do. When I told him that I wanted to put everything we had seen down on paper, as the sergeant had requested, he gathered me up in his arms in an all-mighty hug, and said he would be with me all the way.

A few hours later Kurt and I kept our appointment down at the RCMP station. Sergeant Doyle was again very generous in his thanks. In a strange way I felt a great relief. Everything was finally out in the open, for all the world, friend or otherwise, to see. We no longer had to watch what we said depending on who we were talking to. We could use our phone without any fear of who might be listening on the party line. Best of all, I knew that Kurt would never again be welcome among the Gang – or at least what was likely to be left of it. He had made his choice, and it was me.

In so many ways I felt like we were entering a new phase in our life together. I could tell that Kurt felt the same way. When we finished signing all the police papers, he told me I deserved a treat, and took me for ice cream and coffee. He said that the coffee was for me, and the ice cream was for the baby.

The following day I was puttering around the house, and Kurt was working out in the barn, when the phone rang. It was Corporal Tim Holden, relaying another message from Sergeant Doyle. He suggested that I might want to come by Mavis Drake's office at a quarter to five that afternoon. There were no more details, but the corporal hinted it would be well worth the effort.

Kurt, covered in dust, suggested I go without him. We arranged to meet for a beer at our favourite pub once whatever was going on had ended.

Mavis Drake's office was full when I got there. There were tears in Mavis's eyes, but it did not seem that she was distraught. Emma Jones was holding her hand. I saw Clint, which was no surprise. I was slightly surprised to see that Judy Strome was also there. With Judy, nothing ever seemed to change. She was as beautiful and well-dressed as she had been for as long as could remember. I could have sworn I saw her wink at Corporal Holden, who had the decency to look slightly uncomfortable. I was wide-awake and yet somehow I felt as though I were in some sort of dream. Then Tom Doyle started speaking.

"You should all know that the news people in Saskatoon are aware of what's about to happen. I've been on the phone with CFQC TV and CKOM Radio Saskatoon, and they're on the way down to Grandeur. But I wanted to meet with Mavis and the rest of you before the news hounds arrived. Everyone here, in their own way, has helped solve this murder. I'm sure there's going to be a lot of idle rumour and gossip swirling around town over the next few days, but you deserve to hear the story as it really is."

The sergeant gave a nice dramatic pause before continuing. He was enjoying the moment, and it was hard to blame him. "I am a man of motives, and believe me, the iron is red-hot. About an hour ago we finished showing our suspect all the evidence. He was visibly shaken. In fact he was so shaken that he collapsed in his chair. And a few minutes ago he confessed. Rudy Schreiber has confessed to the premeditated murder of Richard Drake."

There was a stunned silence. Out of all the members of my husband's former Gang, Rudy was probably the person I would least have expected to be capable of murder. I now knew for certain that my suspicion must have been correct: not only was it Rudy's voice that I heard coming from inside the grey car on the morning that Wolfgang had paid us a visit, but it must have been Rudy who threatened me on the phone later that same day.

The sergeant had more to say. "It's clear now that a strong bond developed between Punch Stuka and Rudy before Punch went to jail for the murder of Mabel Wickham. Clint found an original diagram of the device that destroyed Richard's helicopter among Punch's papers. And we found an identical diagram among Rudy's papers, covered in his own greasy fingerprints. I'm sure there will be people who wonder why Rudy kept this sketch after committing the crime. But if I've learned one thing in all the years I've been investigating crimes, it's that criminals tend to be a cocky bunch, especially when they think they've gotten away with something. Rudy could never have predicted that we would be able to recognize a sketch like that, even if we ever did find it. But we did recognize it, and for that we have Clinton Drake to thank. It was Clinton who went back to the crash site when the Transport experts were all saying that there was nothing suspicious to find, and it was Clinton who then found the fragments of the device shown in the sketch. Clinton also made all the trips, between here and Regina, and here and Oklahoma, to prove how such a device would have worked, how it brought Richard's helicopter down. Without those fragments, we would never have had enough evidence to charge Rudy with murder, let alone get him to confess."

Everyone in the room was now looking at Clinton, who was blushing, maybe for the first time in his life. But suddenly Tom Doyle turned to me. "Of course we can thank Joan, and her husband Kurt, for the last and most decisive piece of evidence. Without them we would never have been looking for the bag that contained pieces left over from the construction of the device. Those pieces were covered in Rudy's fingerprints, too. And when the lab proved that those pieces were a definite match to the fragments of the device that killed Richard, we had all we needed. There was no longer any doubt. And that ultimately is why Rudy gave himself up. So thank you, Joan."

I didn't know what to say. If only Kurt could have

been here, I thought. I was so proud for both of us.

Sergeant Doyle's story was not quite done. He filled us in on all the other little threads that had gone towards weaving the case against Rudy Schreiber: Sadie Kessler's information about the tension between Russ and Wolfgang Kessler about the grey car; Emma Jones' clear-headed testimony about the exact chain of events that led to the crash; Judy Strome's testimony that served to clear Rex Doncaster; even Rex himself, for coming clean about his whereabouts that night. The sergeant also hinted that there were others who might soon be facing charges. Rudy still stubbornly refused to implicate anyone else, but it was clear that he had not gone out to the hangar that night on his own. At the very least, Wolfgang's attempt to hide key pieces of evidence suggested he knew very well what Rudy had been up to. But was that enough to convict the old man of being an accessory to murder? Only time, and the crown prosecutor, would tell.

Sergeant Doyle finished with warm praise for all the other RCMP officers, both from Grandeur and far beyond, who had executed the search warrants that finally broke the case wide open. It was by far the single largest police operation in the history of the town. "And hopefully we will never see a larger one," was Tom's somber closing remark.

Then Clinton Drake asked to be allowed to speak. His words were few, and to the point. He praised Tom and his staff. It was clear that Tom was really moved by the tribute. Mavis Drake moved across the room to Clinton and hugged him, murmuring kind words through her tears. By this time I think everyone in the room was struggling not to cry. But my last shred of self-control was melted away by what happened next. Mavis separated herself from Clint and walked over to me. We held each other tight, sobbing, and spoke words that no one else could hear, and which I would never repeat.

A few minutes later Mavis's office was empty, as we all scattered back to our lives. I phoned Kurt to let him know I was ready, and within twenty minutes the two of us were sitting down to our beer. Kurt signaled the waitress to bring me a small one and another pint for himself. Ordinarily I would have had a full pint myself, but Kurt would not hear of it now that I was pregnant. I immediately felt that there was something strange about the pub this afternoon. It was so subdued: everyone seemed to be whispering to each other. Kurt looked at me. "What's going on here?" he asked. I laughed in the sheer joy of the moment. "Kurt, the killer has confessed! Rudy Schreiber has confessed to the murder of Richard Drake!" Kurt's eyes widened and he took my hand. Within a few seconds tears were trickling down his cheeks. "Dear God, Joan. Tell me everything."

When I had got halfway through my story, who should walk by but Judy Strome and Tim Holden, now out of uniform. Up until then I had no idea that Judy and my husband even knew each other, but it was obvious from the way she greeted Kurt. In any case Judy and Tim did not stop at our table for very long before moving off to their own.

Kurt did not interrupt me even once as I spoke. But he was still holding my hand, and the message coming through was beyond words. The two of us, together, were going to be all right. Our love had never been stronger. And to top it all off, we were going to have a child. Our eyes locked across the table. "I love you, Kurt," I said. Kurt gave my hand a little squeeze, leaned over for a quick kiss, and then flashed me the impish grin I knew so well. "We'll be fine, Joan. With you on my side, I can't go wrong!"

CHAPTER FORTY-SIX

Emma Jones Pringle

Garth and I were taking the plunge in more ways than one. Together we decided to buy a farmhouse and some attached land. When we found the right place, we made an offer and it was accepted. This was just as well. After all, we needed somewhere to live when we returned from our honeymoon!

Yes, Garth and I were getting married. Christmas came and the invitations went out with the Christmas cards. It was a winter wedding, but the church was full and the ceremony fantastic.

The best thing I ever did (well, the second best) was to let Mavis mastermind the reception. She had the idea of using the showroom down at Grandeur Ford, which apart from being a convenient space also happened to be the place where Garth and I had met. She rigged up a walkway leading from my reconditioning department so that I could make a fitting entrance. It was all rather a blur. I was so happy, I spent most of the evening in a daze. Yet there was no way I would ever forget the toast that Mavis gave as my maid of honour. She handled it with real class and said so many lovely things that I cried. I did not know it then, but Mavis had one more trick up her sleeve. When Garth and I arrived at the Bessborough Hotel in Saskatoon, we were informed that we had been upgraded to the honeymoon suite. We turned to each other and laughed. That Mavis!

The three days we spent at the Bessborough were heavenly. Our love took preference over everything: movies, dancing, even eating and sleeping. The only diversion the two of us needed was each other.

I knew that I would be flooded with questions as soon as I got back to work after the honeymoon. Even if I had wanted to, it's not easy to avoid talking to your boss. Sure enough, Mavis wanted to know all the details. "Was your honeymoon suite round or square?" was one of her first questions, made in a voice that was intentionally louder than it needed to be.

"Square, you silly goose. Why do you ask?"

"I was trying to calculate how long it would take Garth to corner you."

I giggled. "Be careful, Mavis, or Garth might not have the nerve to face you when I tell him about your smart-ass remarks. But seriously, we both want to thank you so much for the honeymoon suite."

"It wasn't just me. Clint had one of the staff in his Saskatoon office do some devious detective work, and when they found out where you were staying he made the arrangements to upgrade your room."

"Well, it was wonderful, and if Garth and I don't see him first, please tell Clinton how much we appreciated it. By the way, when you do see Garth, be gentle with him. He's a bit shy about my pregnancy, I'm afraid."

All of a sudden Mavis's tone changed. "While we're on the subject of Clinton, there's something else you should know. I've asked him to think about buying into the business. He's already our accountant, and he knows the potential here as well as anyone. So my guess is that in a month or two we'll have another new salesman." The way she said it made me think that there was more on her mind than sales.

On February the fourteenth, Richard Valentine Drake came into the world. Half of Grandeur and all of Mavis's staff were over the moon with excitement. Clint brought Melanie into the hospital when the baby was only a few hours old. She was mesmerized by the sight: it was worth a million words, and if anyone could come up with a million words, it was Melanie. I could still remember her father calling her "his little chatterbox."

Generally I prided myself on my ability to keep a straight face, no matter how funny the situation. But there were still occasions that demanded more control than I could muster. One of these arose when I happened to be standing beside Garth's Ford Demonstrator in the parking lot one afternoon. At that instant Mavis pulled into the parking space beside me. She was obviously overflowing with some kind of news.

"Emma, please don't tell anyone, but Clinton was just in my office," she began.

"That's not very unusual," I teased her.

"Shush, you devil! Anyway, he was saying how he had been wanting to get into his aircraft for days, and this was the day. So he was walking away, then he stopped in the doorway of my office. He seemed all flustered. He reminded me how I had not had a real holiday since I left England, and how he hadn't had one since he came out of the air force. Then he completely floored me by saying, 'If I were to book you a holiday to some exotic place, could Richard Valentine and I tag along?' Can you believe that, Emma?"

I didn't have a chance to answer, because Mavis couldn't stop talking. "Well, after Clint said it, I was in a flat spin. He left before I could say anything. Right away I got in my car and took off to think. Anyway, that was half an hour ago, and I've been driving around Grandeur in circles ever since. Why I came back now, I don't know, because I still have more thinking to do. I've decided I'm going to drive out to the Flying Club. Maybe I'll catch Clint before he takes off. Even if I don't, I can always talk to Glenys in the office until he gets back from his flight. Yes, that's what I'll do. It'll give me plenty of time to think. Isn't that right, Emma? Anyway, I'm off. Bye."

With that she revved up her car and was gone. "Bye, Mavis, I love you," I yelled as she sped away. What an amazing turn of events, I thought to myself. I couldn't wipe the smile off my face all the way home.

CHAPTER FORTY-SEVEN

Mavis Drake

It had been nearly twelve years since I was pregnant with Melanie, and in that time I had forgotten many of the tricks of the trade. Fortunately I had no shortage of support from my friends and family. In fact there were times when I wondered if there had ever been a pregnancy with so much attention paid to it. Almost every customer who came into Grandeur Ford and Farm Equipment knew the story of my conceiving shortly before Richard's death. I had even heard rumours that some of the gambling types had started a pool about whether it would be a sister for Melanie, or Richard the Second. By the thirteenth of February, I suspected that strange things were starting to happen with my anatomy. That night I had Dad drive me to the hospital, and in the early hours of February 14, 1964, I gave birth to a little baby boy. Since it was Valentine's Day, it seemed only fitting to give him a very special middle name. So "Richard Valentine Drake" came into the world: my new Richard, and a real Valentine. I knew that his father would have been thrilled.

Emma was the first visitor to see my new baby

later that morning, and she brought Garth and Clint with her. The two men were both rather awkward. This was understandable. They were both touching on forty years of age and neither of them had much experience of babies. But Emma had already told me that Garth suggested they forget birth control on their honeymoon. "You can guess what happened," Emma whispered to me, just days before I checked into the hospital. "I may be a rank amateur, and rather an old amateur at that, but something tells me I'm pregnant." We had hugged, delighted by the idea that our babies would be able to grow up together.

Melanie was definitely the most excited of any of my hospital visitors. Her teacher had said she could leave school for an hour before the noon break, and she moved so fast that she practically dragged Clint down the hospital hall. When she burst into my room I could not hold back my tears. The nurse dutifully brought the baby for Melanie to see. It was beautiful to see them together. Melanie chattered nineteen to the dozen, and despite the "I've-just-had-a-baby" weariness, I felt that I had passed another milestone in my recovery from Richard's death. And why not? Richard was not dead: he was here in my arms. I thanked God for bringing me this miracle.

In a previous conversation with Clinton I had raised the possibility of him becoming a full partner in Grandeur Ford. We discussed it again for a good solid hour while I was in the hospital, and I could not help but notice that Clint seemed more interested than ever. He explained the work he was doing with the income tax people, work related to Richard's death. He said that as soon as these matters were settled, he would give me a definite answer.

Within three days I was out of the hospital. Within a week I was back at my office. I only spent three hours there that day, but Clint gave me a shot of criticism for "rushing things." In response I gave him a little hug for caring.

It was not long before word of my return got out, and as if by some strange magnetic force the well-wishers started dropping in to see my new baby. Clint told me, somewhat apologetically, that the word was also out that he might become a partner in the business. He had already discussed the partnership with his parents, and his dad was so enthusiastic about the idea that he had offered Clint any financial aid he might need. "So the upshot is, I'm interested, and I'm prepared to sign the papers as soon as you're ready." I felt relieved and rather excited. I knew I was doing quite well at running the business on my own, but what a help it would be to have a chartered accountant as a partner–especially now that the baby had arrived. Truly, I could thank the Lord for giving me a life with Richard, and for letting Richard have a twin brother like Clinton.

I was well aware of the talk that had begun to filter through town regarding Clinton and me. It seemed that even the grandmothers were not immune; whenever Clint's name came up, both my mother and my mother-in-law would smile knowingly and their voices would change. This was to be expected from Grandma Drake, because she was Clint's mom, but to be subjected to it from my own mother was rather surprising.

The sixteenth of June, 1964, was a bad day for everyone concerned. It was the first anniversary of

Richard's death, and I hugged my little baby a little tighter that day. Richard Valentine was just slightly more than four months old. I had arranged to have a little article printed in the local paper in memory of my husband. It was signed, "From his loving family, Mavis, Melanie, and Richard Valentine Drake; Jim and Edna Drake; Clinton Drake; and Dan and Jean Clifton." After reading it Clinton gave me a little hug, and thanked me for my thoughtfulness.

Nothing could stop time moving on, and I was fully aware of the importance of raising my daughter and son in a "live and let live" atmosphere. Between Clint and the four grandparents, my children had no shortage of loving attention. Melanie was as full of spirit as ever. "Do you know my friend June?" she asked me during one of her chattier spells. "Well, June wants to know if you're going to marry Uncle Clint." It was tough, but I managed to keep a straight face, and tried to change the subject as quickly as possible. Melanie wasn't finished, though. "You know, Mom, both me and June thought it was a neat idea." Then, thankfully, she chattered her way into a different topic.

I knew that Clinton Drake had become a huge part of my life. After all that he had done for Richard and me, I had come to see what a truly wonderful man he was, and my respect for him was enormous. But my memories of Richard continued to block out the idea of falling in love or having sex with any other man. I was sure that there would never be another man in my life who could match Richard. On the other hand, I knew that I was still a good-looking woman with a healthy figure. It was natural that I might have drawn an admiring glance or two from Clint. And if any man could begin to match Richard, it was Clinton, his twin. There was no doubt that Emma would have scooped him up in a heartbeat in the days before Garth came on the scene. She had told me how she used to fantasize about Clinton to the point of blushing. Looking at Clint, that was understandable.

I realized that Clinton was on my mind an awful lot. In fact I was doing very little to get him out of my mind. Emma wasn't helping. She continued to extol the wonders of Clinton Drake, obviously for my benefit. Whenever this happened I did my best to switch the topic back to business, but the thoughts lingered. They forced me to wonder if I could play up to any man, even one as great as Clinton. I didn't know what I would do if some man tried to make time with me. Yet it was bound to happen one day.

As if Melanie's little chat about me marrying Uncle Clinton wasn't enough, there was a much bigger surprise to come. One day Clinton walked into my office. He seemed no different than any other time he had walked into my office: clean-shaven, hair neatly-combed, and handsome as usual, he launched into a report on an impending deal that required my approval. Once we had settled it he turned to leave, but then turned back rather sharply. It was then that he suddenly lost his composure. There was an awkward silence that lasted a few seconds too long before he found his voice again. "Mavis, you haven't had a holiday in years. I haven't had one since the war." Now his colour was rising. "Melanie has four grandparents who would gladly look after her. If I booked you on a holiday to somewhere, could Richard Valentine and I tag along? You don't need to give me an answer right now. Take a week to think it over. And if the answer is no, don't worry about it." Clinton was fidgeting almost uncontrollably. "Now, if you don't mind, I'm going to go for a little flight in my plane down the Saskatchewan River." He turned and almost ran into the door frame in his haste to leave my office.

I was stunned. Knowing Garth was in the showroom to look after business, I gathered up Richard Valentine and headed for my car as fast as I could. I had to get away before I had a chance to spill the beans to Emma. I knew exactly what she would say. She would pat me on the backside and say, "Go girl! Go right now!" As I fixed Richard in his car seat, I tried to collect myself. What was I to do? I wasn't blind. I knew that Clinton had been a godsend to me. But up until a few minutes before I had never thought of him as anything more than an unusually good-looking and decent brother-in-law, uncle, and friend. I hadn't let myself think of him any other way. So why had this offer hit me the way it had? Suddenly I was aware that Clint did not deserve to be a bachelor. He had invited me into a situation that could only lead to intimacy. And strangely it was a notion that did not shock me. It scared me, but it did not shock me. I desperately needed some time alone to think.

I backed out of the parking spot and started to drive, aimlessly, with countless and conflicting thoughts constantly crisscrossing my mind. Before I knew what had happened, I found myself back in the parking spot at Grandeur Ford. I had just pulled on the handbrake when there was a tap on my car window. Emma was smiling in on me. It was just as I had feared. As soon as I was out of my car the whole story of Clint's proposal was pouring from my lips. At the end I begged Emma to keep it to herself. But she was in no condition to tell anyone anything at that moment. My chatty friend was speechless for maybe the first time in all the years I had known her. She seemed to have fallen into some sort of trance, and there was a joyful, almost angelic look on her face.

"Sorry, Emma, I've got to go, I've got to think. My mind is in such a whirl." I got back into my car, still hesitating about where I was going to go.

Finally Emma spoke. "I love you, Mavis."

Her words had an immediate steadying effect on me. She was such a genuine and wonderful friend. Even without hearing it, I knew what she wanted me to do. More importantly, I knew now what I wanted to do. I turned my car towards the airport.

I arrived at the Flying Club parking lot to see Clinton leaning into his car. There was an empty spot beside him and I pulled into it. Rolling down my window, I called out, "Richard Valentine and I needed some air, too, and I couldn't remember whether you gave me a week to think, or if I was too 'weak' to give you an answer."

Clinton scrambled out of his car. "What are saying, Mavis?"

I laughed as I had not laughed for so long. "Clint, I'm saying yes. So go and book us a holiday somewhere, and let's make it soon."

The End

ISBN 142511825-9

9 781425 118259